Mask of Malice

Never Trust A Stranger

ELLEN NOEL

ISBN-13: 978-0692263945
ISBN-10: 0692263942
Library of Congress Control Number: 2014913673

P.Y.P. Publishing, Elizabethton, TN

Dedicated to all those who have shown me love and support.

Mask of Malice

It was a rose placed in my palm
On the brink of a brightened dawn.
I saw him place it in my fragile hand
Complete and pure just as the dance.
So red, so soft, bending sweetly
Through my fingers flowing freely.
Its boundless beauty consumed and swooned me
And as I basked in bliss that would be
Alas I looked and my love was gone.
The dance I danced, I danced alone.
My fingers trembled from the burn,
Fragility became a tearful scorn.
I peered into my calloused palm
On the eve of that broken dawn,
And there I saw no reddened rose
But in its stead a bleeding thorn.

INTRODUCTION

MAY 21, 2013

Detective David Burke paced nervously in front of the three story mansion on the outskirts of beautiful Berea, South Carolina. Late as he was, he was not yet ready to make his grand debut. *This is my moment*, he thought as he stepped into the light filtering onto the walkway. Large gables hovered overhead, blocking the moon from the street so that the only visibility streamed elegantly from the stained-glass windows on the third floor. Standing in their lighted hues of lavender and blue, David felt like he was on a magnificent stage, preparing to create the performance of a lifetime and collect his crowning prize. Inhaling deeply, dewy fragrances of rose and lavender blooms graced his senses and restored calmness to his jolted nerves. He looked out across the sparkling lake and admired the majesty of the estate captured in its reflections. All things mortal paled in comparison to its sustained grandeur. The men inside were no more mortal than he and he guessed they might even bleed more easily. They did not have the training or the spiritual ally that David possessed. It was the edge on which he would gamble leaning tonight as he finally closed the case that would change his life, and hers, forever.

He took long, fast strides to the Explorer parked in the grassy shadows of the courtyard, feeling ready at once to carry out his plan. Scanning his bag for a quick inventory, he counted the items they would need to start a new life together- plane tickets, passports, and fifty thousand in cash. Tucked neatly beneath the stacks of bills, he pulled out a Colt .45 and attached the silencer. Bullets in, and he was back on foot, marching with intention toward the front door. The plan was set on replay in his mind, urging his body to move faster until the cold metal of the bronze handle was felt inside his palm. Shaking off the last of his nervousness, he turned the scroll slowly until he heard the click of the released latch. The late spring breeze was warm and wet against his back as he peaked into the unlit entrance hall, laced in haunting shadows. He took the first step inside, his pistol held firmly in front of him with long, locked arms. Slipping into the shadows of a marble statue, he held his breath and listened. Laughter and jeering could be heard upstairs, but the first floor was as silent as the death it would soon shelter.

Deciding the time was right to go head first into the kill, David stepped from behind the shadows as the laughter came to an abrupt halt. Instinctively, he knew the silence was dangerous, with foreboding tensions pressing through the ceiling. Seconds felt like hours to David as nervous perspiration stung at his skin beneath his shirt. He turned his head in all directions, straining to see through the shadows if anyone might be coming in his direction. He jumped reflexively to the sound of three gunshots thundering from directly above him. Hitting the ground and taking cover behind the oversized statue, he checked for bleeding or injuries, sure he had been shot. *Sadie,* he thought in despair, as he turned on his heels and bolted in the direction of the fired shots. He used his height and strength to dash up the elegant spiral staircase with as much speed as he could manage. His black oxfords clanged loudly against flashing images of his betrothed, not scared or in distress, but dead. Blowing his cover lost its relevance against the pandemonium of bloody phantasmagorias, all featuring his fair Sadie cold, lifeless, and gone. His lungs were burning with exacerbation, his legs shaking with fear of losing her. He could not move fast enough or hard enough through the halls. The doors all looked the same in the ambient light provided by the sconces. All of them were the same white blur, with the same darkness behind them. At last he reached the end of the hall, and the only door pouring light from its seams, and forced his way inside.

Panting and nearly fainting, he scanned the room quickly for any sign Sadie might still be alive. Blood spatter covered the white leather sofas, plush carpeting, and even the walls. From the doorway he could see a stream of steadily flowing blood. It was the only thing in the room still moving, and David walked hastily to find its origin. He stopped cold in his tracks and the panic that had driven him forward now drove him to his knees.

She lay on her stomach across her captor, their bodies equally still and lifeless. Her tiny hand lay limp against the floor and in it she held a small dagger. Her clothes were saturated red with blood and her glassy eyes cast open. He reached down to feel for a pulse, trembling with fear that he had found her too late.

1

"You can't be serious. You can't really think I did this. Come on, James. You have known me for almost twenty years now. I have devoted my career to stopping assholes like these; you can't really believe I am one of them." Detective David Burke looked at his boss with pleading eyes. His face was worn with the grief and worry the last few months had brought on him, made evident by the deeply set lines between his eyes and the scruff on his chin. He sat sulkily in his chair with his head between his hands; his posture slouched so that his chin nearly rested between his knees. His white button-up was tinged with sweat stains down both sides and the tail, now untucked and resting across the crotch of his dingy brown trousers, was wrinkled and a couple buttons had gone missing. A brown neck tie adorned intricately with embroidered gold diamond accents hung loosely around his neck in two parts. It was hard to say how long it had been since he had slept, or even showered. He had been so overwhelmed with the reality of losing everything that he couldn't even remember when he had last eaten. His heart felt as though it was being ripped out of him through his stomach and had been this way for so long that he could no longer tell which one was actually hurting him the most.

"David, you know this is hard for me, too. I know you have done a good job for us. Hell, you are one of the best when it comes to solving a case no one else will even pick up. But the allegations are serious and the evidence is strong. I'm sorry, but the NYPD just can't take the bad press. As much as it kills me to say this, you are a liability to us at this point." Sergeant James Marshall kept his voice gentle but firm, a task that was difficult to do considering his naturally coarse, bellowing tone. He stared at his friend and could feel his shoulders slump with disappointment. Sitting before him had been a man of esteemed character who had come to him an eager kid almost twenty years ago and quickly moved up the ranks. He had, himself, taken David under his wing and watched him grow into a man of integrity and strength. Telling him about the transfer to some unheard of town had killed him; still it was better than seeing his old friend in a hunter green state-issued jumpsuit before a jury.

"Listen, David, this is better than the alternative. I worked hard to get you a transfer rather than prison time. Please, just take this offer and start a new life in North Carolina. You will still keep your badge and solve different cases. Put all of this behind you and begin fresh. Look at you. You are falling apart here. I want to believe you would never take a woman from her home and sell her like these dirt bags we put away. I really do. But all the evidence says otherwise. The new car and absences from work to take expensive vacations are being funded somehow and I know it isn't from your salary here. Can you explain that away? Or can you explain why your DNA was found on that rape victim from two months ago that was beaten nearly to death? David, we have a long history but I can't look the other way on this one. I am offering you a second chance to make things right." Sergeant Marshall let out a heavy sigh that caused his tall muscular frame to further slouch as he sat on the corner of the desk only inches from where David sat hunched over in the black vinyl chair in his office.

David's eyes were focused intently on the navy blue uniform folded neatly on the desk. Atop the estranged uniform rested the badge he had failed to uphold and respect. He couldn't explain anything away and he knew it. The Sergeant was right about everything. He should take this chance and be grateful he was not spending the next twenty-five years in prison for what he had done. Kidnapping, rape, battery, and human trafficking. Who had he become? He was ashamed and would give anything to take it all back, to undo the last year of his life. The fact remained, however, that he couldn't. It was his honorable past that was buying him this second chance and any smart man would quietly walk away and never repeat his mistakes in his new home.

David exhaled a heavy, trembling sigh saturated with remorse and fatigue. Feeling utterly defeated, he rose slowly to his unsteady feet. "I suppose you are right, old friend. I'm just so sorry." David did his best to stand erect and push his shoulders back as he stretched out his hand to say farewell. "Thank you sir for twenty wonderful years and teaching me all I know. I will never forget you. You are the father I never had." He looked longingly at the man who had taken care of him since his first day on the force. This was a man everyone admired, who lived every second honestly and humbly without a double life or second identity. With James Marshall, everything was simple and could be taken at face value.

"Best of luck to you, son," Sergeant Marshall said warmly. "And, uh, David? Don't forget to shower before your first day. Look sharp, and always look ahead." He swallowed hard to fight the lump in his throat that nearly caused his voice to crack.

David nodded weakly and quickly dropped his gaze to the gray carpeting as he turned to walk away. His legs were trembling beneath him and everything felt out of focus and detached. He was acutely aware that his blood sugar was in the toilet and he needed to eat. He didn't care really if he ate or not. With everything closing behind him at the door to the Sergeant's office, it really didn't matter if he got hit by a bus on the way home. *Actually*, David thought sulkily, *it would be a welcome escape.* He was sure the news of his screw up had already spread to Newland, North Carolina, where ever the hell that was. They would probably already have their own opinion formed of him long before he arrived there. No shower or clean shirt would change that. At least he would be isolated, far from the temptation surrounding him in New York. He was guessing from the looks of the place online, he would be far away from everything.

Each footstep felt heavier than the one before as he trudged the concrete steps to his small apartment on West 57th. As ramshackle as this apartment was, it was home to him. Everything was exactly where it should be. Every magazine was organized numerically by volume number and date of publication, each DVD had been carefully alphabetized, and even his dishes had a specific arrangement. He had spent years perfecting every inch of that dump to his liking. He didn't like change, not in the slightest. He panicked if his mail was late, for God's sake. Here he was now, crumbling beneath the reality that everything in his life was changing at once. The anxiety and stress was too much to bear. As he picked up his first empty box and began to place each magazine according to title and volume, it occurred to him that there was only one cure for such stress. If he must dismantle his entire life in one night, he must not do it sober. And an occasion such as this called for only his finest Cognac.

"Remy Martin Cognac Black Pearl Louis XIII! Hello, beautiful. You started it all and now you will help me end it all." David cheered as he held the bottle in the air with his right arm. The $55,000 bottle of Cognac had been a gift from the Rose Academy to celebrate the commencement of a wonderful relationship between the wealthy underground society of men who trained and sold beautiful women and the NYPD detective that would protect them. In the beginning the very thought had disgusted him. But after the gifts kept showing up at his apartment door, it seemed only natural to at least meet with the people responsible for such extravagance and wealth.

David tilted the bottle and swallowed hard. He grinned in reminiscence of the first time he had walked into the dilapidated warehouse about a year ago. He was greeted by a short slender man with thick black hair greased straight back and a flashy smile. He sported a Gucci suit with a silk shirt underlay, alligator shoes, and a sparkling blue diamond band that couldn't be missed as he held out his right hand with confidence. About his neck was a solid gold eighteen inch snake chain which held securely to a black rose woven at the base of it. While his appearance was over-the-top indulgent and flashy, he obviously had something that David didn't: money in abundance. He would later refer to this man simply as Ray.

The interior of the warehouse was as unremarkable as its exterior. Slate gray and rusted walls settled over floors made mostly of dirt and broken concrete. Poorly lit and widely open, the place had an eerie appeal that made the detective excitedly curious. Steel rafters overhead played a comfortable home to countless webs and rats' nests. The air was thick with the smell of calcium, rust, and mildew. Across the back wall was a succession of closed steel doors, each separated by a thick wall made of concrete blocks. Each door had a number painted on it from one through ten and just beside the number was a list of heavy locks. It was obvious these doors were meant to hold something in rather than something out.

Ray had said very little throughout their walk to this area. But, upon their arrival to their destination, he turned and with enthusiasm said, "I urge you to keep an open mind, Detective Burke. What you will see here will change your life. This is a whole different enterprise. Remember, these are not just women. They are trained performers, finally understanding their purpose in life is to serve us. Can you think of any woman who has ever really cared about what you wanted?" No, he couldn't. "How about a woman who knew when to shut up and let you be a man?" Again, no, he couldn't even name one. "I am guessing that's a no, then? Women are like a good dog. They just have to be trained, groomed, and once in a while they may need to be reminded of who their master is. And what do you do with a well-trained dog? You either keep it or sell it, right? The women here been trained and are ready for the market."

"I agree that there are times when women should learn to keep their mouth shut. And a little submission wouldn't hurt, either. But my wife was not a dog. She may have been a lot of things, but she wasn't some dog that needed training. I am not sure I really agree with you on that," David said in defense.

"Well, Detective Burke, perhaps I should explain it a different way. At the Rose Academy, we realize that every woman has her inner rose. It is just hidden by the thorns of her personality. These thorns are typically a product of feminist movements, liberal rights parties, and a generally hostile society. They cause women to believe they have rights they really shouldn't and as a result we end up with torn households where no one can identify who is really in charge. We see women giving men a list of things they have to accomplish in addition to 40 hour work week. Men are cooking, raising children, working, and rubbing the feet of their women before they go to sleep. That is not the way it should be done. Women were a gift to men, for the pleasure of men. Now, I don't entirely blame women for this. It's just a product of bad teaching. They don't know any better.

Their minds are so weak, and they are easily influenced. That is why they *need* us, David, to show them the error of their ways and teach them who they really are and why they really exist. The purpose of the Rose Academy is to shave away the thorns and reveal the delicate, flawless rose underneath. I realize this can be a bit overwhelming, and it certainly is a new point of view, which is why I want you to meet one of them so you will better understand what I mean." Ray reached into the inside pocket of his satin-lined Gucci dress coat and withdrew a ring of keys. The sound of each lock as it turned with the key created a hushed echo which seemed to ricochet endlessly off each wall and back at him.

He should have arrested him then and there, taken down his whole operation. He wouldn't be in this mess if he had acted on his better judgment. He would have been a hero instead of the shmuck getting drunk surrounded by half-packed boxes and wondering what to do next. But, he hadn't. His curiosity had overcome his better judgment and he had gone along with all of it. Perhaps if his wife had not just left him broken and miserable, he would not have been so quick to agree. Perhaps if his broken heart had not been patched by the lavish gifts provided by the high-rolling Ray he would not have been tempted to stay. Perhaps. But for the defeated, yet tempted, David Burke who stood there in the warehouse before door number three "perhaps" was nothing more than a whispered suggestion. The same word now felt more like a piercing scream which might leave him deaf.

The final lock released with the clanking of steel and the door was pulled open slowly. David had half expected to see a woman chained and bruised in despair, her clothes tattered and dirty from weeks in this unusual prison. However, he found himself pleasantly surprised by the delicate and humble lady he saw perched quietly on the bench against the back wall of her concrete chamber. He held his breath as he took a step back to take in the beautiful image before him.

She could have been no older than 20. She sat still, as though in a portrait. Her long blonde hair fell in smooth waves about her face and shoulders, rays of sun through the dusty glass twenty feet above her kissed the crown of her head and reflected back to his eyes in shimmering delight. Though her shoulders were held back and perfectly straight, she held her face slightly to the ground, her calm blue eyes cast submissively downward. She wore red lipstick that accentuated her natural pouty lips, held loosely together as though it were their purpose. Her alabaster skin appeared delicate and the blush of pink across her high cheek bones gave the air of innocence and discretion. Her thin and delicate frame was modestly covered by the white chenille dress which donned it. The lace bodice was fitted to her lovely curves then relaxed below the waist to the length of her crossed ankles. Her bare feet peeked at him just below the seam to reveal a small black rose tattooed on the inside of her right foot.

He felt his body begin to sway and realized he hadn't yet exhaled. "She's...she's...wow. I mean, gorgeous." David stammered. He forced his bewitched eyes to look away in an attempt at regaining his composure. "Can I talk to her?" He asked feebly, immediately regretting the pathetic tone in his voice.

Ray bucked up and stood taller, obviously proud of himself. "Of course you can. This one is named Eyelah, at least until she is placed in her home. Then they may name her whatever they wish. She won't speak back until you give her permission. Don't be alarmed, it's just a sign of good training. You may talk about whatever you please, and you may kiss her anywhere you please. But, my rule is this. There will be no penetration unless you purchase. It just isn't fair to the other clients. You understand." Ray spoke with rehearsed confidence as he motioned for David to come toward the girl. It was apparent he had quoted his disclaimer dozens of times before, at least.

David nodded in agreement and walked carefully toward her. She still had not moved and if he could not see the shallow rise and fall of her chest, he would have been inclined to believe she were a statue rather than a living person. With less than a foot between them he could not resist the urge to touch her. His hand was shaking slightly as he first laced his fingers through the shimmering waves of her hair. The smooth, cool strands felt like of silk flirting with the heat and roughness of his palm. His hand continued through the silken pleasure until he found her chin which he easily manipulated upward toward him. He felt a heightened pleasure in doing this and was unsure if it was because he had met no resistance in his manipulation or because of the strikingly submissive affection in her face. Her blue eyes had met with his, long lashes cast shadows over them illuminating her humble nature. Her features were relaxed but ready to follow his command. She did not speak, as promised, but in her expression she told him he was her master.

Indeed, it had been awe-inspiring and the best feeling he had ever experienced. Eyelah had stolen his reason and he was enchanted. He felt sure then that Ray was a saint and Eyelah was the perfect example of how every woman should be. It hadn't taken more than this one encounter to convince him to help Ray in his holy mission of changing the modern shrew with her liberal rights and sharp tongue into the perfect woman. It was a service to all men. His life had been a whirlwind of these beautiful women ever since.

Well, until now. Now it was all gone. The NYPD had found him out and amazing, high-rolling Ray had jumped ship to God knows where. There were no beautiful, well-trained and submissive women here. Just lonely, pathetic, drunken Detective David Burke.

He picked up the last full box and laid it carefully against the wall by the door. He lined up the corners to form a neat stack in line with the boxes beneath it until he was satisfied and lay back onto the bare carpeted floor of his empty living room. He could feel the room spinning around him and was reminded he was still very drunk in spite of the late hour. The constant spinning in his eyes quickly spread to his gut like a virus and threw him onto his hands and knees, heaving painfully. He was bitterly reminded of how little he had eaten the last few days as he could only manage to produce a few tablespoons of burning yellow bile regardless of how hard his stomach punched at him. It seemed to steal the last of his energy and his shaking body collapsed face-first into the pool he'd just ejected.

He rolled onto his back panting and wiped his face off with his sleeve. "What have I done? What have I done?!" David's eyes began to burn with resurfacing tears and his words were choking with a bitter mix of vomit and mucus in the back of his throat. "Oh, God. God? Are you there? God?!" He screamed in desperation. His thoughts were saturated with his constant sobs. David had never felt so confused, ashamed, or alone in his life. He was glad his mother was dead. It would surely kill her to see him like this. He couldn't recall when it had gotten out of his control or at what point he had decided to go beyond protecting them to actually helping them train the girls. That was his biggest mistake. Even worse, he had begun to take pleasure in breaking them in. As David's eyes became heavy with exhaustion, it became resolutely clear to him. He was sure that God would not hear him now. While dancing with the sinners, he had become damned among the demons.

2

Sadie sat up straight in a gasp, her dark eyes wide open. Her heart raced wildly and with enough force to make her thin body tremble. The pounding thud could be felt in her tightly clenched throat and with every beat her airway seemed to be pulled more closely together. She tried to swallow back the tight clump that had formed from fear but couldn't manage to pass through the pasty dryness in her mouth. Her head turned slowly from side to side and as her eyes adjusted to the darkness of the room she was reminded of the safety of her familiar surroundings. The moon poured through the window, kissing the outline of her lone dresser against a long and shadowed wall. A large mirror perched atop the dresser reflected its tranquil light back onto a black guitar case lying on the floor, still open from the night's amusement.

The crimson sheets were warm and soft beneath her palms as she traced their edges to where Cuyler lay sleeping. His body was perfectly still except for the steady rise and fall of heavy breathing. His face was calm and made her aware that she was safe here. Broad shoulders slanted across the bed to strong arms which still held tightly across her waist. Their weight and gentle heat spoke of passion and serenity and called her to find security in them. This was an idea she happily embraced as she settled back next to him. She laid her head on his chest and listened to the steady repetition of his heart, trying to match his rhythm with her own. Her fingertips danced along his smooth skin, tracing each line of every muscle and then across the shadow of his neck to his lips, soft as an amber rose painted in the corners of her soul.

She was lucky to know him, to be so close to him, and to love him like she did. His every touch was a whisper of Heaven. It amazed her that even as he slept he could make her nightmare disappear. Sadie inhaled his sweet scent deeply and relaxation swept across her. Her thoughts took her to every memory they had shared and she wondered how he could love someone with her past. His contagious laughter that had ignited her first attraction to him had become her drug of choice now. His smile overflowed with optimism and kindness for all of mankind and was her permanent intoxication. She sighed with a stifled laugh as she reminisced of his energetic demeanor in every conversation and in every interaction with this man. After three years, it was hard to imagine a life without him. What quality could her life have without his passion, his generosity, or his patience as its greatest part? She felt sure her life would be as a song without melody in his absence.

She softly brushed the lace of his long dark lashes and wondered how the world must look through those blue-gray eyes, so shaped with hope and humble honesty. In the height of his excitement, Cuyler would have eyes made of both ocean and ice with the gray interlacing the blue in breath-taking hues. Her lips turned their corners into a blushing smile as she thought of those nights they made love for hours and his eyes would turn to a deep green with sleep envy. Better still, when he played his guitar and sang words he could never say aloud, they would blush with the color of the endless sky. With eyes such as these, the kind of eyes that cast out demons, she would never understand what made him speak to her three years ago at the bus stop leaving Bethesda, Maryland.

It was an unusually crisp and damp night in June. Fireflies danced to the quiet hum of katydids and crickets. In a town of sleeping saints, Sadie had sat alone in her shame and melancholic state. She was then a hopeless wonderer in search of some spirit less fragmented than her own. Her pain had long since given way to a discomforting numbness, the gift of the morphine surging through her veins. Appearances meant very little to her shattered esteem. Her black hair lay in loose knots over her eyes, damp with the freshly fallen dew. Her face had rested in her net-covered palms over her black leggings and denim cut-off shorts. On her feet she wore black converse sneakers, worse for the wear with holes along the sides and the white trim tainted brown with travel.

"Ya know, they say when you leave a place a permanent impression of your life remains there forever. If all that we are is where we are going then what does that make of us when we leave?" Sadie lifted her eyes slowly to the direction of the deep, smooth voice that had engaged her; unsure of whether or not the voice was a vivid hallucination. First in her view were a pair of camel-colored construction boots that looked almost new except for the mortar dust caked over the toes. His jeans hung heavily over the laces, forming creases at the ankles and knees. He wore a black t-shirt which was torn along the seams and collar and had a picture of the iconic Kurt Cobain across the front. Long auburn hair fell in curls over his shoulders and nearly touched his waist. His eyes were a pale blue-gray and wide open with cheerful anticipation of her answer. They complimented his pearly teeth exposed in flashy show behind a welcoming smile. Although she had found it strange that a man would be hanging out near bus stops alone in the middle of the night, it was really no different than her being there also. Besides, there was something inviting and kind about him, something that made her spirit lift slightly.

"More fragmented than the moment before it, I suppose." She had answered him with a wry smile that couldn't be stopped from creeping across her face. Sarcasm was a nasty habit she had acquired as a defense mechanism to keep everyone away. What he had done next surprised her most. He wasn't brushed away by her jaded cynicism as most others in her life had been. Nor did he look at her with course disapproval, but laughed instead.

"Right?!" he said through his chuckling and then he simply took a seat beside her. They had spent the night together on the bench- two perfect strangers enhancing the stillness of the midnight at a bus stop in Bethesda. He had stolen her attention with his laughter and her heart with his unwavering optimism and sense of humor about life. As six a.m. approached and the bus pulled to a stop in front of them, he posed one question that changed her life forever. "If you really have to leave, would you leave with me instead?" They had been together ever since.

She felt his warm body begin to shift and her attention was redirected to the cool air of their small apartment in downtown Elizabethton, Tennessee. She raised her head so that her eyes were slightly lifted to see his. He smiled sweetly through his sleepy gaze and cupped her face in his gentle hands. The calloused wear of his trade as a mason brought a strange reassurance to the pearly texture of her cheek. She dropped her eyes to gesture in the direction of his guitar leaned against the wall closest to the bed.

"Play for me," Sadie whispered, her dark eyes dancing in a playful plea. As he strummed his guitar clumsily in the midst of the cool November night, she watched the moon wash across his face and wished they could stay lost in each other forever. In that moment, she forgot that forever never comes for the wistful dreamers of a heart-driven moonlight.

3

The morning came with excitement filling the one-bedroom loft apartment. Sadie and Cuyler rushed to gather their black luggage from the utility closet and frantically stuffed them with an assorted variety of jeans, shirts, hoodies, and toiletries. They had planned the trip months ago, yet in their typical form had not prepared in the slightest. Their plane was leaving in less than two hours. With a forty-five minute drive to the airport and fifteen to check in, they had only an hour to pack and prepare.

"Ireland! Can you believe it? We are really going to do this aren't we?" Sadie cheered in high-pitch. She was dancing around the room with no particular rhythm in celebration that all their hard work and saving had finally paid off. Cuyler danced around her, waving his arms and laughing boisterously. He was an Irish man himself, and moving there meant learning about his heritage first hand. They were moving to the very house his great grandfather had lived in and the experience was sure to be rich.

"This is crazy! Oh my God, I can't wait!" Cuyler shouted with enthusiasm, wrapping his long arms around her from behind. "You're so beautiful and I wouldn't go with anyone else, my sweet Sadie."

Her dancing slowed to a gentle sway of her hips and she turned to face him. She lifted herself onto her bare toes so that her mouth was only inches from his. Her arms reached around the nape of his neck. "I love you," she whispered. Her long knitted skirt sashayed across her ankles freely with the movement of her hips and her fingers matched their movement through his long, soft curls. She could feel his hands pressing against the small of her back to bring her closer to him.

"The plane! Cuyler, we are going to miss our plane!" She laughed and teasingly pushed him away, stumbling over her open luggage resting in the middle of the floor. She quickly found the zipper and pulled it tightly across the front against the resistance of apparel overflowing from inside.

"Ha! Are you ready? Let's go," he said, barely forming the words through his laughter and amusement of her clumsy display.

"Are you kidding? I'm always ready," Sadie replied with confidence. She pulled her black hair back into a long slick pony tail and slipped into her knee-high black boots. The six-inch heels put her at the perfect height to match his six foot frame.

The two of them walked briskly down the creaking steps of the aged apartment building. In its current state, it would be hard to believe the Abernethy Building was originally built in 1926 as an extension to Courthouse Square during a time of heightened growth and prosperity. The musky smell of aging wall paper came together with the dust stirred by their hurried steps to thicken the air and sting their senses. It would not be with great sadness they said farewell to this place. It had been the place they called home since they'd boarded the bus in Bethesda. However, its dilapidated conditions no longer reflected its former prosperity and fueled their motivation to leave.

At the end of the second flight, they reached for the metal bar across the door. "Let's do it together. This is the last time. Are you ready?" Cuyler asked, his blue eyes fixed on her with restless hesitation.

"I'm ready," she replied. "On three- one, two, three!" With that, they pushed the metal bar and with a resounding jolt the door gave way to the brisk sun of the outside where their cab was waiting for them. The driver was a middle-aged, heavy man with a thinning hairline and toothless grin. He popped the trunk for the couple to put their luggage inside.

"Are ya headed to the airport?" His voice was raspy and carried a thick southern accent that slowed each syllable into two.

"Yes sir. Tri-Cities Regional Airport please." Sadie giggled at Cuyler's mature intonation. He was simply adorable when he tried to be sound official and polite at the same time. He caught her giggle and countered with a poke at her side.

She was awestruck at how happy he made her. This bliss was certainly a far cry from her mother's suicide five years prior that had piloted her depression and self-destruction. She was only sixteen then and had known nothing of life but the alcoholism of her father which consequently laid the marks upon her mother. Her mother had done everything to protect her from his abuse but in the end her sorrow pressed a Derringer .38 special to her temple and pulled the trigger. The cream carpeting in her bedroom was stained red with blood and there were small pieces of brain matter still hanging from the exit wound when Sadie found her. It was after that day that being numb seemed the only answer and the needle-supplied morphine surging through her veins became the best method. The prickling burn reminded her she was still alive and the sedation helped her not to care. She hadn't spoken to her father since that fateful meeting between her and Cuyler. Now she knew she never would again. She was leaving everything from her past here in the states and starting a new life with the only man who had ever shown her true happiness.

"What are you being so quiet about over there?" Cuyler's deep, subtle voice broke her thoughts and she looked up at him to answer. Behind his sweet smile was a hidden hint of worry. She didn't know how long she'd been staring blankly out of the window. She saw signs for the airport and realized it must have been almost the entire drive.

"I was just thinking about how amazing you are and how much I love you, of course," she said affectionately. His expression relaxed and the worry was gone. He leaned down and kissed her on the tip of her nose.

"I love you, too," he reciprocated. His smile widened as he pressed his lips to hers. The car jerked to a stop and cut short their embrace.

"Okay. We're here," the cab driver said dryly. He popped the trunk again and allowed his passengers enough time to unload their things before asking for his fare.

The faces inside the airport turned to look at the couple as they walked through the doors to go inside. As Sadie and Cuyler stood in line at the check-in counter, she couldn't help but notice her body temperature climbing as sweat began to bead around the nape of her neck. Cuyler seemed to be suffering the same discomfort and she could see damp circles surfacing on his gray t-shirt. This tiny airport was so buzzed with life that nearly everyone stood with elbows touching. Jim Morrison's face was almost completely saturated with Cuyler's sweat when they stepped up to the counter.

"Fill these out and attach them to your bags. The drop off is over there," the clerk said, pointing to his far left. He had obviously had a long day. Fatigue illuminated the bags under his eyes and frown lines around his mouth. His square frame was hunched over and made him appear at least three inches shorter than he really was. He had long since passed the point of being polite. He made brief eye contact before dropping his eyes again to the computer screen in front of him. "Do you have any carry-ons?"

"No sir. Not this trip." Sadie said cheerfully. Her eager tone only seemed to irritate him further. He motioned for them to move ahead toward the luggage drop-off without another word.

The two of them walked hand-in-hand through the crowd and dropped their two suitcases onto the large black belt in front of them. Sadie watched them disappear into the dark tunnel twenty feet away. The next time she would see those bags she would be in Ireland. She loved to move around and see new places. That was possibly one of the most amazing things about Cuyler. He also loved to try new things and see new places. For him, life was an everlasting adventure. Before meeting him Sadie had merely existed from one day to the next. Now she knew what it was like to live and he was the breath that supplied life. The new life he had shown her had been nothing short of perfection.

As their bags slipped completely out of view, Sadie heard the overhead speakers click on with three chimes. An official, robotic voice without name or face instantly gained the attention of hundreds of mumbling faces as he reported there would be a delay in their flight until the storm passed. She had not even realized it was storming. She looked outside and saw the snow coming down heavily against the windows. Already, a thick blanket had coated the runway. From the looks of it, she would not see Ireland or her black canvas suitcase for quite a while.

"Tennessee is always full of surprises. Did you look outside?" Sadie placed her small hands on his shoulder and pointed to the window behind him.

He turned around slowly to look in the direction of her pointed finger. His face showed first his surprise then his usual amusement. He laughed loudly over the noisy grumblings of the passengers around him. "I guess we will have to find a way to amuse ourselves for a while. It looks like we could have hours to fill." His eyes turned to an emerald green through a wicked slant. Sadie knew exactly what he was thinking. He licked his lips and leaned toward her, his large masculine frame completely dominating her slender feminine physique. His arms wrapped around her and held her tightly. She could feel his muscles tighten across her waist and back, pressing her chest against his and making it difficult to breathe.

"Do you remember our first walk through downtown Elizabethton?" She asked him. She knew she had to change the subject or the only place they would be seeing tonight would be the Washington County Jail on an indecent exposure charge. Wouldn't that make a most excellent phone call to his mother? She could just imagine it now. His mother was at least number three on the chart of sweetest people in the world. But when it came to her precious baby boy, she could be likened to a grizzly guarding her young cub. The thoughts of his mother getting angry with her made her stomach coil and she tried to shrug it off. "You knew the entire history of the town. I love listening to your stories. You made me fall in love with it immediately."

"Yeah, well I never want to just be a name on a tombstone. I want to be remembered for generations after I'm gone. How can I expect that to happen if I don't show those before me the same respect? It's important to remember and appreciate them. You know?" Cuyler's body stood taller with his enthusiasm. "I can't wait to show you Arklow. It's beautiful there. You are going to love it. The waves crash against the rocks with authority and yet the grass grows along the banks with graceful prose. It's spiritual there, and the history is so rich! Ah, I have so much to tell you and show you. Just wait, baby, this is going to be the best adventure we've ever had!"

"But aren't you going to miss your favorite place in all of Elizabethton? I think I fell in love with you under that willow tree." Sadie giggled, realizing how silly it would be to anyone else to have a favorite tree in any town but Cuyler had an appreciation for all things unique and beautiful. Delightfully, that included her and trees of significance. "It was the first moment I realized that I could never live without you. Will we visit it again someday?"

"Beautiful Sadie, we will go anywhere our whims take us. We have nothing but pure and untainted time to share with each other." His hand fell to her stomach at the sound of it grumbling. "Are you hungry? I can get you something if you like," he said tenderly.

"Yeah, I guess in the rush this morning I forgot to eat breakfast." She placed her hand over his and laced her fingers through it. "I do want something, but I don't want you to go away. I love having you close to me like this."

"I will be right back. It won't take me long, and you need to eat. I can't have my beautiful rose going without anything, can I?" She loved it when he called her that. It was a nickname she had earned on their third date when she stood in an open parking lot dancing in her usual free-spirited nature. The name actually suited her since she loved anything having to do with roses. Everything about a rose signified beauty and grace. Each petal was soft to the touch and delightful to the senses with their sweet fragrance and enchanting colors. Yet, they had thorns also and, try as they might, would never be able to stop intruders from bleeding among them. In them she saw the representation of her own life so lovely and delicate with the tendency to bleed within.

"Okay, but hurry back. I will miss you," she said as he walked her to an open space near the window. A chilly breeze radiated from the window and felt soothing in the heat of the small airport. She placed her hand against the cool pane to absorb its frigid delight. It was stifling with so many bodies crawling over each other and the air was thick with strangers' perspiration.

"You know I will." He smiled tenderly at her and playfully kissed the crown of her ebony hair. His right hand grazed across her cheek and her hair slipped gingerly through his fingers as he turned to walk away.

As Cuyler rounded the corner and disappeared from view, she felt a chill run down her spine and the fine hairs stood on end with the burning pressure of someone staring at her. She turned her head cautiously to find the person responsible without drawing a lot of attention to herself. Sadie glanced casually over her left shoulder and saw a man smiling at her under the thin, silver rims of his glasses. He was blunt about his eye contact and began walking confidently toward her. She couldn't explain why but something felt wrong. Perhaps it was his direct and unwavering lustful stare that frightened her. She felt breathless and wondered how long he had been there. She wanted to run but it was too late. He was already standing in front of her.

"Hi," he said casually through thin lips and a flashy grin. He was a man in his late twenties with sandy blonde hair cut in a curtained swoop that rested on the borders of his long fair

lashes. His rounded almond eyes were jade green and complimented his peach skin tone. His square jaw was accented by
an intentional five-o'clock shadow. A well-tailored gray suit fit
perfectly on his six foot, two hundred pound frame.

"Hello," Sadie replied in a cool polite tone. She craned her
neck in an attempt to see past him. She was looking for Cuyler,
or at least an exit strategy.

"My name is Kendrick. I work in photography and sales. I
am sorry if I startled you." His accent was thickly southern in
spite of his up-scale appearance. His hand uplifted to offer a
friendly handshake.

Sadie lightly accepted and quickly withdrew her right hand
back to her side. "It's okay. I'm just waiting for my boyfriend,
Cuyler." She didn't want to be rude. She had a tendency to overreact to the advances of strangers. She smiled at him apologeti-
cally and tried to shrug off her paranoia. "Can I help you with
something?"

"I was watching you with your boyfriend. I didn't mean to
stare but as an artist I must tell you something. You have the
most amazing features. The two of you, actually, would make
a beautiful portrait. I hope this isn't too forward but I would
like to take your picture. I don't normally walk up to a complete stranger asking for something like this and I sincerely
hope I'm not freaking you out right now." He reached into
the inside pocket of his jacket and pulled out a tattered black
leather wallet. Flipping it open, he handed it to her. "See, this
girl here is my daughter. And that lovely woman standing behind her is my wife. They have been behind me one hundred
percent with my photography business but my wife is tired

of carrying all the weight for us. This trip to Tennessee was my last chance at finding a picture worthy to sell. I am flying home tonight and if I go back empty-handed then she is leaving. She already told me. I know this sounds crazy but you could make the difference for me if you would just stand over there and let me take your picture." His left hand gestured to the fire escape door on the other side of the room.

Sadie started to say no, but the pleading look was difficult to deny. It was just one picture, maybe two. Maybe it would be something of a tiny adventure to tell Cuyler about when he returned with the food. She could picture him laughing wildly at her for being heroic simply by leaning against a door. "I can't stay over there long. Cuyler won't like me disappearing on him. Just a few, okay?"

"Yes, of course. Thank you so much. You don't know what this means to me. Hey, after we take them you could give me your email address and I could send them to you. What do you say?" he asked, raising his eyebrows eagerly.

She was walking beside him now, away from the security of the window, weaving through the crowd. "Is this the door you wanted me to stand in front of?" Sadie touched the painted metal frame of the door. Chips of peeling paint felt cool and sharp beneath her fingertips.

"That's the one. Just sort of lean against it and look down. Let your hands and shoulders relax toward the floor." He watched as Sadie repositioned herself and tried to relax. "I know it's strange to do this in the middle of the crowd like this. No one is watching though. Besides, you look beautiful. Just pretend they aren't there."

Sadie again shook her arms and took a deep breath to try to relax. She closed her eyes and thought of the night before. Lying in her warm bed next to the man she loved was the most relaxing thought she possessed. The crowd began to disappear and she could no longer hear their pointless ranting about weather-spoiled plans. Even the stagnant smell and heat vanished completely. She had become so lost in her imagination that she had not noticed Kendrick standing only inches away. His hot breath pushed across her cheek and startled her. Her eyes jerked open with alert intensity.

Without warning, the door flew open behind her and she was falling backward with nothing to catch her. Her boots slid helplessly against the ice beneath them and her arms flailed wildly for something to grab hold of but desperate fists only clenched the brisk wind around her. Just when she thought she might hit the ground below her, she felt two large hands wrap around each arm and hold her in position, suspended and helpless inches from the pavement. With sudden realization of her immediate danger, Sadie knew she had to get someone's attention. With all of the breath she could manage, she forced out a piercing scream that lasted only a second before a man with a thick black beard reached toward her and pushed his heavy hand hard against her mouth. Hot tears streamed from her eyes and collected between his fingers and her cheeks, then ran beneath his palm into her mouth. Her lungs were burning and her arms were losing feeling from the strangling grip of the men who held her. She jerked angrily against them and kicked toward the bearded man as hard as she could. He only jumped back, laughed, and stared hard at her, locking her eyes with his black and soulless expression. She wanted to believe that if she could just hold them off a few minutes more Cuyler would find her, or Kendrick, anyone.

"A lively one, eh? I know just the right place for a girl like you. That's enough of this, boys. Get on with it," he barked out in a northern accent. He broke his eye contact with her and gave a signal to the men holding firmly to her aching arms. Sadie looked up at them to see what the signal had meant. The bearded stranger removed his hand from her mouth. She inhaled deeply to scream, but was disarmed by a blunt and forceful pain across her right temple. Her ears were ringing wildly as she tried to process what had just happened. The ringing quickly dimmed to silence, her body fell limp against the ice, and Sadie's world faded to black.

4

Sadie slowly opened her eyes and tried to focus. She squinted with reluctance beyond her piercing headache and tried to see past it to make out any shape in the darkness around her. She was shivering convulsively and the constant muscle tremors made her entire body feel as though it might break inside her. The cold, wet floor touched its grainy texture into every inch of her body and she realized she was naked.

With the darkness cloaking her heavily, Sadie tried to steady her breathing into only slow shallow gasps to make as little noise as possible, for fear of missing some small clue as to her whereabouts. She lay perfectly still and listened intently for any sounds she might recognize. At first only silence roared in her ears so loudly it seemed to deafen her. A high-pitched drip fell behind her and the sound echoed to her side with resonance. It's tinkling made no distinct pattern but fell in uneven clusters, echoing into what sounded like a puddle beneath it. For the first several seconds, each drip immediately sparked a jerking reaction in her gut until the jerking gave way to a constant tingling in her spine. She had become completely absorbed by the presence of the drip, ever unsteady and replacing her mania with a more dazed, obscured demeanor. With each resonant sound came a strange reassurance that, like the drip, her heart was continuously still beating also, however unsteady it felt.

Then a shuffling to her left made her jump and spin around in its direction. Sadie, now crouched low with palms to the ground and feet ready to flee, found herself paralyzed by fear. The shuffling was light and accompanied by frequent scratching sounds like tiny nails on metal. Sadie could think of a million things that could make each sound and in the dark, as she was, her imagination was wild with ideas. She concentrated, tried to be rational, and only one thing came to mind: rats. Her throat clenched as her eyes widened and her mind zeroed in solely on the shuffling only a few feet from her and edging closer. The scratching seemed to multiply into thousands all around with the constant echoes bouncing back at her. Her eyes were hot with the humid mildew in the air stinging against them, yet she could not close them. Every thought raced tirelessly telling her to run but her muscles refused to move her in any direction.

The constant shifting and grating sounds were quickly increasing in volume and if the sounds were indeed rats then they were against the dirt beside her now and perhaps only inches away. Sadie wished so much she could wake up, that this would only be a nightmare. She held her breath in dread of being the prey and wondered if her predator could see her, hear her, smell her fear seeping through the moisture in her pores.

She felt something sharp graze across the top of her left foot and break through her paralysis. Heart in flight and muscles tensed, she was on her feet and prepared to flee in any direction that still held ground to run on. She screamed against the raw hoarseness in her throat and took her first few steps. She was pushing hard into the blanket of nothing ahead, her arms in front as though she might push away the nightmare of her surroundings. Her lungs burned intensely with each heavy breath as she gained enough speed to feel as though her feet barely touched the mud beneath them.

Without warning, her right ankle was jerked forcefully out from under her and her chest crashed against the ground. The pain was sharp and fast across her ribs and into her neck. Her naked skin burned with the sudden offense of the abrasion and she could feel the warmth of her own blood surfacing over her right side. Sadie screamed a shrill and terrified shriek, pulling with all her strength against whatever had hold of her.

"Let me go! Oh, God! No! Let go!" she choked out as loudly as she could. She could taste the blood on her lips trickling onto her tongue and between her teeth. When her right leg could not break free on its own, she reached down to push the aggressor away. Her hands were frigidly cold and their chilly tingling exaggerated as they scraped against the sharp metal edges around her ankle, slicing her tender fingertips. Her hands withdrew from the pain's source at once and fell with weight against her quivering knees. In the damp and dismal darkness,

Sadie needed no light to realize she was not being held by a person at all but by cuffs attached to a thick steel chain.

A chill swept across her skin and seemed to penetrate through her, to each aching nerve. Ascending up her spine and into her chest, the chill became a clenching vice crushing her and stealing her ability to breath. The burning across her side intensified as she pulled her knees into her chest and the raised hairs on her legs stuck into the raw scrapes. In this moment, Sadie felt everything. Each cell of her body seemed to weep with the sorrow of her detriment. What was lost and had yet to come, what was now and could not be undone- these thoughts became the demon melting her soul into a painful sob of tears she could not control.

Sadie closed her eyes in defense of their burning, which felt like fire in spite of the cold dampness around her. Images of Cuyler filled her imagination. She saw the warmth of his eyes as he had stood before her at the airport. Brilliant with their deepest shade of blue, the glow in them reflected his love for her and his endearment was secured in his smile and gentle touch across her cheek. She imagined his long hair, soft beneath her fingertips, and could almost feel the warmth of his body against hers. Her shivering began to subside and her sobbing calmed to a steady flow of sorrow. She wondered how long it had taken for him to figure out she was gone and if he might be feeling the same sense of hopelessness with her disappearance. Oh, God, how she wished she could turn to him now. Desperately she longed for him to tell her it would be okay, that she would wake from this nightmare and be back in his arms by morning.

"So, you're awake? Sorry, the accommodations may not be to your standards but you must earn where you sleep here." The voice was startlingly deep and strongly southern. She had not heard him until he spoke and though his stern intonation felt like stakes across her spine, she kept still. She opened her eyes slowly and saw a faint light creeping across the mud floor about fifty feet away, making visible heavy imprints which led to the dark brown leather boots of the stranger standing just out of arms' reach from her.

She didn't know what to do, whether she should respond or be quiet, and her mind felt increasingly more like a chaotic clustered mess. If she spoke and that was the wrong thing to do, he could easily kill her from where he stood. If she did not speak, he could consider that rude or offensive and kill her out of frustration for her lack of cooperation. With chains around her ankle she would not be able to run. So Sadie sat, dumbly staring at the dim stream of light, frozen by her uncertainty.

"Not much to say yet, I know. It's better that way for everyone. Women really shouldn't say so much anyway. All that mindless nonsensical fluff you spin out into the air is nothing more than a dangerous web of ideas created to entrap men and confuse them into thinking you matter. Well, my dear, I am here to save you from all the misled mendacities society has taught you. I am here to show you a new life of subservience and grace. And you will embrace it because I will kill you if you don't." The stranger paused and turned to face her then crouched down so that his face was only inches from hers. The light behind him cast shadows across his face and the only feature which could be clearly seen was the hollow glare in his eyes as they narrowed to emphasize words Sadie barely understood. "Don't cry. I will make you beautiful again. You will thank me in the end, you'll see." His voice had softened as he spoke but his body language remained assertive and strong with large shoulders squared directly with hers.

He reminded her of a military-trained commanding officer addressing his newest recruit. His words were direct and had meanings beyond what was spoken. He seemed cold and unforgiving, yet trained and professional. It was a strange combination that left Sadie conflicted on whether she should be terrified for her life due to his threat on it, or reassured that there was a light at the end of this if she cooperated. Sadie couldn't even make eye contact with him. She wasn't sure this was really happening, or that he was even really speaking. The only clue that kept her alert to the fact of this strange reality was the tireless weight of the chain resting on her feet. What was he telling her to do, exactly? And what did he want her to say? Did he ask her something? She couldn't be sure.

"Okay. I understand this is all quite strange to you. You are confused. You don't know where you are or why you are here. That's why I am here. I am your Keeper. Right now, I have been sent to be your guide, your teacher, and your personal trainer. My name is Clayton. You may call me Keeper when I allow you to address me directly. That is a privilege you will need to earn," Clayton stood upright and towered above her crouched shape in the shadows. He walked around her smoothly as he spoke and each step caused a heavy echo in the dark space surrounding them. At times, Sadie could feel mud splashing off his boot and onto her arms as he marched, steadily and repeatedly encircling her. "You have been hand-selected to join an elite training program. We are the Rose Academy. It is our mission to strip away the thorns of your personality and replace them with the qualities that make women desirable, useful, and valuable. We provide a superior product and service to our consumer. That product is you and the service is whatever they ask you to do. Upon graduation, you will be the dream-come-true for every reasonable and wealthy man in the world. That is assuming you actually graduate. I am an easy-going kind of guy. As long as you do as you are told and show me an honest effort, we will get along just fine. Today is the first day we have met so I will forgive your mannerisms just this once. It is my hope for you that you will cooperate, learn, and grow into the beautiful woman of your potential. If I do not see sufficient progress that is to my liking, then I will punish you. Some of these punishments will be the loss of conveniences such as food and clothing. Other times, the punishment may be more severe. In the end, if you cannot be taught then you will be dead. This decision is mine and punishments are carried out at my discretion. So, for the next several weeks anyway, I am your new God. I will require that you do not speak until I ask you to do so. That is a cardinal rule here. The second rule is that eye contact is made by invitation only. You will learn by experience what that invitation looks, sounds, and feels like."

Clayton stopped his circular pace directly in front of her and took one knee so that his face was close enough that Sadie could smell the stale coffee on his hot breath. She held her breath and looked down, afraid of offending him. His voice deepened to a threatening low and he spoke just above a whisper. "And the last but most important rule is this: you must remember that I am in charge. Your job is to serve me, to make me smile, and to take care of *all* of my needs. What I ask of you is exactly what you do. You do not ever protest. You do not ever ask questions. Move quietly, follow directions quickly, and remember your place. Do not show me any emotion I have not asked you to display. It really is simple, even for a woman's delicate brain. Do you understand so far?"

Clayton paused and stared at her. She could feel his eyes burning a hole through the side of her head. None of this made sense. Everything was happening too fast and she didn't know how to respond. To her, it felt as though she was staring into someone else's life through dingy acrylic glass windows, unable to see more than a two dimensional view of unbreakable, unchangeable danger. The image seemed unrealistic to her, perhaps distorted by hunger, fatigue, and subnormal body temperatures. Remembering what he had told her about waiting for permission to speak, she kept her gaze to the floor and gently nodded. She would have time to figure things out later, but in this very moment her first priority was merely to survive this encounter with Clayton. Hopefully, she could appease him enough that he would leave her soon and she could start figuring out where she was and how to get out.

"Very good. That's an excellent start. We knew you would be the most adorable toy to play with. We've been watching you for days. Did you know that? We watched you with your little boyfriend- taking walks, holding hands, making *love*. Lucky bastard." His left hand began to travel the surface of her face, along her jaw then to her neck. "You are beautiful," he whispered as he traced his fingers down her collar bone, and just touched the tip of her nipple before allowing it to fall lightly against her inner thigh. He continued to stroke the inside of her thighs as he spoke. "Your long legs and cute ass are not even your best qualities. It was your amazing smile that flashes with the promise of fun, and your big, sad eyes that told me the smile was just a mask to conceal the real woman underneath. I could feel you, Sadie. You were begging to be saved. That's why we picked you. Well, that, and we know how much more breathtaking you will be once you are rid of all your imperfections." Clayton chuckled, obviously remembering something she couldn't. She didn't recognize him at all, and yet he had been around her for days?

"You look surprised. Ha! Did you think it was a coincidence that Kendrick wanted you by a door? Or that he was even there? How much sense does it make really to take pictures of a complete stranger in a crowded airport by a fire escape? Come on now, Sadie. We knew you'd go for it though. Kendrick has a face that is hard to refuse. Even if you could refuse him, you could never refuse his wife and child could you?" Clayton threw back his head, bellowing with laughter. He was a glutton of his own humor.

Sadie could think of few things worse than this. She wanted to cry out, scream, and run all at once. Still, she knew there was no way out of this while she remained on a chain. There could be more men just like him waiting outside the door. She closed her eyes and tried to stay quiet and still, as he had told her, relaxing her face to hide her disgust for him.

"You know what? I think you have been such a good little girl, listening so quietly and following directions so well, that

I am going to reward you with a kiss. That's what only the best girls get on their first day." His voice had changed to almost childlike. Sadie wasn't sure of the diagnosis, but there had to be one created just for him. This man, with his mood swings and delusional way of thinking, was dangerously insane.

He leaned in and pressed his lips to hers. They were warm, soft, and wet against her and he was gentle in his embrace. Again not wanting to offend him, Sadie kissed him back. She followed his lead and only moved if he moved, pressed if he pressed. The seconds felt like hours and she was sure he would never let her go. Finally he pulled back, smiling and obviously pleased with her.

"I am going to give one more gift, Sadie. Here are some clothes I brought just for you. Keep this up and you will be eating at a table and sleeping under a blanket in no time. I might even lay next to you for a minute or two." Sadie could see all of his extremely white teeth showing in a perfectly straight line as he smiled at her. She could already feel herself hating him more with every word he spoke. Still, she couldn't deny that, by comparison, food and blankets sounded nice. If it would get her off this chain and out of here, then so be it. Even if she had to lay down with him, it beat sleeping with a hundred rats in a mud hole.

Clayton walked briskly toward the dim light of the half-open door and came back with a small brown paper bag. He laid the bag down beside her and stood up, again his towering figure cast a long, dark shadow over her crouching frame.

"Stand up, Sadie. I want to see you wearing it before I leave. It's a gift and I want to enjoy it," he said assertively.

Sadie stood slowly. Her legs felt stiff and sore, and the soreness radiated up her right side and into her face. With the sudden change in position, Sadie felt dizzy and her headache was exaggerated ten-fold. She steadied herself and lifted the contents out of the bag. Without saying a word, she began to pull the black silk over her cold and aching frame. She was grateful for the soft fabric, as she could imagine how much worse it would hurt to put anything rough over her fresh abrasions. The slip was a spaghetti strap trimmed in lace that hung low, exposing the top of her breasts. She gave the bottom seam a gentle tug. It barely covered her.

"Beautiful. Just as I had imagined." Clayton pressed his hot hand firmly against her back and drew her into him. "I will be back in the morning and when I walk in I want you to stand with your hands folded in front of you and your head bowed. This will be your pose from this moment forward when in my presence." Clayton watched as Sadie moved her hands forward and folded them gently in front of her. He smiled with approval and took a step back toward the dim stream of light to better see his watch. "Time is up. I am leaving. See you in the morning. Oh, and welcome home."

Sadie stood frozen in her humble pose as heavy footsteps faded across the dirt floor and concluded with the loud thud of a closing door. An ever-present chill sharpened itself into her bitter skin, but she hardly felt it now. She felt strangled by the tears in her throat but somehow could not remember how to release them. She knew of loneliness now, as it had never been known before. Fear of the unknown had always haunted her, but with Cuyler by her side the fear had been nothing more than a mystery to be solved or a territory to explore. Now, standing in solemn darkness that numbed every sense, the unknown was a heavy weight composed of razors, slicing her wits and leaving her soulless.

She closed her burning, tired eyes and imagined a place much better than this, where chaos was a collection of tinkering percussions meant to add life and vitality to her existence. This memory was from the first months they were together. Even as much as had happened since then, she could remember every detail of that night. She could hear with such vivid recall the strumming of his guitar, each string unique and elegant under the direction of his careful fingertips. She began to sway against the chain and imagined its rattling as her addition to their song. The warmth of his arms around her, holding her closer with each sway, the sweet smell of his cologne, and his gentle kiss against her black hair embraced her as they danced. Her body began to relax and she lowered herself to the ground, under Cuyler's guidance and support. His hand laid her head gently upon the floor beneath him, his eyes locked into hers and plead for a way to express his devotion to her.

Sadie allowed herself to be lost within the memory, to have this pleasure in spite of her suffering. She began to realize the power that can be felt within a memory can shake you, awaken you, or drive you. In the most hopeless moments, the same can help you to stand or rock you to sleep. These are the times when those who live within a memory become the most important, most pivotal, and most influential. In her sorrow Sadie found perfect bliss within her memory and, as she drifted into sleep, she could hear each word he had spoken to her that night as

they made love between crimson sheets. It was a strange epiphany to her that as much as that moment was her distant past, it
was also her elemental present and just as it had altered her life
then it was saving it now.

"Sadie, I love you. I have always loved you. Even from the
first moment I saw you, I loved you then and I will until the
end."

5

DECEMBER 2012
NEWLAND, NC

Cuyler felt the steering wheel vibrating hard against his palms and looked down to the speedometer. He was pushing ninety miles per hour and still felt like he wasn't driving fast enough. The more police stations he could manage in one day, the better his chance at finding her. He glanced over at the stack of flyers sitting in the passenger seat, the end result of two hours of photocopying earlier this morning. He had traveled north the last two weeks as far as Massachusetts then across to Maine and back down to Tennessee. He was heading east this week, from the state line of North Carolina to the coast. Then perhaps he'd come back across South Carolina.

His Ford Focus whined under the stress of climbing the steep grade at this speed. Looking through his mirrors, everything looked like a colorful blur. He was reminded of a Van Gough painting called "Olive Trees" in which the trees' subtle green hues nearly blended with the darkened blue of the night sky. That sky, much like the one he pressed toward now, seemed to cry for those beneath it as the trees reached pleadingly into its darkened blanket for comfort, or perhaps release. Thinking of that painting brought fresh to his mind the memory of his sweet Sadie as she had looked upon it in awe at an art gallery in Asheville, NC. She had nearly cried as she traced her fingertips through the trees and into the sky.

"I wish I could touch the sky," she had said with a flinty smile. "Just like these trees. To reach into it would be to feel liberation in its purest form. It must be the example of tranquil sovereignty."

She had a talent of giving everything around her a story, a uniqueness, a life all its own.

This was a gift she had shared with him many times. Like the evening they had spent by the covered bridge in Elizabethton. He had originally intended to share its history with her. She had listened intently, smiling at every word he spoke. At the end of his long narrative, however, she had pointed to a family of ducks and started giving them all names, voices, and personalities. The tall willow wept its green leaves into the creek front, creating the perfect shade over the grassy null below it, and offered them a refuge from the heat. They had sat for over an hour simply creating a duck-sized drama. He had laughed so hard that evening at her ridiculous banter.

Cuyler chuckled quietly beneath the roar of the engine that had quieted since the terrain had leveled as he crossed the

North Carolina state line. His mind was constantly filled with memories like these. Sometimes he would smile with reminiscence of her graceless beauty. Other times he would laugh aloud at something she had said. Some made him cry until he collapsed in his own tears. After days of being awake, the collapse was almost a relief. It was the only time he slept. Perhaps the worst of times was when his memory seemed so vivid he would get lost in it. He would even turn to answer her, or touch her, and find that no one stood beside him.

He slowed down to make the sharp left turn into the parking lot of the Avery County Police Department. It had been a quick drive into Newland but he was glad to get out and stretch just the same. He inhaled the cold, sharp wind as he stepped out of the car. "Ok, Sadie. Let's hope for the best." He said to the stack of flyers as he grabbed a few off the top.

The inside of the police station was warm and the temperature coupled with the overwhelming number of chairs and an oversized laminate counter made the room feel cramped and stuffy. Cuyler reached for the small silver bell and gave it a gentle tap. A standard-issue secretary with blue-gray curls appeared from the room behind the desk. She was obviously trying to swallow her breakfast and still wore a few crumbs of it on her lips. The crumbs stuck firmly to her red lipstick as she spoke.

"Can I help you, son?" she said in an irritated, raspy voice expected of an older woman tired of being interrupted.

He was so tired of being polite to women like her, always eating and never listening. "Yes, ma'am. Are you the secretary? I have some flyers here and…"

"We don't put up sale papers in here. If you don't have a good reason to be here, then leave. We are busy." Her demeanor shifted from a display of irritation to disgust with one look at his haggard appearance. She had not hesitated to interrupt him with her assumptions about what he was carrying. "And I am not the *secretary*, I am the nurse." She turned and started to waddle back into the room behind the counter.

He was absolutely fuming and stunned at the same time. His Sadie was missing, possibly dead, and all she cared about was feeding her face. Of course he looked rough; he hadn't slept in three days. Neither had he shaved. He had barely eaten. How could he be expected to look any different than he did right now?

"Wait. Please. You don't understand. I am not selling anything. These flyers are for my girlfriend. She's…"

"We aren't going to sell anything for your little girlfriend, either." The old woman did not even turn back around to meet Cuyler's desperate eyes before disappearing into the back room.

"She's not selling anything. Just listen to me." Cuyler began to raise his voice before he could control himself. He was so exhausted his fuse was virtually nonexistent. After several seconds with no response coming from the back room, Cuyler's fist landed with a resounding thud against the laminate counter in front of him. The silver bell crashed to the ground and the event echoed dully in the room to sound more like a bicycle being hit by a truck instead of an angry man in a lobby.

"What is going on in here? Can I help you with something?" A deep and sturdy voice came from behind him and Cuyler turned to see a tall man with broad shoulders who looked to be about 20 years his senior. He stood in the doorway in a defensive position with his right hand hovering over his holster. Still, in spite of his stance, his face appeared more irritated than threatened by Cuyler's temper tantrum.

Cuyler took a deep breath and tried to calm himself. "Yeah, actually you *can* help me." His voice was still shaking from frustration suffused with fatigue. "I just want to drop off this flyer. My girlfriend is missing and I made these flyers with her picture on them. I was hoping you guys would hang one up in case someone sees her."

He held one of the flyers up high so the armed man could see it from his position across the room. The picture was taken a couple months ago at a dinner party held to raise money for a local charity. He had told her that as the significant other of the headliner for the event, her attendance was mandatory. The truth was, however, that she was terrible at getting to know new people because she would crawl inside herself and shut down the minute more than two strangers entered a room. Forcing her to go to the dinner party was his way of forcing her into a situation in which she would have to socialize and communicate with more than one person at the same time. It had worked, obviously. At the moment this picture was taken, she was caught standing among three other women, her smile wide with laughter and her eyes sparkling with the buzz of a good time. Of all the pictures they had taken, this was the one that best represented the Sadie he loved.

"Missing, huh?" His hand moved from its position over his gun and his tall, large body visibly relaxed. He began walking toward Cuyler with long, easy strides. "My name is Detective David Burke. I may be able to help you. Let me see what you have there."

He took the flyer from Cuyler and looked it over for several minutes. His features hardened slightly as he stared at the image of the smiling Sadie. His weathered face then frowned its creases until his brows nearly touched as he read the date across the bottom of the page. "Missing since November 15th? A month has passed already."

Cuyler stood frozen and completely unable to respond. He had not realized that it had been exactly one month since that day at the airport. He had concentrated all of his energy on finding his beautiful rose, and his thoughts had pressed him forward. His mind was constantly flooded with thoughts of their happiest memories, of holding her and touching her, and of their reunion once he found her. He even fantasized about what he would do to those who took her from him. But with this man's acknowledgment of time, the memory of that fateful day came flooding back to him like punch to the chest, crushing all the air from his rattled lungs.

His right hand had been the last to touch her. He looked down at the same hand now and could still feel the silk of her ebony hair as it slipped through his fingers and the warmth of her skin against his palm as he touched her cheek. He replayed their last moments in his mind like a CD that skips. The last image of her that imprinted in his mind was her smile, sparkling with adoration, hope, and trust. She had trusted him to protect her and take care of her. On that day, he had let her down. He left her alone and vulnerable and for what? A crummy airport breakfast? He wondered if his beautiful rose was lying in wait for saving or did she now lie withering?

"Are you alright? You look terrible." Detective Burke stated in a matter-of-fact tone, breaking the long period of silence between them.

Cuyler shook his head as if to clear the memory and looked up at the detective who stood staring at him with genuine concern. "Yeah, I guess I am. Actually, I do feel kind of dizzy." Cuyler held his head between his hands. Everything around him was spinning wildly and it was suddenly very difficult to breathe. He could feel a sharp pain across his chest that radiated into the side of his head. The heat in the room felt intensified and centered on him, like being trapped in a fire. It was a combination which made his mouth feel like cotton and his stomach flip upside down. "I think I might be sick. Where is your restroom?"

"Down the hall, first door on the left." Detective Burke replied, pointing toward a short, well-lit corridor just beyond the desk.

Cuyler rushed toward the door, still holding his head between his hands. Detective Burke watched the young man duck into the bathroom and shut the door quickly behind him. He turned his attention back to the flyer. He had seen a lot in his fifteen years as a detective for the NYPD before transferring to this dump. After all that had happened back in New York, he found it very ironic that a case like this one had just fallen into his lap.

Newland, North Carolina was a town forgotten by everyone, even God. It was the type of town that when he said he was at the red light, everyone knew exactly where he was. There was only one. The views were great, striking even. Mountains encircled its some two thousand members with majestic prose. Streams ran openly against the rear of large gardens, lined by towering willows, oaks, and pines. Every family seemed interconnected and no person here a stranger unless, of course, you were from New York.

The pace here was always slow, and the greatest excitement this forgotten town ever saw was the homecoming parade on Football Friday in the late fall. Compared to the Big Apple, this town wasn't just sleeping. It was in a damn coma. No small-town bullshit could surprise him, of that he was sure. At least he had something to do- a most welcome change from hanging posters of lost dogs and picking up slouchy, skateboarding teenagers when they skipped out of class.

David huffed uneasily at the flyer and couldn't shake the feeling this would be no small town affair. There was something that gnawed at him and he wasn't sure if it was the allure of the woman in the picture or the potentiality of excitement he had been craving that wouldn't allow him to look away. David knew full well the risk of helping the young man find his lost love. The temptation could prove to be too strong for him to overcome, especially if his instincts proved to be right about her captors. This beautiful girl was exactly what Ray sought after. She was the right age, height, and weight. He knew, also, that Ray would love that smile and the perfect contrast of her alabaster skin and dark hair. She looked like a living snow white.

Still, moving here was about second chances. This could be his second chance to make things right between God and himself. To do something good for this girl could not undo all the pain he had caused, but maybe it could lessen the severity of the marks against him. After all, no one in the NYPD could track a missing person like he could. Surely, after all he had lost because of his involvement with Ray he would be strong enough to overcome their enticement this time around. He stood rubbing his chin in his hands for several seconds, trying to decide if he was ready to jump into the pits of hell again, when he heard footsteps approaching heavily against the white tile floor.

"What is your name?" David asked authoritatively.

"Cuyler Byrne." He said weakly.

David looked at Cuyler. He was clammy, pale, and in dire need of nutrition and rest. It was obvious he wouldn't last much longer in this condition. He couldn't, with clear conscience, let him keep driving in this shape.

"Well, Cuyler, I can't let you leave. At least, not until you get some rest. It isn't safe." David let out a deep sigh. He could see the visible disappointment and protest sweep across the young man's face.

"I can't lose the time, Detective. I have to keep searching. I can't stop, I can't just give up." Cuyler's voice broke into a cry as his head collapsed helplessly into his trembling hands. "I let her down once. I can't let her down now. I can't. I can't."

"I know you want to keep going for her, Cuyler. But if you don't take care of yourself, you will fall before you ever reach her. Come home with me, rest and eat, and we will discuss how I am going to help you find her. How does that sound to you?" Detective Burke laid a heavy hand on Cuyler's shaking shoulders. It was hard to watch a grown man reduced to such a pathetic display. He knew now, more than ever, he had to help. Hell, it was the right thing to do and God knows, with all the mistakes he had made already, he owed it to himself to try. Cuyler agreed with a nod and turned toward the door to leave.

"Carol I am taking the rest of the day off. You know how to reach me if you need me." Detective Burke waved to his nurse and she acknowledged his gesture with a forced grunt before disappearing once again into the back. She was as round as she was tall with blue eyes deeply set in wrinkles disclosing she had to be in her late 60's, although David had never had the nerve to actually ask her. She disgusted him with her loose skin hanging over her arms when she moved them and bulging through the knitted floral fabric of her scrubs. Whether her shift had just started or was coming to a close, she always looked a frazzled mess.

He turned his attention back to Cuyler. "Just leave those flyers here with Carol. She knows what to do with them. Do you think you can drive about two miles east of here? My apartment is just there," David said, pointing down a narrow winding road. His voice had softened to a tone saturated in sympathy.

"Yeah, I can drive," Cuyler replied weakly. "I will follow you. Thank you, Detective Burke. You can't know what this means to me." He climbed into the front seat of his focus and started the motor.

6

The gentle popping of the fireplace and its warmth radiated over Cuyler, bringing the comfort of an old friend. He pushed what was left of his steak and eggs around the white ceramic plate with his fork as he stared into the flames. Their dance was without rhythm or pattern and left him entranced in their bright hues and flagrant movements.

"Here, this will help you get some sleep. It will help ease your headache, too." Detective Burke handed him two pills and watched as Cuyler rolled their oval bodies between his fingers, continuously staring into the fire. He sat them down beside the plate of half-eaten food.

"So, you want to tell me what happened? What were you doing when she vanished?" Detective Burke took a seat on the sofa across from Cuyler and sipped his coffee while he waited for him to respond.

Cuyler swallowed hard to push back the sadness welling up in his throat. This was not a memory he wished to relive. "We were at the airport in Blountville. She was standing by the window because it was so crowded in there, with everyone travelling for the holidays. I knew it was a place I could easily find her again when I returned. She was hungry and I went to get her some breakfast. When I got back…" he ran his hands into his hair and his face flushed bright red. Detective Burke could see how this was torturing him. He could only imagine the guilt he must be feeling.

"This wasn't your fault. How could you have known?" David asked, attempting to reassure him.

"Maybe. But I shouldn't have left her there. She told me to hurry back. I should have just taken her with me. Oh, God, what have I done?" Cuyler couldn't hold back the tears any longer and buried his shame in his sleeve.

"What else can you tell me? What happened next?" David knew he had to get him to remember facts. "Even the smallest detail can solve a case like this one. Focus for me and try to remember anyone who looked suspicious to you or who may have been following you around."

"There was this guy in a suit. He had dark blonde hair that kept falling into his eyes. He stuck out to me because I had seen him around our home town a lot the last couple of weeks. He always seemed to be wherever we were. It was strange. You think that is the guy that took her?" Cuyler jumped up from his chair and started pacing in front of the fire. "I can't take this. Just sitting here isn't helping. I need to go find her."

"Okay, I understand you want to rush off. But, actually, this is helping. Just trust me." Detective Burke let out a heavy sigh and stood up to face Cuyler. "Let me tell you something about myself. I have spent most of my career as the lead detective in cases just like this one for the NYPD. I have put more people like that guy behind bars than anyone on the force. I know what I am doing and we are going to find your Sadie." David paused for a moment, trying to choose his words carefully so he did not reveal too much. "I know of this ring of criminals who seek out girls just like Sadie. She fits the victim profile for this group of people perfectly and this situation reeks of their work. They select women based on particular qualities that make them unique, like their eyes, hair, skin tone, and talents. Then they follow that woman for weeks, sometimes months, so they can get to know more about them. They want to know who their friends are, their relationships, and habits. When they are satisfied that she is perfect for them, they will usually take the woman from a crowded place, like an airport. If she is with them, this is good news. It means she is most likely alive. But it has been a month already, so she is running out of time. They try to sell the girls as soon as they can, usually within the first 3 months if possible. I can help you, but you cannot act brashly. I need you to focus and do exactly as I say so we can bring her home safely. Do you understand me?"

David looked Cuyler square into his eyes. Lightening crashed into the stormy seas inside them with anger, frustration, and desperation. "Alright. I will do whatever it takes. Just tell me what you need. I love her, Detective. I can't stand the thought of her being sold like some animal. She's been through enough already."

David reached over and took the pills off the table. "First, you need some rest. From the looks of you, it's been days. Take these. When you wake up, take a shower, and you will be able to think more clearly. Meanwhile, I am going to run by the station. I need to do some research. I will be home in a few hours. Just make yourself at home. There are blankets in the closet and the spare bedroom is just through that door." David watched as Cuyler swallowed the pills he had given him. He grabbed his keys and his coat and walked to the front door.

Cuyler didn't say anything as David left. He just sat back down and stared blankly into the open flame. His mind was filled with frightening images of Sadie's abduction. He was surprised any stranger could even get her to have a conversation, let alone leave with him. There had not been a trace of her left behind, and no one he had questioned recalled even seeing her. He wondered where she could be and how Detective Burke could ever find one woman among millions.

What if she was already sold and relocated overseas? He had heard of sex trafficking. He knew it was a problem in large cities that were overridden with crime, but never imagined it could affect them. In his mind, he could see her alone and scared, unsure of what to do or whether anyone was going to save her. After all she had come through in her life with beating addiction, escaping an abusive father, and letting go of her mother, it could not end like this for her. He could not let it.

With the pills beginning to take effect, Cuyler's eyes felt heavy and hot. His muscles were relaxing and the pain in his chest dissolved into a comfortable numbness. He lay down on the couch, stretching across its length entirely. For the first time in years, Cuyler closed his eyes and began to pray.

"God, I don't know if you have forgotten me. I don't know if you can ever forgive me. I don't know if I even deserve to live right now. But I do know that you are there and you can hear me. I am not asking for anything for myself. Please, please, take care of Sadie. Look after her, God. Do what I should have done in the first place, and protect her. And, God, lead me to her."

Cuyler took a deep breath and opened his tear-filled eyes. Within the flames he was sure he could see her looking back at him.

"Sadie, I know you are out there. I can feel you. I feel your fear and your pain. But I will not let you go like this. I will find you. You are my love and my life. I will not give up on you. I have to believe you can feel me, too. It's just me and you. Where ever you are, it will always be me and you. I love you." In his silent sobbing, Cuyler's mind began to fade beneath the sedation and he drifted into a deep sleep.

■ ■ ■

David brought his Silver Ford Explorer to a short stop. It was only half past twelve, which meant he had approximately one hour before Carol came back from lunch. He had to act fast if he was to get the information he needed without raising suspicions. He slipped the key into his office door and turned the handle in one smooth motion.

He laid one of the flyers Cuyler had made down on his desk. He felt certain he knew who had her. The true question was where were they hiding her? The Rose Academy had several Keepers' Houses across New York, but he had never encountered a new enrollee from this far south. That could only mean one of two things. Either they were forced to relocate completely after he screwed up back in New York, or they had grown exponentially. Given that Ray had seemed to vanish into thin air after David's arrest, the first option seemed more likely.

Finding the new headquarters was about more than just saving the girl. He really didn't know why he should care so much about her anyway. Hell, he didn't know her and had only just met Cuyler. However, this did give him a golden opportunity to get even with Ray for leaving him high and dry in New York. He just packed up and left at the first sign of trouble. After all he had done for them and the sacrifices he had made to their profit, they owed him. *No one fucks over David Burke,* he thought with frustration. The more he thought about it, the more he liked the idea of finding Ray and evening things up a bit. This time, he would do what he should have done in the first place and shut him down for good.

The problem of time still stressed the situation. A month would have given them plenty of time to travel to almost anywhere. If Ray was still running the same game, he wouldn't have gone more than roughly two hundred miles in any direction. The risk of transporting a new student would be too great to travel much farther than that.

He also knew Ray loved the city. It gave him plenty of noise to hide any screams of the girls before they adjusted. Most large cities had an ample supply of abandoned warehouses, bars, and at least one rough neighborhood, giving him the opportunity to blend with the crowd and draw less attention to himself and his Keepers.

David grabbed his papers off the printer and headed for the door. He wanted to get home before Cuyler woke up. The sedative should hold him for a while, but he couldn't take any chances. The burn off rate could vary greatly from person to person and the effectiveness of any drug depends on so many factors. This young man had stumbled into his life at the most perfect time, when he had more free time than he knew what to do with. He had tasted a variety of ways to entertain the spare hours. Thus far, the list included tediously alphabetizing his impressive collection of magazines, books, and DVD's, reading the Bible he had taken from the Corner Street Church of God, and uttering passively versed prayers that slapped the ceiling almost every night. Surprisingly, he had always found alphabetizing and organizing very relaxing, which helped to reign in the frustration caused by the Ping-Pong prayers. But his favorite new hobby was reading the stolen Bible. He discovered it to be more effective than any sedative on the market for sleepless nights. He reasoned that by falling asleep with it in his idle hands, the effort was clearly visible to God, and surely the Almighty would take notice eventually. Meanwhile, it couldn't hurt to put a little action behind all the sleep-reading by helping Cuyler and, if all went well, putting an end to The Rose Academy.

David was relieved to see Cuyler's blue Focus still parked in the open parking lot beside the apartment complex. He walked quietly up the stairs to the front door and turned the latch slowly in an attempt to minimize the noise associated with coming home. The idea of calling the small apartment home clenched his chest with helpless irritation, but the ritual of hushing the associated sounds seemed to dull some of the irritation to a bearable nagging rather than the strangling otherwise experienced. He peaked into the living room and saw Cuyler was stretched across the length of his burgundy and hunter green plaid sofa still soundly sleeping. He laid out his papers on the coffee table and put another log on the fire. The temperature had dropped significantly in the last few days and he couldn't yet afford to turn on the electric heat. The transfer had cost him more than status. It had cost him a twenty-k cut in salary. So log fires it had to be until further notice. Every time he put another log on that fire or woke up to an icy house, his regret edged closer to anger. Shrugging off the disappointment of his double life reduced to one miserable existence, David settled in with his documents. He had always loved a good mystery and the personal nature of this one made it all the more exciting for him.

Cuyler struggled to open his eyes. He felt disoriented somehow, as though he had been trapped in a terrible nightmare from which he couldn't wake and it had left him exhausted. His dazed and sleepy eyes slowly adjusted to see Detective Burke thumbing through a small collection of scattered papers. His concentrated eyes narrowed as he turned the page, measuring and circling, calculating, and circling again. He had not noticed

Cuyler watching him and for several minutes he continued with the same pattern, until he jumped up and ran into the kitchen.

Cuyler could hear banging and rattling of dishes. With the door now left open, a sweet aroma filled his senses. Pineapple ham. His stomach growled with audible rigor. He smacked his lips together. All he could taste was stale cotton between his pasty lips. He couldn't help but wonder what exactly Detective Burke had given him, or how long he had been sleeping. Whatever the time, he wanted filled in on what the Detective was working on so diligently. He decided it was best to make his presence known if he was going to get the information he desperately needed. Sadie had always said there would come a day when he would see that time was too valuable to sleep it away. Who could have imagined this would be that moment?

"Detective Burke?" His body felt like iron cast as a mold against the couch. Rising to a seated position was a slow process.

"Oh, good, you are awake," David said with rushed excitement. "I have been waiting for you. We have a lot to go over. First, though, you need a shower. The bathroom is just inside the guest room. I already put towels and soap in there for you."

"Thanks. What time is it? How long have I been sleeping?" Cuyler rubbed his tired eyes. They felt as dry and stuck together as his lips. Standing up and walking to the window, noticed the light had dimmed considerably outside.

"It's almost six. You slept about seven hours I guess. Not as much as I was hoping you would get, but it's better than nothing." David said dryly.

Cuyler made his way slowly into the shower. He stood still and let the hot water blanket over him. The pressure pushed his long curls over his shoulders and into his eyes and he reflexively closed them. Instantly, Sadie was there. Her long fingers delicately interlaced his hair between them. Her eyes met his and he was lost in their depth. They were faded by the light to a gray hue which startled him and locked him motionless in their capture. The warmth of her smooth, porcelain body pressed against his stimulated every inch of him. His fingertips touched lightly on her parted lips then moved to embrace her. Their lips met and passion grew between the young lovers. There was no moment dull when each moment shared between them was laced with love and passion for each other.

"Are you still alright in there? Cuyler?" Detective Burke's voice thundered through the door followed by several hard knocks.

Cuyler's eyes jerked open and he realized he must have been dreaming again. He looked around at the bright lights shining through the generic-white shower curtain and reflecting off the equally sterile walls. He let out a heavy and shaken sigh.

"Yea, I am ok. I will be right out." He reached down to and cut off the water. As the last of the water disappeared down the drain, Cuyler felt as though his memory disappeared with it and the regret left a residual sadness in his heavy-laden heart.

"Alright, so I have gone over my notes about The Rose Academy, the group I told you about," David began, looking briefly at Cuyler to confirm his attention. "Using what I know about them I have narrowed it down to about 10 cities they would most likely be working in. I selected them based on some important demographics they all share." Detective Burke was speaking with a lot enthusiasm as he fixed each of them a plate full of ham, mashed potatoes, and steamed broccoli. Cuyler couldn't help but think the Detective must be a bit lonely and at least half of this enthusiasm stemmed from actually having someone to entertain. "I already printed the maps and circled the cities I feel would be our best bet. Additionally, I printed some demographical and statistical data on each city to help you become familiar with the area before you travel."

"Sounds great." Cuyler's voice reflected his eagerness with due inflection. He looked over the map in his hands for several minutes, tracing each circle and wondering silently if Sadie would be found there. "Listen, Detective, you really can't know what this means to me. Thanks to you, I have a reason to think this is going to have a happy ending. I am scared but I'm also hopeful and that's more than I thought possible."

As they ate, Detective Burke told Cuyler about his experience with The Rose Academy. He explained their purpose and how they had almost been shut down in New York by David Burke himself. "We were so close to shutting them down. Then the leader just up and ran. He fell off the map and we lost all leads. Well, until now. Now I have a second chance to put them all away and make them pay." David stared into the distance as he spoke. Cuyler wanted to believe he was a hero, but there was something strange about the story that didn't quite make sense.

"How did you end up down here in this shit town if you were a hero in New York? Why didn't they keep you there to finish the job?" Cuyler asked. His concern was skeptical, though he tried very hard to hide the suggestion of his question.

David sighed with audible frustration and rolled his eyes. He turned his beer straight up and polished off the second half of it before he answered. "That, my friend, is a long story for another night. Let's stick with our goal and that is finding your beautiful young lady." David flashed a broad smile at Cuyler and his eyes danced with eager sincerity.

Cuyler still suspected there was more to the story, more to those dancing eyes than what was being revealed. He could be housing with the devil himself, and it wouldn't matter. This devil was all he had at the moment and it was worth the risk. He decided it best to let sleeping dogs lie for the moment and change the subject.

"Hey, so do you mind if I step outside and burn one down?" Cuyler asked as he stood from the table. He needed a few minutes alone to digest it all. He pulled a menthol cigarette from the pack in his coat pocket.

"Sure, I don't mind. I have something better if you need to relax." Detective Burke chuckled and again flashed his eager smile.

"I shouldn't tonight. Thanks though. I want to have a clear head for the road tomorrow morning." Cuyler returned his smile and stepped out into the piercing cold air. He stared into the stars and tried to process all that had happened in the last twenty-four hours.

Somehow his listless search for Sadie had gained direction and purpose. He now had targets for his aim and a method with which to hit them. He had a plan. He couldn't help but smile at that word. Sadie was all about planning everything.

Undoubtedly, even as she looked into the eyes of Satan, she would have a plan to improve the situation.

Prior to meeting Sadie, Cuyler never planned a single moment of his life. It only took a few months before she had him planning years at a time. She always said that to have a goal and a plan to succeed gives one purpose and motivation. He had never told her, but she was right. Her theories about moving forward regardless of the past and present had changed his life, made it amazing. Now the same theories would be put to the true test and hopefully save hers.

As if meant for confirmation, a shooting star passed across the night sky. He was, at least in his mind, standing next to Sadie. He could see her eyes wide with excitement. She loved the stars.

"I love that the sun is always shining in your bubble, Sadie. I want to be there with you always," Cuyler whispered gently.

"Indeed the sun is always shining, but there are times when I desire a star to wish upon. So, the sky becomes dark and the most beautiful stars shine beside a perfect glowing moon," Sadie whispered in reply.

"Then we could draw our own constellations; tell their stories to each other. Though I doubt any constellation could shine as beautifully as you do, my love," Cuyler said as he stood among the cold staring into the stars. His eyes traced the constellations as he drew them with the hope that somewhere Sadie had drawn her own for him to see.

7

The musky smell of the classroom had become familiar and comforting to her. She could look around this room and see the other girls next to her. Each of them was equally as scared, unsure, and homesick as she. Although they had all been given new identities, secretly they had shared their real names and lives with each other. In the rare moments when they were alone together in their bunks they had managed to build a network of support and friendship. She had been fascinated by their lives and found that with each story came the blessed reassurance she was not alone in her losses.

She drew her greatest comfort in sharing with them her stories of Cuyler and their many adventures with a girl called Lady Y who was especially interested. She had pale green eyes which stretched wide with wonder when Sadie spoke. Her long lashes batted playfully at each romantic scene painted and her frail, tiny body would dance around the room as Sadie sang Cuyler's songs to everyone. Her olive skin was complemented perfectly by black curls loosely hanging about her tiny cheeks. At the young age of thirteen she had lived here longer than anyone.

Lady Y had lived somewhere warm, but she couldn't remember where. Her last memory was of her mother on a sunny day by the ocean. She was building sand castles when her shoulders started to sting. Her mother went back in to get the sunscreen and at that moment a thin man with black hair and a gold necklace had walked up to her. He introduced himself as Ray and began talking to her about the sand castle she was building. She remembered hearing her mother call for her and when she looked away from him, Ray put his hand over her mouth and she had fallen asleep in seconds. When she woke up, she was in this same house where she had remained ever since, but she had never seen that man again.

She had been a gift to the Keeper and he had raised her as his special pet. It was he that had given her a new name. "The Y stands for yes," he explained, "because it is the most important word for any lady of my house to know." She couldn't remember her real name.

Most nights Lady Y did not sleep in the bunker with them, however. The Keeper had a special fondness for her and she would remain with him. There were times Sadie, like the other girls, would be required to stay with him as well. Though Lady Y never said as much, Sadie sensed she was grateful to have time to spend with her friends in the bunks. Sadie was always glad to see Clayton's pedophilic perversion take the night off, but hated him the same for what she experienced every time her name was called to sleep with the Keeper. It was explained by the Brethren on her first day inside the House that the field training was necessary to teach Sadie how to sleep next to her master. She found that she rarely ever actually slept and spent most of the late hours inside his chamber dreaming of ways to escape.

In the beginning she had to sleep in the floor beside the bed. That is where she had first seen Lady Y. It was only a couple days after her capture and she was glad to have a carpeted floor to rest her head upon. She was lying naked in a bowing position on her knees. It was a requirement of sleeping there for new students to learn submission and vulnerability. The Keeper had told her the position left her most important features exposed for the pleasure of her master if he needed them. She had not yet closed her eyes when Lady Y was escorted in by a member of the Keeper's Brethren.

She wore a white lace gown that covered her from chin to floor. Across her face she wore a veil that illuminated the darkness of her hair and the green in her young eyes. The fabric flowed loosely over her newly developing body. She walked with grace and solemnity to the Keeper's bed and he lifted her over Sadie and laid her upon his white satin sheets.

Lightly stroking her, he spoke in gentle whispers. "Lady Y, I have decided to do for you a great honor. As of tonight, I am no longer your Keeper and you are no longer a student. Tonight, I become your master and you are mine, for all time."

Clayton snapped for his Brethren to enter, his eyes fixed on his new prize. The girl remained dutifully silent as he undressed her and Sadie was taken out of the room so they may complete their union. Sadie thought the girl might hate her for not intervening, to which she replied, "No, it makes us sisters and I could never hate my sister."

It had been almost two months since that night. Sadie had caught on quickly to the nature of this place. So quickly, in fact, that the Keeper had taken notice. Tonight she was to graduate into the second phase of training two weeks ahead of schedule. A ceremony would be held in her honor with everyone in attendance. Sadie hated him and everything he represented. She despised his Rose Academy and playing along with his degrading rules. Still, after all the humiliation he had put her through, the ceremony was to be held in *her* honor. She couldn't understand why that made her heart flutter, if only the slightest bit.

Standing now in the empty classroom where she had met her amazing comrades, Sadie felt a strange mixture of hope and loss. She would, after tonight, be transferred to another Keeper. She was going to miss the women very much. They had been her only comfort. Most of all she would miss the wide-eyed Lady Y. Yet, there was hope in leaving the first stage behind. It meant an opportunity to gain more freedom and the possibility of making her escape. In this house the Keeper kept them under video surveillance day and night. She had hope that her new Keeper would not be so strict.

"Novice, it is time to prepare. Come with us." The voice of the Brethren broke her concentration. She immediately brought her bare feet together and walked quietly behind them, head bowed and eyes cast to the floor. It was a response that came quite naturally to her now.

The shower room was always cold and the water tepid at best. She stood silently poised in her humility as the two men bathed her with their bare hands, sliding the soap across her curves and covering every inch of her. She could remember a time when tears would fall as their slippery fingers would find their way inside her at every bath. Now, however, she had grown indifferent to their violations.

The preparation took almost two hours to complete. The Brethren had given her a total transformation. She hated to admit it but part of her felt like a star as she walked in long, graceful strides in the long red dress made of satin, a fabric that was well fit to accentuate curves on her thin body. It was sleeveless with a sash they tied loosely about her neck; the tips of it fell over the low neckline.

The Brethren had fashioned her long ebony hair into loose curls that bounced softly against her back and shoulders with each step. The red lipstick complimented her fair complexion and the elegance of the dress quite well. She was surprised at the end result, never having felt so beautiful in her life. If Cuyler could only see her, if he had been the one she was walking toward instead of the Brethren, this evening would have been perfect. She would then feel anticipation rather than fear, and excitement rather than sadness.

She turned the corner of the hallway into a small room, lit dimly with lanterns and candles strategically placed atop its own bronze pedestal and illuminated a red rose vine fully in bloom and hugging tightly to outlying borders of the mahogany-stained stage. The vine continued upward to create a lovely weave around two large wooden columns at the rear. The rest of the stage was completely barren except for a bronze table and two golden goblets which rested in perfect center. The table was beautifully crafted with traditional Victorian scroll covering the front and claw foot posts. The top of the table was smooth with an oil-rubbed finish. It looked like a shrine built for a god. As Clayton took her left hand, as a gentleman would welcome his guest of honor, and led her to lie upon the table she could not help feeling like the sacrifice to be made to the god of this alter.

Lying upon the cold table, she glanced beyond the stage and could see her friends staring at her with admiration. She could remember a time when she had entered her first class-room here and realized that every Novice had been given the same black slip as she. They were forced to wear it daily as a reminder of the withering roses they were with the promise to one day shed the wilt so they might bloom again. They knew, as well as she, the red dress meant a first bloom and a chance to move forward. Her life was a little bit safer now because of this red dress.

"This is a special night. For tonight this young Novice has achieved her foundation, built with humility and obedience. She has forsaken all those who were a part of the whore she was and has begun her transformation into the prize she will be." Clayton bellowed from behind her. He took a knee and his eyes penetrated her as he spoke. "Novice, you have come far. But you still have so far to go. You have learned that your body is meant for the pleasure of men and your mind for the recognition of the needs of men." As his hands worked their way into the slit of her dress, she was reminded of their first meeting. She could feel his clammy fingers fondling closer, pushing her thighs apart with their ascent. She wondered if he was really going to do this with everyone watching. Her cheeks were burning with humiliation.

"Her very anatomy was designed by God to not only meet my needs, but to please my senses. Her lips are soft because they are intended to caress me and her vagina warm because its intention is to welcome me." She felt two of his fingers force their way inside her. She didn't want to be wet for him, but she could not stop the physiological response of his stimulation.

She could barely make out his words. Shock was breaking her concentration. His fingers slid in and out of her, slowly, with the rhythm of his speech. She closed her eyes to hide her shame. She could not process how this was a special night for her, to honor her. She wondered if the audience still watched and if their eyes were still filled with admiration.

Stop. Don't touch me, you arrogant piece of shit. Sadie's thoughts were as null and void as her tears. Still, she could not stop them from falling. She tried to move her legs to force him away, but they were bound to the table. She looked down and saw two Brethren, one on either side. On their face, they wore black masks that covered all but their eyes and mouth. One of them held something in his hands.

"I can see your curiosity," Clayton said as he held up a red masquerade mask for her to see. It was satin to match her dress with gold embroidery lavishly decorating the outer edges. The eyes of the mask, however, were not open. The inside of the mask was lined in black satin. "I forgive you, Novice, do not be ashamed. That was my gift to you." Clayton smiled as he laid the mask lightly on her face and tied it behind her head. "Now for your rebirth, my dear Novice, as you have earned your mark upon your right foot. It symbolizes your graduation of the Rose Academy and entrance into apprenticeship. The mask will be lifted as your eyes are opened to your new Keeper, as their beauty shall be reserved to him alone from this point forward. But it is more than that. It is death to all that you were, and a rebirthing of whom you were meant to become."

Sadie's chest vibrated with rapid palpitations and panting breaths. Again she was in the dark, just as she had been in the beginning, with her ankles bound to force her surrender. She peaked her ears sharply, attempting to figure out what was about to happen to her. The Brethren were silent except for a small popping sound that reminded her of opening a small box or canister. She could hear him withdraw something from inside it, and lay the items on the table next to her. The fear was screaming inside her body, drowning all but the sound of Clayton's words as he played narrator to her revolution.

"Novice, the Brethren are now prepared to place the mark upon your foot. Be honored and wear your mark with dignity," he spoke with full-bodied authority.

With the same hands that created violation beneath the flow of tepid water, the Brethren held firmly to her ankles. His hands nearly wrapped completely around her tiny feet, forcing them apart and against the table on either side.

The first of the Brethren leaned over her, dipped the needle into the vile and pushed it into the inside of her right foot. The burning surged into her skin. Sadie clenched her fists and tensed her body. Her cry came from deep within her as the needle punctured her time and again, each with slow, deliberate motions, occasionally reheating the needle to burn the image more deeply. Sadie sobbed into the darkness of the mask. Clayton, completely amused by her tender reaction, cackled down at her from where they stood hovering. His laughter echoed in her mind and her heart began to race and boil with rage.

The ember needle pushed the ink through her skin again, with more force. Her sobbing shook through her entire body. She felt her foot being pressed into the table with brute force, abducting her hip against the leather straps. She tried to pull it back and found herself fighting against him. With each power struggle, he would push harder. Then she felt his other hand against her knee.

"Stay still, bitch," the Brethren hissed at her, and pressed his large arms into her with all of his strength focused on her knee and ankle. An audible *clunk* from her hip clipped through her as the joint separated from its socket. The pain felt like hot knives slicing open her leg, penetrating the bone. It radiated into her abdomen with fast intensity. Her anger became a raging madness as she lunged her upper body forward with clenched fists, aiming solely at the man inflicting her.

Strong hands had hold of her wrists, and forced them back upon the table. With the loud smack of her head against the bronze surface, Sadie was still. The red satin mask fell quietly to the floor and she opened her swollen eyes. Her vision was distorted and faded, but she could see Clayton now towering over her from behind, shouting words she could not rightly comprehend. Inconsolable sobs drowned out every syllable, the piercing heat of the needle renewing each frantic cry. The weight of the man on her injured leg overcame her sensibility and all reality was as a broken mirror.

At last the piercing stopped and the Brethren stepped back to admire their work. Sadie now cried in a quiet, broken whisper. Clayton moved in front of her and straddled across her chest.

"Sadie, how very disappointing. Look what you have done. I cannot send you to a new Keeper in the mess you have made of yourself. You are good for nothing like this." He lowered himself and took a seat on her tender abdomen. Her wrists were still held firmly above her head by someone she couldn't see, her legs bound by tightened leather straps around her ankles. She was helpless. Clayton held her face between his hands, forcing her to look at him. "Calm yourself," he whispered as he leaned toward her. She could smell the smoke on his hot breath as he pressed his lips against hers. His tongue forced through her teeth and rolled inside her mouth, against the back of her throat.

A hard thrust was felt against her injured leg and with another loud clunk the pain intensified as the joint snapped back into place. Sadie could not stop the scream from escaping her, even with Clayton pushing his mouth against hers. He sat up and she could see the anger burning behind his eyes.

"I warned you, didn't I? I said to be calm!" he shouted as his right hand came swiftly across her cheek. She was stunned at first by the hit, but had no time to recover as another landed across her other cheek. "I told you," he spat at her between hits, "to shut the fuck up." His hands landed across her throat and he began to squeeze against her trachea, her cries interrupted by a strangling cough.

"Please," she begged with her last gasp of air. The dim light of the candles around her was fading into speckles of black. She was sure she would die here. Her rebirth would be her death upon this shrine.

"Apologize! Say you are sorry for ruining my evening, for being an ungrateful little whore who is unworthy to kiss the soles of my feet." He grabbed her by the hair and pulled her forcefully off the table. "Get on your knees and bow to me!"

Sadie's fear drove her quickly to her knees. Her palms were on the ground, her face against his shoe. *Damn this crying, I can't speak.* She thought. "I'm sorry," she choked out.

"I am sorry for ruining your evening. And I am sorry for being an ungrateful whore who is unworthy to kiss the soles of your feet."

"Beg me," he demanded. "Beg your master's forgiveness. This time, do it in your own words. Show me you mean your apology. I am not sure I am convinced."

"Master, please, please forgive me." Sadie's voice shook with fear. She knew this could mean death if she did not please him. "You are the reason I breathe and my existence is only for your pleasure. I was stupid to forget my place is here beneath you. Please, my Lord, give me another chance. Please, I beg of you mercy though I do not deserve it. I am not worthy. I know that now. I will do anything to please you." Her right leg trembled with the pains of its injury and vibrated throughout her body. She prayed it would not be made obvious to him.

"Perhaps I have been too hard on you, Novice. You may stand." He said evenly.

Sadie stood weakly, trying to balance her weight on her left leg as much as possible. She clenched her teeth to mask the pain.

"I am not going to kill you; that would be a wasted investment," Clayton said sardonically. "But you must pay penance for what you have done. You have disgraced the Rose Academy with your wailing and disobedience. Remove the dress. You do not deserve to wear it."

She did not know when the room had become so empty, but she now realized she was alone with him. She reached up and untied the scarf from her neck. The light fabric fell silently against her arms as she reached up to unzip the satin dress and it slid lightly against her naked flesh to the floor beneath her. She now stood completely barren with her head bowed in humiliation, her hands folded behind her with shame.

He scrolled his eyes over every inch of her for what felt like hours. He silently stared at her as she tried not to move. With each passing second, the silence roared around her, feeding her paranoia and leaving her to wonder what would become of her now. Where was Cuyler? Was he even looking for her? There had been times in recent past when she felt that certain he had thought of her, maybe on some starry night as he drew constellations with his memory. She could not have felt farther from him now and wondered if he had given up, assumed her dead. Tonight, she could draw a constellation for her precious Cuyler: red with the weeping of her soul as it died, standing helpless and naked before a cruel and merciless Lord.

"You are not altogether bad, Sadie," he finally spoke. "However, the new Keeper will not want damaged goods. You made me hurt you and now your eyes are swollen and your leg bruised." He let out a heavy sigh and crossed his arms. He began to circle around her, his heavy boots echoing against the walls of the empty room. "I have considered remediation, but regretfully I cannot return you to your dorm to corrupt the others. It would not be fair to them."

Sadie could feel her sundered heart recoil into her gut. She could feel this was going to end badly. She may have saved her own life with her plea, but there are many things worse than death.

"I have a friend just south of here. He likes it when we take out the trash. To him, our trash is his treasure," Clayton continued with a chuckle. "He has a unique way of teaching that has turned even weeds into roses in the end. Perhaps that is a better place for you. The instruction is individualized to your weaknesses. He is so good, in fact, that even our Dean has admired his work." Clayton stopped his pacing and stood close behind her. "Good luck," he whispered darkly into her hear as he turned militantly on his heels and marched out of the room.

Sadie was paralyzed, trying to process what was happening. The evening had gone very wrong for her. Now, instead of being in a better place, she was going backward into a tighter lockdown. What could lie in wait for her there? What was meant by a unique way of teaching? She could only imagine what was in store for her.

"I have come to prepare you, sister," a young voice broke her thoughts. Lady Y stood beside her, holding a washcloth and a bag of ice. Sadie couldn't speak to reply. Fresh tears welled inside her eyes at the sight of her little sister. Why was it she who must send her away?

"You will be ok, Sadie. You must learn the art of quiet obedience. This life is not all bad, if you do not fight it." Lady Y spoke with sincerity as she gently dabbed the ice against Sadie's wounded face. "It will come with rewards in the end. Take me for example," she smiled, "I have received my reward. I am pregnant."

8

"Get in the van," barked the voice of her tattoo's creator. She crouched to climb into the back of the van and paused at the sharp pain still dominating her right leg. She tried once again to push off of it, but the injured leg gave out and she fell clumsily onto the snow and gravel below her. Her body, trembling with fear and fatigue, scrambled to rise to her feet before the Brethren lost their patience. Above all things, a woman of the Rose Academy must always be quickly, and gracefully, obedient.

"In the van now, you lazy bitch," he growled, pulling her up by her hair and slinging her into the van. She crashed against a steel cage waiting in the cold shadows along the rear of the van. Her mind was spinning, unable to focus on anything outside of the intense pain throbbing through every muscle and nerve.

Sadie wailed with the uprising agony of all that was wrong in her life. She would be taken farther from Cuyler now and she was sure he would never find her. The memories, like splinters into the wounds they inflicted, festered and bled into her spirit until she was septic with their sadness and despair.

"You just won't learn to shut up, will you?" the Brethren yelled at her, grabbing hold of her wrist and pulling her bare legs against the wooden floor of the van. Sadie pulled against him and tried to fight with any strength she could muster. "Damn you. If you want to act like an animal, then I will treat you like one. Get in the cage," he demanded.

"No," she cried, shaking her head and frantically trying to kick the cage away from her. It looked to be barely large enough for a medium-sized dog. She could not possibly fit into it. She wouldn't do it. They had taken her dignity, stripped her self-worth, and stolen life and love from her but they would not reduce her to some rabid animal being sent to its final resting place.

"No," she cried again with more assertion. Sadie sank her teeth into his hand and he jerked back, nearly falling out of the van. She saw him stumbling and thought this might be her only chance to run. She bolted for the door of the van and jumped only to find she had not landed on solid ground but another of the Brethren instead. He had snatched her mid-flight and slammed her back against the van floor. Sadie was too stunned to react. His large strong hands wrapped almost completely around her neck and shoved her back into the cage. The steel door slammed against her face and she heard the turning of its lock and with its final click, her weeping seized to a revering silence. She would never be the same, not now. The final click of that lock would echo through her forever, just like the tattoo of the rose upon her foot. The mark of the beauty within and the thorn without, ever bleeding until the blood had washed out.

The van ride to Berea, SC was an hour long and, crouched low inside her steel courier, she allowed her fingertips to lightly trace the artistry of the Academy's trademark. *A rose,* she thought, *how ironic. I suppose it is the physical display of my youth left to suffer among these thorns. I'm so sorry, Cuyler. I tried to find my way back to you, but what am I to do? I miss you so much. I would give anything to feel the warmth of your strong arms holding me again, or even just to see you from afar, if that is all that could be granted to me.* She sighed. Even her breath was still shaking from the night's unfolding.

She could hear the Brethren laughing coarsely at her expense. One of them had a stick, or something shaped like it. Every couple of minutes he would gouge her battered side through the steel bars and whistle or call her name as though he were calling a household pet. Then the pair of them would laugh out with boisterous cheer. *I would, if I were capable, take that stick and kill them with it.* Sadie surprised herself with a smile as she imagined her brooding over their corpses. She understood, with the most abrasive awareness, that she was going to a place where cruelty and passion walked hand-in-hand. The Academy would be nothing compared to where she was going, otherwise they would not have sent her so badly beaten. Surely death would be imminent if she did not figure something out. *Okay, plan B. When I get there I will take a look around and see what I am up against. There has to be a way out of this.*

The van came to a slow stop and the men got out. Crisp wind filled the back of the van and sent a chill down her spine. Lady Y had only given her a short denim skirt and a black tank top to wear out. She told her a new uniform would be supplied when she arrived. She had seemed so hopeful and naïve, with her cheeks glowing with love for her unborn and a smile that stretched the width of her face. Sadie couldn't understand her. She was so young and vulnerable and yet completely fearless where it counted most. Sadie wished she could be more like her. Lady Y had tried to teach her the best way she knew how. What was it she had said before they left? What was the secret to surviving in all this constant torture? She couldn't remember anything she had said except that she was pregnant. Didn't she understand there are laws against a grown man impregnating a thirteen year old child? Sadie frowned at her frustration.

She heard the locks click once again and the door to the cage creaked open. "Get out," the Brethren spoke solemnly. Their demeanor had made an obvious switch from adolescent to professional.

Here we go, she thought. *Let's see what bullshit ritual I am supposed to play along with now, what humiliation you can put me through, what man I am supposed to bow to and praise for the asshole that he is.* She stood as quickly as she could. The muscles in her hips cramped and in her gut she felt a wrenching hunger. She hadn't been allowed to eat two days before the ceremony so she could look her best in the dress the Keeper had provided for her. She had been promised a meal after her graduation was over but, in light of the evening's downfall, she had been denied that final right.

She walked forward as straight as she could; given the pain each step brought her. Her dark hair fell into her eyes as she hunched and limped along the paved driveway. She was grateful for the chance to hide her face, her shame, her hatred, and her pain. At this moment, she knew without a doubt there was no other way to hide. Her bare feet slid against the ice beneath them, the snow biting at her ankles and stinging her calves. It seemed this walk was taking far too long and she wasn't sure how much longer she could remain standing, let alone walking. She looked up to gage the distance and saw an immaculate Victorian mansion. The gables peaked to part the clouds below them and cast long shadows over three stories of stained glass windows. Each window showcased its own unique light with softened hues of sapphires, emeralds, and rubies like she had never seen before. Their elegance was all the more complimented by the masterfully crafted woodwork of the columns, which served to brace the front porch wrapping around the two visible sides of her new home. Vast gardens spread the property around her and perfumed the night air with sweet scents of Jasmine, Camellia, and Christmas rose kissed with snow and sleeping soundly in the stillness. The moon crept beyond the clouds; its reflection danced to the song of the katydids humming along the banks of a tranquil lake just beyond the gardens. The beauty of it was breathtaking and she couldn't help but to accept its warm invitation, to find hope in its virtuous image.

The door opened to a blinding light. She thought she heard music beyond warm greetings exchanged between her captives, but she couldn't be sure. Her legs had stopped their shaking and her ankles their aching. She floated into the light and was greeted by an ember of warmth. Echoes of images flashed around her, like the dancing of angels cast out by shadows of death. Her senses completely gone and no longer able to hold herself, Sadie collapsed.

"What the hell did you do to her?" a voice called out from a dimly lit corridor. The voice chimed through her confusion as she tried to focus. Footsteps pressed heavily against the tile floor and Sadie was lifted from the ground. Her eyes lost distinctive vision with the sudden shift in position and her stomach reacted with violent blows against her diaphragm. It wasn't until she tried to breathe through the hurling of her gut that she realized her ribs were broken. The pain and pressure of it clamped down on her lungs, leaving her panicked.

"Take her to Dr. Scavway, now! Down the hall, last door on the right," the voice shouted. Sadie jerked in the arms of another man as he ran in obedience to the angry voice. In spite of the sweat beading on the man's arms, Sadie felt arrested in her chill as though the snow and ice had followed her inside. At last the jerking motion stopped and she was laid down on a soft cot, her body falling limply against the smooth, white sheets that covered it. Three men were standing over her, covering her with blankets and shouting blame to one another. *Why do they care if I am dead?* She thought. *God, please let me die. I am tired of this. I can't take any more of their abuse and they will never let me go on their own. Please, God. Please.*

Suddenly, the men stopped their shouting and, stepping back from the cot, stared at the doorway. Sadie heard the clicking of heels approaching and was surprised to see a woman looking down on her. She stood quite tall with dark, wavy hair that fell to her waist and polished, olive skin. Big brown eyes smiled down at her over a curved nose and wide lips. She was absolutely stunning. With her chin tilted upward and assertive steps making her entrance, Sadie was sure she had never needed her beauty to make her presence known or respected. The woman donned a stethoscope, white lab coat, and gloves then made quick steps to Sadie's bedside, where she lay still taking fragmented breaths between the stabs of pain coming from her right side. The woman leaned over her and pressed her stethoscope against Sadie's chest.

"Take a deep breath for me," the woman spoke softly through a rich accent. Sadie couldn't breathe any deeper than she already was, the pain was more than she could handle. With every breath, no matter how shallow, she could feel the splinters of her ribs stabbing into something below them. "Listen, my name is Dr. Scavway. I am going to make you feel all better but you have to cooperate. Can you do that?" She tried to answer but couldn't move her lips. She settled on a nod and stared at the young physician, hoping she would understand. "Very good. Just look straight ahead for me," the woman said. She shined a bright light into Sadie's eyes and stared hard at them, as though she could see through her completely to the table beneath her head. Dr. Scavway frowned and turned off her light. She felt soft, warm hands grab ahold of hers. The touch felt almost affectionate and brought fresh tears to her eyes. No one had held her hand since Cuyler.

"Girl," she spoke, and Sadie tried to look at her. "Try to squeeze my hands with yours. Try to hold my hand." Sadie tried to do as she was told, but Dr. Scavway frowned again.

Her focus was brought back to her tear-stained face. The troubled physician pulled her eyelids down gently before moving to her mouth. She tugged back on her lips and pressed her thumb against the gum line, causing the tingling to intensify. She reached again for her light and aimed it into her mouth and down her throat. With every assessment, her frown turned further downward and the warm look in her eyes transformed into a reproved intensity, deepening the creases between them. The men stood around her and watched in awful silence as the doctor touched, poked, and listened to Sadie's trembling body. She lifted the black tank top carefully over her breasts and gasped.

"Cold," Sadie managed to whisper. Her trembling had become a full-body shiver and the muscles were beginning to cramp. She had never been more grateful for a physical. Just the presence of Dr. Scavway made her feel protected and reassured. She tried to reach out and touch the doctor, to thank her somehow for simply noticing her. The doctor acknowledged with a half-smile and a nod, pulling the blankets back over her. She rose slowly and turned to address the men.

"She has a mild concussion, is severely dehydrated, and I noted some mild frost bite on her the fifth pedal digit which will heal easily with proper care. She also has several broken ribs on her right side. There is significant bruising and pain with respirations. These symptoms, along with her hypotension and tachycardia, suggest a possible internal bleed. The cyanosis around her lips suggests hypothermia, hypoxia, or both." The woman only appeared more beautiful with each word she spoke. The men looked down at Sadie then back to the doctor. Each diagnosis, however gracefully presented, caused them to scowl harder in her direction. Sadie's heart raced with fear. *They will kill me without pause with all that is wrong with me now,* Sadie judged. *Surely they would not waste all that time on me.* "This girl is going to need intensive care and observation by my staff for several days," the doctor continued. "Frankly, I am surprised she has not already gone into shock."

"Very well, Lydia. Thank you for your services," spoke a dark and hollow tone resounding of authority and wisdom. Sadie could only see part of him beyond the physician's shoulder. His white hair was combed back and his eyes a distinguished gray. In spite of being upward in years, he stood proudly with his shoulders back and his chin tilted toward the vaulted ceilings. *Could this be my new keeper?*

"Aside from all of the obvious injuries, I feel she would be useful to us if a full recovery is likely. I will leave her to your capable care," he said with a friendly hand on her shoulder. A glisten on his fourth finger stole Sadie's gaze. Slowly her eyes came into focus and she could see more clearly that it was a gold band with a black rose embedded onto the top.

"Yes, Keeper Shamen. I will begin immediately," replied Dr. Scavway. She gestured toward the door and the men began to file out. The Brethren who had assaulted her scowled at her as they passed, but their scowl quickly faded when their eyes met with the elder of the house. They made their exit quietly and quickly, their pale faces exposed their dread of the dark corridor ahead.

"My dear young girl, they have made quite a mess of you, yeah?" Dr. Scavway asked as she directed her attention back to Sadie. Sadie nodded. This woman seemed safe and so unlike anyone she had met here. What was she doing with these broods? "I am going to give you something for pain. It will also help you to breathe easier. It's called morphine. Have you ever taken it before?" Her eyes were bright and nurturing as she held the needle up in front of Sadie.

She knew the drug all too well. It had once been her only friend during a time of despair. She had made great strides to rid her life of addiction and start a new life with Cuyler and recalled with remarkable clarity how the drug had almost taken her life. The pain of the withdrawals had lasted for weeks. The physical damage had been significant, leaving scars on the valves of her heart as its permanent testimony. It was not just the physical damage that had scarred her. As the drug made its dramatic exit, Sadie had been left with the flood of emotions the morphine had served to deny. They disclosed themselves in one fire-bent rush and had nearly drowned her in their resurfacing.

Throughout all of the shame and bollix of her addiction, Cuyler had been her only physician, counselor, advisor, and friend. It was his hand that held onto hers and would never let her go. She had not had to do any of it alone. Her gratitude for his selfless devotion had kept her sober for the last three years. Part of her wanted to push the needle away and out of her arm, but a much greater division of her mentality reminded her that addiction and recovery were equally pointless here.

Sadie tried to relax as the familiar burn crept up her arm and into her circulation. The tingling in her fingertips gradually made its way into every aching or bleeding segment of her body. She relaxed deeply into the table and searched for something pleasant on which to focus. The flashing of gold under fluorescent lights seemed sufficient. It was the only thing in the room that wasn't white, except her physician. It was a small nameplate attached to the lab coat of her caretaker which read, "Lydia Scavway, M.D. Administrator of Medical Services, Rose Academy." Inlaid into the edging of the gold nameplate was a recession of roses, intertwined, each laced around the next.

Sadie wanted badly to ask the woman how she came to work for such a flagrant organization, such as she perceived the Rose Academy to be. She wondered how it was that the physician showed no signs of abuse, execration, or of having ever being treated as she had. Nor did she appear remorseful for the girl she treated. Exhumed within her umber eyes was only a prosaic affection, warm to the touch without depth or personal interest. Perhaps the physician was conveniently benighted of her affliction and the truth about the "use" for which the girls were healed.

Had Sadie been able, she might have brought her concerns to the lovely Dr. Scavway, who now seemed her only safe haven in a world which entrapped her inside a continuously changing nightmare. The reality was, however, that she was far from able and, as the morphine leaked slowly into her senses, heaviness fell over her tired eyes and she drifted into a sweet slumber.

"Come here," Cuyler said cloyingly as he pulled her down to the pavement beside him. She fell neatly onto his broad chest and rested her head in her palm so she could still see him. His auburn curls were still neatly contained within the gray bandana he had worn for his show, somehow illuminating his bright eyes and adulating smile. Her tan skirt blended well with his khaki shorts and matching shirt so that from a distance they might have looked like one person lying there on the pavement of the Bonnie Kate parking lot.

"You were amazing on that stage tonight, Mr. Wonderful," she teased. "I could watch you perform all night, if I wouldn't miss you so badly." Her eyes danced a perfect reflection of the clear summer sky and Cuyler was lost in them once again. The depth of those perfect eyes left him speechless.

"I missed you, too," he finally whispered through gently parted lips.

"You nearly broke my heart," she pouted at him. She crossed her arms and stuck out her bottom lip for the full effect.

He reacted with a tighter embrace around her thin frame. "No, Sweetness, you can't have a broken heart," he pleaded with playful condolence.

"And why is that exactly?" she countered.

"Because," he responded in deeper inflection, "if your heart breaks, then so does mine. We are one heart, my love."

The couple rested in serene silence for several moments. Their spirits pirouetted with the chirping of crickets and the ramblings of the stream a few yards behind them. The Bonnie Kate Café was situated in heart of downtown Elizabethton, pumping life into the small town with its own unique combination of live music and delicate cuisine. Cuyler had long since been a beloved asset to the café's collection of local bands and independent performers. His voice was bluesy smooth with just enough bite to flatter any classic rock song requested of him. Tonight had been the first time she had seen him perform without his usual entourage behind him. Although his demeanor and character never wavered, he was never more alive than when he held a guitar and stood before a mic.

Sadie admired his courage to stand before a crowd and his abilities to please anyone for whom he performed. She had always dreamed of being able to do that same thing and, if given the chance, perhaps she could muster up the nerve to try. Without a doubt, no matter the hours of practice or size of nerves one possessed, no one could top Cuyler in this town. Given his extraordinary talents, it had been no surprise to her when a crowd of fans immediately flocked to his feet at the first chord. They had not stopped shouting his praises until the last strum; finishing the show with one of his favorites- a bluesy original entitled "In My Head."

Now resting beneath the stars in a parking lot by the river, Sadie and Cuyler enjoyed the absence of the noise and basked delightfully in its swooning silence, until a whining rumble came up from between them. Laughing, they acknowledged their simultaneous hunger.

"Let's get something to eat. Red Chili?" Cuyler asked with anticipation.

"Red Chili it is then," she replied, a bit disappointed. This was one of Cuyler's favorite restaurants and, although the food was amazing, it was also Korean cuisine and the spices always left her bilious for two solid days after tasting any of their fine menu options. It was a secret she held safe with her even now, knowing all too well how much he adored it and how terrible he would feel if he realized his choice restaurant had brought her discomfort.

Their interlaced hands swung in joyous reprise as they skipped through the breezeway. Entering Elk Avenue, the black French-style street lamps provided a romantically lit welcome at this late hour. Feeling no pressure to rush through their night, the couple chose to dance, rather than walk, the entire length of four blocks to where the Red Chili stood with its doors propped open, welcoming its guests with a spicy aroma. They had become lost in their twirling, their laughing, and the natural exultation that comes from being hopelessly and devotedly in love. Sadie stumbled over something wide and stiff in her path, bringing Cuyler down with her in an uproarious laughter.

Finally managing to shift their weight and stumbling to stand erect, they were shocked to see the elegant street lamps had burned out and left portent darkness all around them. Tall buildings cast long, haunting shadows over the deserted Elk Avenue. Music no longer spilled out from the speakers at each corner, and even the Bonnie Kate Café had fallen mute. Wind whirled about them, shaking the wooden benches which speckled the length of the street to offer its visitors rest and refuge in the shade. Sadie watched in horror as the bolts intended to hold the benches in place began to loosen and fall, giving in reluctantly to the pressure of the current all around them.

One by one, the benches flew into the air, smashing without mercy against the surrounding buildings. Breaking glass could be heard from all around them as store fronts shattered against the flying debris that insulted them. With broken glass now added to the compilation of splintered wood and steel which whirled their cruelty about them, the danger they were in left them in shock. A shard of glass speared toward them, aimed straight at Sadie's heart. Immediately Cuyler reacted, knocking the assailant to the ground and slicing his hand open. Ignoring the blood now liberally dripping from his wounded palm, he reached for her arm and tried to pull her away from the obstinate storm. Hail pelted through the blinding rain, reacting with the summer heat to create a steep fog between them. Her arm slid through his bloody fingers and, like a ghost, Cuyler disappeared into the mist and wind. Frantically, she called out for him, desperately screaming above the pounding of the hail and rumbling of the thunder overhead.

Splinters wailed against her back and shoulders, knocking her to her knees. Attempting to crawl beneath the rubble quickly piling up rubble around her, Sadie's hand grabbed hold of the object she had tripped on earlier. As she leaned forward to reach over it, thinking she may be able to crawl over, rather than around, the object, she saw in clear view the face of a young woman. In spite of the rain, she did not flinch or try to run. Her skin was cold, hard, and ash-gray with hints of lavender around the parted lips and sunken cheeks. She stared blankly into the storm whirling above them, hail clapping against her dark, soulless eyes. Her arms were folded modestly across her waist and in her small, lavender hands she held a single rose, red in full bloom. It was as though someone had molded her freshly from clay and left her there to harden in the sun. Only, here she found no sun at all, only the whipping course of a deadly storm. Peering closer onto the dead body in front of her, Sadie realized the corpse was her own.

Sadie released a piercing scream, her wet face stained with the warmth of hollow tears. Bowing on her knees as if to pray, she cried for God to hear her, to lift her out of her sentence and give her peace once again. She was sure the prayer would recherché against the hovering clouds until they were lost all together in their crevice. Just as she began to accept her death in God's silence, Sadie felt a painful jolt of electricity surging through her entire body. Her lungs felt crushed beneath the weight of their air hunger. Every muscle cringed behind the jolt, including her heart which quivered with sharp, painful stabs across her chest. Voices could be heard shouting blurred commands somewhere in the distance.

Another surge of electricity pulled her up from the table and Sadie gasped. Her dark eyes sprang wildly open and searched for something familiar around her. She panted through cracked lips, the short and spontaneous breaths roughing against her dry, sore throat. The room around her was blindingly white and spinning with frigid gusts around her. In her mind was a penetrating confusion of questions she couldn't ask. She couldn't even scream, her voice stolen by the parched burning in the back of her throat.

Two arms reached around her from behind and forced her back upon the plastic cot while someone else secured her wrists against the frame. Her confusion became buried beneath a consuming rage. Sadie tried to scream as she pulled and jerked against the straps on her arms. She tried to kick but the same had bound her at the ankles.

"Shush now, girl," a friendly voice whispered into her ear. "You are alright now. It is confusing to you, I know. Just slow down and take deep breaths." As the voice continued to coach Sadie smoothly into relaxation, her orientation returned and she recognized the voice as the young and beautiful Dr. Scavway. This room then, she concluded, must be the exam room where she had passed out after the morphine. *It was all a dream. Cuyler isn't here and I am not a corpse. It was just a dream.* A knock on the mahogany door beckoned the doctor. She cracked the door open just enough to see who was behind it. Sadie watched intently, but could only make out jumbled whispers filtering in through the thick wooden barrier between them.

"She's awake, that's true," Dr. Scavway said, frowning. "But she isn't ready to be released." She paused and frowned at the whispering of the man behind the door, then replied, "I will have her ready by tomorrow then, but I can't promise anything. Perhaps you could work her gently at first." The young physician drifted her round brown eyes over her shoulder at Sadie then back to the door. "I understand, sir. As you wish."

Sadie watched her walk solemnly back to her bedside, her head hung low and long dark curls falling over the seams of the pressed white lab coat she wore. She sat down beside the bed and took hold of Sadie's balmy palm. The melancholy expression wore heavily on her tired face, as though she had been working day and night only to find out it was for nothing.

"What is your name, girl?" she asked, staring into the floor.

"Sadie," the young patient answered through a coarse whisper.

"Well, Sadie, I must tell you this life for you will not be easy," Dr. Scavway began, heavy laden. "I don't want to release you, but I have no choice. Orders have come down from the Keeper and you already have your first assignment tomorrow." She paused and released a quivering, weighty sigh. "I have been taking care of you for weeks and you have come so far, but you are not yet healed. So, I beg you to be careful and do exactly as they say. You will not survive that again. I am sure of it. I almost lost you twice. I know that I do not know you at all, and you do not know me. I see a lot of girls come in here and most would never have pulled through like you did. I have to believe that you are not meant to die here, and I want you to promise me something."

"What?" Sadie attempted. She wanted to say much more, to reach out and embrace the woman who had brought her back to life. Tied down and still frail from recent weeks, all she could offer was a faint smile.

"Promise me that you will do whatever it takes to reach a full recovery, gain your strength, and get out of here. I had a dream last night as I dozed in the chair at your bedside. God showed Himself to me and told me you would be our saving grace. He said He had sent you here to end all of this. I used to believe in God, angels, and miracles. That was a long time ago, before Kendrick claimed me as his own. Now, I don't honestly know if I believe in anything. Still, something inside me is telling me to believe in you. As far-fetched as all of my babbling sounds, I do believe you are here for a very distinct and important purpose. For that reason, I will always be here. I will keep you alive and as strong as I am able. I can promise you that in return."

Sadie contemplated the words carefully chosen by her caretaker. She understood the gravity of each request, each promise, and each implication. The idea of some protection here from sickness and death was a welcome bargaining chip, one Sadie was confident was not often laid upon the table. Obviously, Lydia Scavway was a prisoner the same as the other girls. The only difference lie in the services she rendered for the Academy. Her position seemed quite welcoming compared to sexual exploitation and yet, looking at the doctor now, she could see the same shame, sorrow, and fatigue she endured. They were the same spirit in that moment; moved and motivated to change their existence into something better, far from this desolate prison.

Sadie gave her physician's hand an affirming squeeze and locked eyes with her new partner and companion. She would be the warrior on the front lines for both of them, she decided. They would find their liberation soon and, if prophecies proved true, their revenge also.

9

The morning sun smiled through the blinds of the exam room, warming her cheeks in spite of the winter nip. She opened her eyes slowly, not wanting to be awake just yet. The time spent under Dr. Scavway's care had strengthened her and given her some solace and refuge against the duties waiting for her just outside the door. She was determined to make this final moment of peace last as long as possible, stretching out the last second to hours if time would allow.

"You are awake. I trust you slept well last night?" Dr. Scavway asked, rising from the white, leather recliner behind the cot. She walked around to assess her patient, her eyes bright and hopeful. She listened with her stethoscope in silence, moving the bell to the usual spots over her heart, lungs, and abdomen.

Using cold fingertips and moving in a clockwise direction, she pressed gently over the four quadrants of the abdominal wall. Sadie winced as she pressed along the right side.

"You will be sore for a couple of weeks still. The good news is, young Sadie, that your breaks are healed and the bruises diminished," she reported with a smile. "I have more good news for you, as well. I couldn't stop them from releasing you to work today, but I did manage to talk the Keeper into a much easier job. I am not supposed to spoil the surprise, though, so I am going to leave you hanging a little bit. Let's just say, you're day will not be difficult and I personally know you will be in good hands."

Sadie reached behind her to push herself into a sitting position. She realized the doctor had done her best to look out for her, and had been pleased with the results of her negotiations. "What happens after today?" she asked, hoping for more good news.

Lydia frowned. "After today you will go back into circulation. I will still follow up with you weekly, but you will be expected to work as the other girls do." Dr. Scavway hesitated, and took a seat beside her patient. "Sadie, do you remember what we talked about last night?"

Sadie nodded, not really sure she wanted to revisit that particular conversation.

"I meant what I said. I will be following you closely, and I will do all that I can to keep you safe. In return, I need you to be obedient, keep yourself healthy and useful, and find a way to end this. I had the same dream last night, the one about you saving us. I am hopeful you are the one sent here to end their tyranny. But, let me caution you this. You must not tell anyone about our agreement. Do you understand? They will kill us if they suspect mutiny. It is essential that you understand this." Dr. Scavway's eyes were pleading and almost panicked. Her hands were wrapped tightly on Sadie's shoulders, the anxiety and anticipation driving her grip.

"I understand, Lydia. Don't worry, I won't tell anyone," Sadie said after a long silence. "How am I supposed to get us out of here, though? I didn't know such a level of cruelty existed until I met these men." Sadie dropped her gaze, sure that the physician was expecting the impossible and they would all die in here, together if they were lucky.

"Sadie, you must understand how the system works. We have only thirty minutes before they come to get you. We will talk as I prepare you, okay? Try to keep up; I may not have another chance with you like this." Dr. Scavway watched for Sadie's acknowledgement before helping her to her feet. The white tile floor felt like ice and chills escaped all the way up her trembling body. The physician gathered supplies from her cabinet, a brush, lipstick, blush, and an aluminum bucket with a used razor and two washcloths in it. As she undressed Sadie, she seemed as unaffected by the seeing the nudity as her patient did displaying it. *Strange what the human mind can learn to accept,* she thought curtly.

"The first thing you need to know is this is a business, and a very profitable one at that. These men are not here because they hate women, they are here to make a profit. The best way to do that is to train the women at the Academy. They can make as much as three to five million off of one well-trained graduate of the Academy. The women are hand-selected based on certain criteria such as age, height, weight, and talent. As obverse as this may sound, it actually speaks very highly of you to be selected at all." The doctor watched Sadie's eyes narrow at the cruel humor. After a brief roll of her eyes, she continued brushing her hair as she explained.

"As you have already witnessed, the girls are considered budding roses, hindered by the thorns of disobedience, independence, and modernistic feminist ideas society has raised you to believe. The purpose of the Academy is to reprogram you into the more traditional trophy wife that men secretly desire. They cater to the demands of the wealthiest men in the world and have served many famous clients such as musical celebrities, actors, and even two U.S. Presidents. They have international support as well with clients serving in the United Nations Council, the Embassy, and many, many countries. If you had completed the ceremony, you would have been moved to an Apprentice House, where the girls learn from each other and have 'pretend masters.' It involves a lot of role play, rigorous exercise, and strict nutrition. The days there are extremely busy because you must learn the fine art of silent, unquestioning obedience. It is there that you perfect the skills needed to stop thinking of anything other than your master and his anticipated needs. You are then put up for sale to the highest bidder."

"What happens if no one buys you?" Sadie questioned aloud, trying to process how her life might have played out differently if she had exhibited self-control back in Asheville.

"You would have no problems finding a home. They would have made an easy three million off of you in a couple of hours. But, if you are on the market for longer than a week then you will be sent to a Recycling House, much like the one you are in now. The Recycling Houses are the dumping grounds for the Academy and, depending on the severity of your discretion or disability, the House you are transferred to could be structured very similarly to the Academy or could be little more than a brothel or prison." Lydia could see the dread on her patient's face as she leaned in to apply the cherry-red lipstick to her full, rounded lips. "You got lucky, Sadie. This place is the Taj Mahal of Recycling Houses. As long as you are quiet and obedient, you shouldn't have any trouble. Occasionally, I see some the girls pretty badly bruised by the clients, but bruises heal."

"So, how much will be made from selling me now?" Sadie wondered. She still wasn't sure what her work would be here. If this was a place of remediation, she may still have a chance.

"You are not for sale to any Master now. They will probably sell you by the hour; usually the going rate is a grand per hour for someone as attractive as you. Ordinarily, the clients are finished well before that hour ends, but the charge still applies. Knowing this, sometimes they will ask you to dance or engage in foreplay to take up part of that time so they don't lose money," she replied in a matter-of-fact tone.

"So, I am just a hooker now?" she questioned with obvious distaste at the idea.

"I guess you could say that, but they won't. They will refer to you simply as a product. They take care of their inventory, that's why I am here. I ensure that you stay healthy, clean, and attractive enough to generate a generous profit margin.

"There are other people you need to be familiar with, too. The Brethren are our immediate supervisors and almost all of them have some military experience in their birth country. They keep inventory, make assignments, and carry out orders and punishments from the Keeper of the House. The Keepers run the House to which they are assigned and must always be shown the utmost respect. They decide whether you live or die. Above them are the Generals, sometimes referred to as Directors. These are the ones that work between the Houses, find and retrieve new girls, and manage the Houses in their district. It is a job with a lot of responsibility because they must ensure that all Houses remain profitable, clean, and follow rules while continuing other duties such as negotiations between the Academy and the Clients, marketing, and recruitment. Most of them are Masters themselves, so they understand the needs of the clients. The General for our district is Kendrick, my husband."

"How did you end up marrying Kendrick?" she asked sheepishly, hoping this wasn't prying too much. She remembered that name from the airport. The reality of that day hit her like a punch to her gut. Feeling as though she might faint from the impact, she steadied herself against the cot.

Dr. Scavway reached into another cabinet to retrieve a black, silk robe. She turned then to the sink and began filling the aluminum bucket with soapy water. Dropping the washcloths in, she gave her attention back to Sadie. "Kendrick purchased me from my father. My father is a minister of the Central Government of India, with the primary responsibility of assisting the Parliament. He met Kendrick while working on a project in the Civil Service department. Kendrick was there doing recruitment for the Academy and that's when he saw me. I was purchased and brought to the states immediately." Sadie took note of the sadness in her eyes. She understood all too well the pain of losing a mother and hating a father.

"The only man above Kendrick is our Dean. His name is Ray. He is the Lord of the operation and can be quite severe at times. Usually, however, he is very nice as long as everyone is doing exactly as they should. One thing these men all have in common, Sadie, is they love money. They are business-minded and profits are all they care about."

"Then how is it that you expect me to shut them down? There are so many of them and if I don't make a profit they will kill me, right?" Sadie was becoming more disheartened by the second and her focus was spiraling down the drain with information overload. She had just been brought back to life less than two days ago and her will was lost among the sea of names and ranks she had been appointed to overthrow.

"Well, yes, but you don't need to worry about that. You will turn a profit. Don't even think about going to the police. Most of them work for Ray so they won't help you. At least half of the physicians do, too, and the minute they see your tattoo, you are as good as dead. You are going to have to be smarter than that. Remember, they are still just men. As cunning and strong as they are, every man has one weakness that turns his brains to mush and drops his defenses with the drop of his pants- sex. They can't say no to a pussy that's wet and ready. It is the only time you will find them weak. Do you follow what I am telling you?" Dr. Lydia Scavway smiled at her masterpiece with adoring expectation.

"Yes, I think I do," Sadie said after a long pause. *So what? I'm supposed to sex them to death? That would likely kill me first,* Sadie thought sarcastically.

"Ok, we have two minutes. Slip this on." Lydia slid the silky robe over Sadie's narrow shoulders. It draped gracefully over her breasts and reached just above mid-thigh. "You look seductively tasty, my dear," she said approvingly, admiring the finished product. "Just remember what I told you- be silent, be strong, and be smart."

Just then the door flew open and Lydia immediately fell to her knees, her head bowed, and her eyes downcast. Sadie silently wondered if she should do the same. She started to kneel when a firm hand held her in place. She cast her eyes to the floor, desperately trying to figure what to do next.

"You may kiss me if you wish, Lydia," the man said in a smooth, southern accent. *This must be Kendrick,* Sadie figured although she hadn't yet mustered the nerve to look at him. *Is he the one Lydia was referring to when she promised I would be in good hands?*

Lydia leaned forward and kissed the top of his slick, polished boot. "Thank you, Master," she said softly, rising to the traditional pose Sadie had learned at the Academy. Her body poised gracefully facing Kendrick, her hands were folded in front of her, and her eyes cast to the floor. Sadie was surprised by the affectionate way Kendrick looked upon his wife. He gently weaved his fingers through her silken curls, smiling with honest admiration for her.

"I am going to take her now. You have done a beautiful job, as always, my precious pet. I will be back just as soon as we are done. I have missed you," he spoke to her calmly and sweetly as his right hand moved along her curves concealed by her lab coat. Lydia looked up to meet his lustful gaze through black lashes. She offered a smile to her Master in acknowledgement of his promise, and stepped aside gracefully.

Kendrick gripped Sadie's arm loosely and ushered her out, directing her down the hall with easy pressure on her back. She walked lightly, focusing the impact of her weight on her toes so as to keep her steps quiet. The length of the hallway, she judged, was roughly twenty feet. Plush violet carpeting stretched its entire length and complimented the antique white walls nicely. Brass sconces with crystal globes provided brilliant LED lighting, drawing attention to the elegant, timeless art decorating the walls. She noted the collection included some favorites of her own such as Ophelia-Mellias, The Baths of Caracalla, and Cave of the Storm Nymphs. Victorian art had suffered a terrible reputation in her mind as primarily being a list of boring, aristocratic portraits until she had found these paintings online. She smiled slightly, remembering Cuyler's excitement when he finally found some Victorian art to share with her. She never considered herself a master of arts or literature, but recognizing these paintings made her feel more confident here.

At the end of the hall, boasting within a ten by ten canvas framed in heavy brass was a striking piece she did not recognize. It was of a nude woman straddling a white stallion. While the woman was completely nude, her right arm had been drawn folded over her breasts and her body angled so that part of her body remained a secret to the hungry observer. The white stallion was elaborately decorated in an elegant red and gold turnout blanket that flowed from the animal's shoulders to train the ground below them. About its head was a matching halter with golden leads loosely resting in the left hand of its rider. She sat solemnly perched upon a richly brown leather saddle, her melancholy nakedly displayed for the wealth of gloating spectators.

They stopped their trot in front of an inordinate mahogany door with scroll detailing intricately carved throughout its surface. It stood open to the hallway, inviting its guests into a room much like the office they had just left behind only instead of being wall-to-wall white, this room was decorated in warm shades of apricot and sage. The walls were lined with metal cabinets and black granite counters. In the center of the room, affixed atop slate gray tile flooring, were a white cot covered in plastic and a short black stool. Sadie was directed by Kendrick to lie down on the cot, and she did so without hesitation. *Be quiet and obedient,* she told herself as she positioned her body supine against the sticky plastic.

Kendrick whistled to gain the attention of the Brethren who, from the thud of his heavy steps, Sadie guessed must be at least two hundred pounds. She stole a quick glance at him as he struggled to situate his large legs and buttocks on the creaking stool.

"Left arm," he grouched at her. She laid out her left arm, palm-side up, into his gruff hands. He reached for the equipment behind him and pulled out a tattoo gun. "Be still," he grunted and pushed the needle into her inner wrist.

Be silent, be strong, be smart. Be silent, be strong, be smart. She kept repeating to herself. Since her addiction, she was unrealistically afraid of needles. Although sure they would love to see her overreact, giving them an excuse to exercise their cruelty, she remained determined not to lose control. *Be silent, be strong, be smart.* She closed her eyes and chanted silently to herself.

In a manner of minutes, he released her arm and was done. With her left wrist held securely in her right hand, she peered down at the fresh ink and red, swollen skin. The irritation was a result of the dull needle he used inside his rudimentary equipment. Still, clearly could be seen three numbers: 4-4-9. She wondered what the numbers meant, and guessed they were used similarly to those tattooed on Jewish captives in prison camps. Her name would be made obsolete by use of the number, stripping the remainder of her identity in just a few short strokes of a needle.

Kendrick pushed his dark blonde hair out of his eyes and pulled her by the top of her arm to stand. The two exchanged a simple nod, indicating that part of the process was complete. They made a quiet exit back into the hallway and turned the corner.

Sadie found herself standing before a set of French doors, complete with white lace panels and brass scroll knobs. He opened the door and gave her a gentle shove inside. Sadie was surprised at how gentle he was being with her. He had not offered to hit her, shove her down, or even raise his voice. His congeniality could only be due to the request made by his lovely wife. She couldn't help thinking he had true feelings for her, in his own way.

Another man greeted Kendrick warmly as they walked into the carpeted room. This room was very large and set up like a sanctuary, with a high alter and vaulted ceilings. Stained glass windows stretched well over ten feet high and showcased hues of sapphire blue, emerald green and ruby red. She realized these were the same windows that had caught her attention when she first arrived that bitterly cold night. The sun shone translucently through their shades, providing a solemn ambient light that stretched across the violet plush carpet, until it bowed humbly at the raised alter at the head of the room. A mahogany-stained podium stood proudly front and center and showcased a Celtic cross deeply inlaid into its anterior facing. *Could it be possible they have church in here?* She wondered skeptically.

She stood behind the two laughing men, shamelessly naked before the alter, with nothing except the black silk robe draped over her shoulders. Nudity had become a most natural existence in recent months, to the point that she barely even noticed it, even when standing before God. Their conversation faded at last and she was redirected to a short, plump photographer busy fixing the set with various props, drapes, and costumes.

"I want you over here, doll," he bubbled through his fat cheeks. He blinked continuously, either in response to the stinging sweat as it beaded into them or, perhaps, it was just a nervous habit. Sadie couldn't be sure, but she hoped to God she wouldn't have to begin her first day touching his clammy, malodorous body. The brown sweat stains beneath his pits soiled down to his large, round belly that always seemed to be getting in the way of his short, stubby arms.

She did as she was told and stood by the black, velvet rug stretched over the floor. He raced over to her, fluffing her hair and pinching her cheeks with his wet, clubby fingers. There were white crystals stuck to his palms, she noticed, that kept getting stuck to her single strands of her dark locks and pulled at them painfully. *Is that glaze all over him? That fat bastard has been in here eating donuts over naked, miserable captives like it's just another day at the office. Where does the Academy find these assholes? I never realized moral depravity was such a commonplace quality.*

"Just, uh, kneel down on the rug and look sexy," he said, spitting a piece of soggy donut on her upper lip that he had been storing in his cheek. Thanks to the fresh lipstick, it stayed in place. Sadie tried to control her face so as not to insult him. "Sorry," he blushed, and wiped it away with his sweat rag. She thought of his offensive-smelling sweat transferring from his brown, crusty rag onto her mouth and swallowed hard to keep from vomiting.

"Jesus, Darrell, you have to tell them exactly how to pose," Kendrick barked, sounding quite annoyed at the dumpy photographer. "We've been over this, they are just women. They don't know how to do anything until you train them." He took fast, managerial steps toward the awkward pair, now both kneeling on the rug.

Kendrick grabbed Sadie's hands and roughly positioned them, one on each thigh, pulling apart the fingers. He then reached between her legs and pushed them apart until her labia were clearly exposed and strained apart from the stretching of her legs. Taking a few more quick steps, the Director stood behind her now. She felt his large fingers tangle in her hair as he gave her head a solid yank, extending her long, graceful neck and pushing her breasts forward at the same time.

"Now snap the picture," he commanded.

Darrell scrambled onto his feet as quickly as his clumsy nubs would allow him, and scurried to face Sadie with the camera. The flash snapped into her eyes several times before Kendrick held up his hand, signaling for the dim-witted Darrell to stop. Her arms were then held above her head, shackled to an iron bar propped on church hymns to hover about two feet over her. This time he tilted her head so that her chin rested on her left clavicle and her left ear lay easily against her suspended arm. As before, the flashes came in a quick series of at least ten, before her limbs were rearranged again.

Through the streaming of position changes and flashing lights, Sadie's mind drifted to an outer darkness, translucently flickering in and out, until she became as a puppet on strings. Bending this way and turning back again, all movements were simply that- a body in motion without conscious thought or reckless longing for anything different. In some of the flickering, her mind grew heavy with desire to be home, safe with Cuyler in their musky one bedroom apartment. But it is alarming how much a single wish can weigh, its dreams dispelled within the mind of its helpless host. Its scaly fingers encroach upon the heart, penetrating every fiber until the body aches continuously for it, all the while knowing such yearning is in vain.

Sadie's inundated mind yearned solely for her freedom. As the flickering faded and eventually ran out, a slate of gray veiled across her eyes so that she now saw only its flatness before her.

All depth, color, beauty and horror dissolved into the even gray; the flashing of the fat man's camera no longer burning her retina. The veil then stitched its way into her ears. Dull insults, harsh tones, and sharp commands that had been a source of her melancholy disposition became no match for the evolving aegis, which made all sounds a blended muffle. Turning its direction further inward, her weighted wish still pressed its helplessness upon her determined to keep her within its clutches. Yet the veil was stronger than any unattainable thing, such as a wish, and curtained her mind in its bland protection. With the claws of her wish removed from her heart, the coolness of the cloak extinguished the burning beneath.

Gone were the feelings of despair and pain, humiliation, and confusion. In its stead, Sadie found the wasteful bleeding of such emotions had slowed beneath the chill, keeping time now only with the pendulum of her gray transcendence. She smiled slightly at the stone that had replaced her heart and, looking up into the camera's focused lenses, Sadie granted leave to her sequestered soul. The last of all that gave her life left her to bask in the slate veil of gray. Unforgiven is the one that abandons the sun to welcome the night, who finds strength in banding demons, falling with dark angels, and abating what is right.

10

"Detective David Burke,

"I am leaving Lexington. I have been here for two weeks and searched every bar and warehouse I could find. There is nothing here but the usual dollar-store hooker. I don't want to give up on finding her because I still believe her to be alive. The problem is where would I even look within one city? Is there a city I have missed? I have been to Louisville, Lexington, and Berea since February. Before that, I was in Virginia combing through every street between Abington and Roanoke. All of which have been a disappointment.

"She haunts me in my sleep. I dream of her for hours just to wake and reach for an empty place beside me in another dingy hotel. I see her at every street corner, in every store. I feel like I am losing my mind, or maybe it was gone the day she disappeared. I can't tell if it is hunger, fatigue, or grief that affects me most. It's like being caught in some damn illusion that doesn't stop, no matter how much I drink.

"Two nights ago I was casing a bar downtown. I stared at this girl with long dark hair who stood with her back to me. She was talking to a man outside, and it looked as though they might be in an argument. I couldn't make out what they were saying, and I didn't care. All I saw was that long dark hair and convinced myself it was my Sadie. With leaps and bounds of hope I ran to her from behind and grabbed her, all the while yelling, "Sadie, it's me. I found you. I found you."

"Somehow, even when the girl was fighting against me, I still could not accept that I had made a mistake. All I could believe was this girl was my sweet love and we were together at last. Well, I was euphoric until her boyfriend punched me square in the left eye. And still, all I could utter was her name over and over. It's all I had left.

"When he hit me I realized something. It is possible that her name may be all I will ever have. Most days the gun beneath my seat looks more appealing than waking one more day without her. Is this all just a futile mission? Am I fervently searching for a warm and caring woman, so filled with life and compassion, only to eventually find death has already taken her?

"Crazy questions go through my mind all the time. But the one thing I can never question, never doubt, is... Her breath is my breath, her heartbeat my own. Her existence is the mainstay of mine. So I must know that even as I breathe, so does she. We did not find each other by chance; it was fate. I have always known she and I were joined by something stronger than us. It is that same unnamable force that allows me to see her, however dark the void that stares back at me, and to feel her ivory skin against my palms even though it is only the air that lies there now.

"Have you ever experienced that point of resting that isn't really sleeping, yet it isn't awake either? It is those short moments before your conscious mind slips away completely, yielding its authority to the subtle subconscious. This is when I see her, truly see her. During this time she is not a vivid hallucination adorned by what I remember; I can see her as she is now. I see the pain and anger behind her blackened eyes. She looks alone and frightened- her body thin and frail. I can hear her whisper to me, too. She wants so much to tell me where she is, but all I can hear are whispers. There are no syllables, only beautiful notes strung together by the quivering of her lips.

"I am sure by now you are convinced I have gone completely insane. Being on the road for months has not been easy, by any account. Staying in city after city with no place to call home takes its toll- that goes without saying. I have been trying to make money and resources last out as long as possible, but I am down to my last fifty bucks. Actually, I am sitting here staring at it on the night stand beside me. Ha! Good thing I sold the car already. I wouldn't be able to keep gas in it anyway. I guess it's safe to say I am going to have to find some work somewhere if I am going to keep this search going.

"I have met some great people out here, but none that I trust like you. I was hoping I could stay with you next week, just for a few days. I could really use the rest and maybe I could look for some per diem work while I am there. I hate to ask anything of you after all you have done for me. You have supplied my leads, taught me all you know, and even wired me money on two occasions. I can't tell you how grateful I am to you. I mean that as sincerely as any man could to another.

"There is one other reason I would like to come back. Sadie's birthday is only a few days away, March 17th. I don't think I can face that day alone. I am using the last of my money to buy a bus ticket down. According to the schedule, I will be there March 16th. I will call you from a pay phone when I get in town. I am mailing this letter through overnight express, hoping it will get to you before I do so my call is not a complete surprise. I can only hope it finds you well.

Thanks again,
Cuyler"

David laid the letter down on his desk and stared at the photo of Sadie. She looked so perfectly posed upon her knees, her dark eyes cast upward behind her hair, as though she were kneeling only to him. Kendrick was truly a genius with a camera and always had been. Still, he could tell by the looks of this girl that he hadn't needed any special angle or lighting. Cuyler was right; this young woman was uniquely crafted. She was flawless in her physique, gorgeous beyond comparison.

"Mr. Burke," the raspy voice of the office nurse interrupted his thoughts. "You have a phone call, line one. Says he's some photographer from New York."

"Thank you, Norma. Send it through." God, how he hated that woman and her tacky red lipstick, which always seemed to be trapped in the wrinkles around her lips, spreading across her face as she formed each drawn-out syllable.

He let the phone ring a couple times before picking up the phone. "Detective Burke here."

"Well, old friend, hello! I must say I was delighted when I heard from you. I do hope all is well and there are no hard feelings between us," the familiar voice came through the receiver.

"No hard feelings. I understand you had to protect your investments. Although, I have to tell you, I miss being in business with you," David replied in his most convincing voice. He could just imagine how he was going to get even with them all, and he didn't care in what order. Kendrick would make a great first for him.

"Did you get the package I sent you?" Kendrick asked casually.

"Yes, actually I was just looking at it. I like what I see. When can we meet to discuss this further? I would like to see the goods you have in stock." David almost had him. Just a few minutes more and he would have a location.

"Well, I have to warn you. All I have now is refurbished goods, which is why you will have the opportunity to try it out before you buy it. I will be having a showcase tonight at a private residence near you, if you are interested in stopping by." Kendrick's smooth, southern accent felt like coming home. He was part of the original crew that initiated the first academy. His unique charm was undeniable and had won them hundreds of girls with minimal effort.

"That sounds wonderful. I am free tonight. Will you be in attendance?" David asked with more anxious energy than he had intended.

"I am in New York for the next two weeks or more. We had some unfinished business and a few items we needed to bring down to one of our other stores. The economy has been tough on everyone and we have had to relocate to more remote locations. I forwarded the address and details to your cell. You will be our guest of honor tonight, sir. I hope you like what we have to offer." Kendrick's voice reflected his broad smile.

"Perfect, I got it. Until next time then," David said in his most reassuring tone. He heard the click come through the receiver, signifying the call was disconnected. David couldn't shake the disappointment of Kendrick's absence. That changed everything. He could still case the house tonight; make an appearance to ensure his place among them, and perhaps even look for young Sadie.

"Norma, I am finishing up here and heading home. If you need me, you know how to find me," he shouted through the door she'd left ajar. He gathered his papers off his desk as he impatiently waited for her reply.

Picking up Sadie's photo once again, he paused and gently tapped his finger along the contours of her face. He hated the arousal she gave him, hated himself for wanting her. This woman belonged to Cuyler, a man who would risk his health, his life, and trudge through every dingy whore house to find her. *She belongs to Cuyler, not me, because I don't deserve her. I could never deserve a girl like Sadie.* He gingerly placed her inside the folds of Cuyler's letter and slipped them both into the envelope with a heavy sigh.

Norma still hadn't acknowledged his departure as he closed the door behind him and walked hastily to his Explorer parked at the end of the lot. Even with the short walk, the March wind felt like it was cutting through him. He had always hated winter- the wind, snow, and cold rain. All of it cut him to the bone. Now that he was always alone, winter was somehow colder, and darker, than it had ever been.

With spring just around the corner, the temperatures had warmed only slightly. According to the locals cold rain and wind would be the norm until around mid-May. He could not tell if it was the weather that caused the ever-present chill in his heart or if it was prolonged guilt and disappointment that fostered his depression.

The drive home was short and mechanical, just as everything he did in his daily life. He came home, hung the keys by the door, slipped off his shoes, locked the door behind him, and headed for the shower. It was always the same routine, day in and day out. Always the routine was accomplished in silence, with not even a mouse or a roach with who he could converse. The dull ramblings of the local news helped to overcome some of the silence, but he still longed so much for someone with whom he could be close. It was embarrassing for a man his age to have these feelings. *Stop being a pussy. What woman would want someone with your past anyway?* He was a monster after all.

As he undressed and stepped into the water, his thoughts drifted through memories as they often did. Sometimes he would remember his wife, what it was like when they loved each other, before the fighting and the anger. She always surprised him with her love in the most gentle of ways- in a note left by the bed or delicately running her fingers through his hair in the morning to wake him. He could remember what it was like to hold her, and how she fit so perfectly in his arms after a long day of training. Her smile would never let him give up on anything. The sparkle in her eyes let him know how much she admired him.

He wasn't sure at what point he had lost all of that admiration. He couldn't remember now what had made him so angry all the time or why he had started hitting her. Somehow, after the first hit, he was simply addicted to the adrenaline and the power. He was ashamed of it every time and felt genuine remorse for his actions, but he couldn't stop even when he knew it was wrong. She was right to leave him. He deserved this loneliness.

And then the memories of the girls would come rushing in like an old friend, warming his body all over with a sudden surge of excitement. Damn, they were so beautiful and the authority and power he felt was such a rush. Some sick part of him loved the recycling houses, like the one he would be attending tonight, because he didn't have to be so careful with them. The graduates of the academy must be handled with care so they remain unmarked for the higher bidders. The recycled girls, on the other hand, could be used however he felt. He hated to admit it, but it still gave him a chubby to remember the looks on their faces when he would corner a pretty one and then get off inside her.

No, you sick bastard. Shut up. Get out of my head. I have changed. I am not that man anymore. God, I am praying for forgiveness. I am praying that you take my demons away. God, I am weak and sick. Please, give me strength. I don't have to feel this way. Please, take my desires from me so that I may focus on saving Sadie. Cuyler deserves to be with her. They deserve a chance, God.

The shame and disgust he felt made him almost sure God couldn't hear him. He had been to church many times since moving here and had prayed faithfully every night. He asked for forgiveness, for justice, for peace. He begged God to give him some sign that his prayers were heard and not just bouncing off the ceiling. He hadn't seen so much as a rainbow for reassurance. Maybe there was just no hope for someone like him. Perhaps his soul really was damned for all he had done and his name permanently struck through in the book at Michael's Gate.

David paced nervously in front of his closet as he dressed. His strides got longer and more intense as he contemplated what he was about to do. "I am going to just go there and look for Sadie. That's all my mission is tonight. That's it, David. Don't touch the girls; don't even end up alone with one. Just look for Sadie." He pulled her picture out of his front pocket and took a deep breath, "Damn, why does she have to be so beautiful? Maybe just one girl wouldn't hurt. They need to trust me again, after all, and what better way to show them I'm still one of them?"

He slouched down on the bed and buried his head in frustration. What was he supposed to do with all that temptation right in front of him? He couldn't stay completely away from the women there or his cover would be blown. But what if the women for him were like alcohol for an alcoholic? If he had one, he might turn into the man he had left in New York.

Straightening his jacket, he walked casually to the mirror. He had chosen a lavender button-up with a black suit, no tie. He had to admit, he looked pretty damn good. "Ok, David," he said to his reflection, "Here's the deal. You don't have to hurt anyone. Your mission tonight is to look for Sadie and to find out where all the assholes are hiding that fucked you over. That's it. But, let's be honest. You look fucking amazing tonight. If you happen to notice a girl that looks hungry for it, well, it's only fair to give her a little taste." David flashed a grin at himself as he grabbed his keys and wallet, "It's a party, David, loosen up."

The GPS was guiding him farther and farther away from town and as he made a left onto Flat Springs Rd, he reached for the roach in the center console of his SUV. It was the last of some hash he had confiscated from a kid on a skateboard in exchange for his freedom. He had saved it for a night like this one, with his nerves almost getting the best of him in spite of his pep talk in front of the mirror. He took a deep breath and held it through three switchback turns before exhaling.

His eyes were still a bit hazed over when the GPS announced his arrival to his preprogrammed destination. "I guess this is it, then," he said to himself. He stepped out and took a look around. It was the perfect location, remote and surrounded entirely by dense forest. The house was modest and discrete, two levels, and enclosed by a chain-linked fence. He could hear the crowd inside laughing over the dance beats leaking through the open windows.

"David fucking Burke! Been too long, old friend," a familiar voice shouted to him from the open front door. "I've been waiting for you. Come in!"

David stared at him, stunned. If he were not directly addressing him, he might not have actually recognized this man. He had grown out his beard and traded his slicked-back hair in for a much shorter buzz cut. He must have gained at least twenty pounds around his waist line, maybe more. He stepped inside, still unable to actually speak and trying to wipe the guilty expression off his face before it was noticed.

"Hey, brother, I'm really sorry about leaving New York like that. It was nothing personal you understand, just business." He stretched his hand out to David the same way he had when they had first met.

"Yeah, no, I understand. Hell, I would have done the same thing. You did leave me in a mess though. But, hey, let's forget it. It's good to be back." David tried to sound casual and gave his old partner a firm handshake.

"Let me make it up to you then. You have your pick tonight, on the house. Will that help to settle things up between us?" he asked expectantly.

"It's a start," David said with as a smile swept across his face. What luck that he should be greeted by none other than the one man he hoped to track down- Ray. "I am so glad I ran into you. We have so much to discuss." David gave him a reassuring wink.

"Ah, tonight is about pleasure and making amends my friend. We will discuss business, yes, but not tonight. Tonight you are my guest of honor and my personal mission is to find you pleasure." Ray put a hot hand against his back and motioned toward a dimly lit hallway in the rear of the house.

The two of them walked confidently through the crowd of smiling faces. Men engaged women in pleasant conversation as they encouraged them to keep dancing and throwing back the drinks. Most of these women were brought here believing they were attending a house party, completely unaware they would wake up tomorrow morning chained in someone's basement, naked and prepped for admission into the Rose Academy. They had been hand-chosen for their spirit, beauty and easy gullibility. The reality was, however, that at least two-thirds of them wouldn't make it past the initial Keeper and would either be sold back into a recycling house or killed in a fit of anger. These flinty types didn't usually work out very well in the program, and Ray didn't ordinarily use them unless Kendrick had to be away for extended periods of time. Judging from the volume of girls here tonight, numbers must be very low lately. That could not be good news for Sadie.

They finally made it back into the master suite. "I picked a few I thought you might like. They have been anxiously waiting for you," Ray said with a grin. He turned to face them, "and I know they are so excited that you are here. They even told me they want to do whatever it takes to make you happy. Right ladies?"

David watched as the drones nodded their heads. He looked at them with their broken spirits and could almost feel the pain radiating from their bodies into his. He wondered how he had ever been blind to their humanity before this moment.

He walked in front of them with authority, pretending to make his selection. Each girl looked so young; two of them could not have been older than fifteen. Their bodies were thin and undernourished, and he noticed small, round scars on several of them. How long had they been here? As he reached the end of the line-up, a tall and slender woman whose hair fell in dark waves atop her bare breasts caught his eye. Her shoulders trembled slightly when she inhaled and as he got closer he could see a tear stain the bruise upon her cheek. From the waist down she was dressed in a catholic school uniform, complete with thigh-high stockings and black Mary-Jane dress shoes. Her weight shifted slightly from one long leg to the other.

"This is the one," David said assertively. He grabbed her by the arm as if to claim her as his own. He could feel his guts turning around inside him. *Keep in character, you pussy.* David hardened his face and gave a sneaky grin. "Get those other bitches out of here. We might be a while."

Ray let out a cackle and motioned for the other girls to follow him. They shuffled silently out of the room. "Enjoy that, brother. I had a feeling you'd like that one. Fuck her till you feel better and just leave her there. We will clean her up," he said casually, and closed the door behind him.

David rushed over to lock the door. The girl looked up at him with wide and terrified eyes. He could see she wanted to be anywhere but here, that she would welcome death over this life if only she had a way.

Beneath her sunken and hollow eyes were dark testaments of food and sleep deprivation. Her left cheek hosted a fresh, lavender bruise just above a cut at the corner of her lip that was new and bleeding slightly. Her tiny features were shaking and frail, as if they might break under the weight of her misery and depression. Her breasts, though still round with youth, bore scars of bite marks and cigarette burns. She had been nothing more than their play thing for quite a while. With this much scarring, it would only be a short time before they retired her to the grave of her choosing. The coloring of the scars told him this girl could not be Sadie, she had been here at least a year and Sadie had only been missing for roughly four months.

"What's your name?" David asked in a hushed, soothing tone.

"My name is whatever you call me, my Lord," the girl replied softly. Again, she shifted her weight, wincing slightly at the motion.

"Listen, you don't have to do that. I'm not going to touch you, or hurt you. I really just want to talk tonight." He paused and took a step toward her, gently placing his hands on her trembling shoulders. Her eyes dropped to the floor and her muscles tensed at his touch. "What's your name?"

"Ember, sir," she replied in a hushed tone.

"Well, Ember, you look as though those shoes are killing your feet. Please, sit beside me on the bed. How long have you been standing there?" He motioned toward the mattress that rested on the floor, adorned with a burgundy floral-printed comforter.

She sat down carefully, gracefully, beside him. "He brought me into this room just after breakfast this morning. I was to stand there until you arrived, sir. It was around nine, I think."

"That was over twelve hours ago. You must be exhausted. Here, allow me." David reached down to take off her shoes and lifted her feet onto the mattress. Ember moved easily into a lying position and waited silently for his next request. Her arms were held close to her chest, covering her nipples. He couldn't bare this humiliation for her and cloaked his jacket over her. "It's all I have. I hope it is warm enough."

She looked confused and relieved by his kindness, unsure as to where it came from and where it was going. "Thank you, sir. It is perfect."

"Tell me, Ember, how old are you?" he asked as he laid down next to her, propping his head on his wrist so he could see her.

"I am 19, sir." Ember closed her eyes as silent tears again highlighted the lavender on her cheeks.

"I know this is not what you are used to. I have been to these places before. All I want from you right now is to hear your story. I mean, how did you get here? It's ok to tell me because I do not work for Ray anymore." He reached to her and gently moved a dark curl out of her eyes. They were the color of a vibrant coral shore struck with lightening. It was the first time he could see them clearly and looking into them now was like looking into the gates of heaven and realizing you are in hell.

"Yes sir, as you wish." Ember sighed shakily and looked up at him. The fountain of youth could be discovered in her lips as she spoke. "I am from New York. I was supposed to go to NYU in the fall of last year. I was going to be music major. I loved to sing and could play five instruments. I had a full scholarship." She smiled only slightly as she reached into a recent past that seemed quite distant. "My mother is a singer on Broadway and my father is a successful writer. I had the world at my feet and so much to look forward to. All I wanted was to follow in their footsteps. I needed some photographs taken for my scholarship. That is where I met Kendrick." Her voice became broken and again the silence fell heavily between them.

"I am sorry this happened to you. How long has it been since you left the Academy?" David asked in part because he wanted to know more about her, but mostly because he wanted to know he had nothing to do with her demise.

"I was in the Academy for three months before I became pregnant by a brother of my Keeper. He told the Keeper I seduced him. I was removed as soon as I started to show and placed in a warehouse on the outskirts of the city." She began to cry as she wrapped her arms across her stomach. She took a deep breath and wiped her cheeks. Immediately they were wet again with fresh tears. "I was laid on a cold table, my arms and legs strapped to the sides of it. The same brother then put something inside me that made the contractions begin. I only pushed a few times before delivering. I suppose he wasn't old enough to survive, and that is his blessing. He threw him into the trash can and I was moved again. I was so tired and the room was spinning. I passed out. When I woke up, I was in the back of a van headed south. I have been in and out of that van ever since."

David found himself at a loss for words. He had not seen the cruelty she described practiced. How could it be real? How could Ray be so heartless? His mind was racing with at least a thousand more questions but all he could manage was to stare into her burning eyes with his mouth gaping, unable to produce even a breath, let alone a form a question.

"Sir, may I ask you something?" she asked in a hushed tone.

"Yes," he managed.

"Why are you here if you do not work for Ray and you do not wish to be pleasured?" Ember dropped her gaze and her face flushed with embarrassment.

"I am looking for someone. She is a friend of a friend. Her name is Sadie and I have her picture in the coat pocket there. I was hoping you might know her." David reached over her into the pocket that held Sadie's picture. He handed it to her and watched as her fingertips tapped along the edges of a lost and soulless Sadie, so naked and broken her pain could be felt even through the printed image.

"I cannot say. Please, forgive me. It is forbidden to discuss this with you." Her trembling began again, this time from fear of reprisal at her disobedience. He watched her body tensely draw into itself, preparing itself for his anger.

"I will do anything for you if you help me. I only want to save her from what you are going through now. Please, Ember, tell me where she is and I will take you out of here, too. We will leave tonight." He realized he was begging but he couldn't care less anymore. The longer he stayed in that small room, atop filthy mattresses with this beautiful woman, the more he yearned desperately to end her misery and Sadie's. Damn the revenge, Ray, and Kendrick. Damn them all straight to Hell. He just wanted to make this right, beginning with this girl tonight.

"That's really kind of you, sir. I don't want to leave anymore. It's too late for me. Look at me. I am mutilated for their amusement. I will never be the woman I always wanted to be. The writer, the singer, the talent- it's all gone from me now. But Sadie, she's sweet. She's a fighter, too. Did you know that about her? She still has some spirit left in her. It's not too late for her. My soul was gone long before I even met her." Her voice trailed into another heavy silence. David couldn't understand how she could see herself as spiritless when, in those eyes of fire and ice, all he could see was fire.

"Ember, where is she? I need to know. I have to get to her before Ray does," David pleaded.

"Did you know they are planning to kill me tomorrow? This is my last night, my last assignment. Ray told me as much when he left me this morning. It will be my last service to him, to die at his hand. Do you know what it is like to be handed your exact time of death and feel like it is your duty to die exactly as you are told so that your captor may have one last pleasure out of you?" She stared penetratingly into him, both accusing him and reaching for him. He had never been more sure of what was right. It was as if the Heavens had opened and God Himself was shouting into his ear.

"No, I don't. Honestly, I hope I never do understand exactly what you feel. But more than that, I hope Sadie doesn't.

Tell me where she is and I will take care of you. You have my word." David held out his hand as a gesture of his word.

She nodded in agreement. "She is kept by the Fourth Keeper. That is where I last saw her. It is Ray's favorite house, the same house from which I was chosen. Those girls mostly entertain the elites of the Academy because of their unique beauty or skill. However untrainable they may have been, they still serve purpose to the Academy itself. It lies just outside Berea, South Carolina. I don't know the exact address, just that I could look out the window and see the reflection of the trees across the lake. That beautiful view used to save me from them. When I was taken from there, my soul remained floating upon the lake and dancing through reflections of those trees."

"Thank you. I will find her. And when I do, I will make sure she knows it was you who saved her life." David kissed her gently on the hand and ran his fingers through her dark tangles. His hand caressed her bruises as he climbed on top of her and straddled her. "If you are ready my beautiful girl, I will keep my end of the bargain." She nodded and smiled at him. His hands moved quickly to her throat and he wrapped them tightly around her tiny neck. As he began to apply pressure, he watched her eyes locked bravely into his. She did not struggle, panic, or cry. Contrarily, he found only peace in her.

Within his mind, thoughts were battling. The cheering banter of his body's celebratory invigoration was aroused by her powerlessness. Watching the life leave her at his command, relenting to the strength behind his muscular frame created a heightened euphoria that tingled through him in the most ex-hilarating way. He could feel it surging into his fingertips and rip the current through his heart, electrocuting his judgment and leaving the raw heat to petrify his good intentions. The feeling was desirable and consumptive, and it grew stronger with each convulsion of her body as it reacted to the crushing pressure over her airway. Her physical reaction only encouraged him to press harder until the resistance was finally broken with an audible snap beneath his palms.

As he removed his hands from her fragile, broken neck he could not stop staring into those amazing eyes. He had expected them to be dull and vacant, hollow somehow. Now as he gazed into them, knowing there was no life in her, it was odd to see them glowing brighter. Ember had caught ablaze and the fires of her freedom would never again be extinguished. The electricity left his body and chills ran atop his skin until it ached. *It was only to save Ember and Sadie,* he reasoned. *She wanted me to do it. She was going to die anyway. It is okay, David, you didn't do anything wrong.* He wanted to believe he had not just enjoyed himself, but the need for convincing disappeared when his eyes fell into his lap and the evidence of his pleasure was stained across the front of his gray slacks. Hanged before the jury, David was lost inside the noose. With all of him he wept. He wept for the singer, the writer, the lover, the dancer; for the hopeless, the stripped, the fearless, and the damned. It was for all these things, and for the life given at the hands of the lifeless. David wept.

11

Cuyler stepped off the bus and inhaled the cool, fresh breeze of the Appalachian Mountains. A perfect sixty degrees beneath a clear, bright morning sky. Under better circumstances, the weather would have been invigorating and motivating. Today it just clipped the edge off his exhaustion. Even so, he was glad to be back in Newland. There was a comforting appeal to being close to his friend again surrounded by familiarity.

He slid his last two quarters into the slots of the pay phone and waited for the dial tone. This had to be one of the last towns on earth that still had pay phones. It was moments like these, when no cell phone could be afforded and your greatest need is the security of accessibility that made him grateful some places were so resistant to change.

"David, this is Cuyler. I am in town. I realize I am earlier than expected so I am going to walk around town and try to find some work. I will catch up with you tonight." Cuyler returned the receiver to its rightful place and took a look around. Where could he go to find a quick few bucks? The constant growling in the pits of his stomach reminded him of his neglect. He felt almost nauseous from the hunger but didn't have two pennies to rub together, let alone enough for a meal.

The street to the left looked as promising as any other. He walked with brisk indifference at the stores he passed. Each one reminded him of those in Elizabethton- old, musky antique malls, one after another, with the occasional diner sprinkled in. His thoughts trailed back to better times, happier times, when Sadie walked by his side.

"Oh, Cuyler, look at this!" Sadie said in awe as she lifted a polished silver antique tea set from the table. "I love its character and charm. Look baby, it even has roses engraved along the front. I could be like one of those ladies with their polished beauty." The silver reflected its brilliance against her face but could not compare to the natural gleam in her eyes on that summer morning.

Cuyler had rolled his eyes and laughed. He had not absorbed her beauty the way he now wished he would have. He had not told her that her love for all things old and new created an aura around her that could not be expanded; that she could not be polished beyond the perfection she already embodied. But she didn't mind, she just laughed with him. "I love antiques," she said sweetly.

"Oh? And why is that?" he asked, holding fast the secret that he loved them just as much.

"Because," she smiled, "there is a sweet serenity in things remembered."

Cuyler wiped a tear from his eye. *Things remembered. Oh, Sadie, sweet Sadie, where is our serenity now?* He could not help but feel as though he had failed her. If David was right and the Roses stayed within two hundred miles, how was it that he had not found her? But, then again, who was he kidding? He was one man against a giant army. When has one stone ever caused a giant to stumble?

An orange and black sign in the window ahead caught his attention. As he got closer, he could make out the words that read "Help Wanted." Brushing the wrinkles smooth with his hands, he tried to stand tall and confident. He opened the door and took a seat at the counter.

"Hi there, handsome, what can I get ya?" the waitress greeted him between the rolling of her chewing gum through her teeth. She was the smallest woman he had ever seen up close, standing a proud five feet tall and barely one hundred pounds. The chopped layers of her fire-red hair fell with chaotic cheer into her emerald eyes and danced playfully against her fair complexion. Every feature was delicate and small, yet sharp and self-accentuated. *Like a pixie,* he thought.

"Just a job application, please," Cuyler said after clearing the rasp from his throat.

"How about a cup of coffee? You look like you could use one." It was amazing that her voice sounded as soft as he imagined a pixie's might. Cuyler nodded and she tapped off lightly on her toes toward the back. She was back in seconds balancing a steaming cup of coffee in one hand and an application floating lightly in the other. He could almost see the wings sprouting from her back. *I really have lost my mind completely*, he jabbed at himself.

"Don't take off with my pen, handsome. It's my favorite one," she winked at him as he took the pen from her child-sized hand. He forced a weak smile and nodded.

The application was very basic and only asked for general information. Still, what was he supposed to write in the line requesting his address? Drifter? Detective Burke's information would have to do for now. He turned the application over and signed the back page.

"Finished already? Let me see how you did, handsome," the waitress said with her hand held out as she smiled warmly at him.

He handed the application over as he asked, "Is there a manager I can speak with? I need a job badly."

"Well, handsome, you are in luck because I am she," she paused a moment and chuckled at the obvious shock stained upon his face. "My name is Serenity, proud owner and manager of The Fire's Keeper. We are a diner Monday through Friday, during the day, and become an acoustic coffee house on Friday and Saturday nights with live entertainment and a great vibe." She paused again, carefully assessing his reaction. He was sure she could see the fatigue wearing shamelessly on his face. His mind felt clouded, and she talked so fast. He didn't have time to react before she asked, "Do you have a name, handsome?"

"Cuyler Byrne," he announced, touching his chest in ownership. "I'm sorry, I guess I am just a little worn out from the bus ride down. It sounds like a great place."

"I like to think so, Cuyler Byrne. I only have one position open right now. Basically, your job would be to cook the food and wash dishes on your down time. Do you have any experience with a grill, Cuyler?" It was a strange conversation. She was saying words that meant business with an inflection that could easily be interpreted as playful and airy.

"No, I don't, but I am a fast learner and a hard worker. I can learn it if you give me a chance. Or start me washing dishes. Whatever you need me to do." He was all but on his knees. He had not expected to have an interview so soon and felt, however irrationally, that his entire life was hanging in the balance of her decision.

"Alright, Cuyler, here is the deal I will make you. Today you will work for your supper. It's just a trial run, sort of an audition, to see how you deal with the heat. I will feed you first, though. You look like you haven't eaten in days!" Serenity reached up to touch his arm and her fingertips slid down to his hand. She gave him a gentle squeeze before gesturing toward the empty chair beside him. "Please, have a seat. I will fix you a sandwich your taste buds will cry for!" She tapped off toward the kitchen.

Serenity. That was name of divine appointment if ever he had experienced it. It could not have been for not that he had met her. She had brought physicality to his thoughts and it was no coincidence. As broken as he was, he could not stop his eyes from following her as she danced and spun through the kitchen. She was an attractive woman who had a contagious spirit about her. As ashamed as he was to admit it, even to himself, his heart had warmed when she touched him. He had not been close to any woman in a long time. That innocent touch, which had lasted only seconds, had left him a bit jumpy.

He looked around as he sipped his coffee. It was fairly large for a downtown diner. A rounded wooden stage sat quaintly on the left by the main entrance. There would be just enough room on that stage for a guitar, a mic, and a warm body. Several tables with three to four chairs were gracing the spacious dining room, their oak stain a nice complement to the slate tile on which they rested. The walls were adorned with various artistic remnants of cultural diversity. They were subtly placed yet remarkably undeniable.

"Here you are, handsome," Serenity interrupted. "Tell me what you think. Pretty great, right?"

"Oh, wow," he choked out between bites. "Serenity, this is amazing."

"Thank you," she said with a theatrical bow. "Chomp, chomp, my dear. There's much to do!" she sang as she flinted away in her fairy fashion.

The rest of the day rushed by with a storm of dishes and dirty tables. The constant crowd, noisy chatter, and bustling of the staff was an invigorating rush for his body and a much needed rest to quiet his mind. Whenever his thoughts would begin to wonder into the hopelessness of his situation, and Sadie's, another order would come in or a table would clear and Cuyler would again find he was too busy to focus on anything other than the task at hand. Closing time came about quickly and, as the last party got up to leave, his spirit felt elated. He could not recall a time in his recent memory when he felt so productive, so useful, and so… happy.

"Cuyler Byrne, you are a gem. Here is your schedule. I am going to need you this Friday night. Be here at six so we can prep. It gets busy fast around here." Serenity handed him a folded piece of paper and pushed him toward the door. "Goodnight handsome. Good work today." She passed him a playful wink and locked the door behind them before skipping down the street.

The walk home was spirited and noisy with thoughts of his new job and the vibrantly sweet new boss that had come with it. There was something in her optimism and spirited energy that was so becoming. He couldn't stop replaying their brief conversations in his mind. She had referred to him as handsome throughout the shift in spite of his haggard appearance. *Handsome*. Of all the names she could have picked, it was *handsome*. And every so often she would find an excuse to touch his arm or bump into him. *Was she flirting with me? No, I must be losing my mind. Look at me, I am a mess.* Yet, she hadn't judged the holes in his shirt any more than she than she had the holes in his speech. He couldn't even begin to understand, let alone rationalize, why something inside him felt lighter the moment she spoke to him. It was like he suddenly felt everything was going to work out. He hadn't felt this way since that day in the airport when Sadie had disappeared.

Sadie. Oh, God, Sadie! Am I really such an asshole that I could just forget about Sadie? What the hell is wrong with me? I am daydreaming about some girl I just met while she is facing unimaginable fear. I'm so selfish.

Cuyler walked up the steps to David's apartment and gave a loud knock against the aluminum door. The temperature had fallen significantly with the sun and the cold breeze swept a chill up his spine. He knocked again, shivering at another cold gust of air.

"Cuyler, I see you made it alright. I was beginning to worry about you. Come in," David offered a wide smile and a friendly hand gestured toward the warmth of his living room. He was glad to see the fire already burning and entered quickly to share its heat.

"Thanks. It turned cold on us, huh?" Cuyler was never good at small talk. A comment about the weather and that was all he had to offer. He stood hunched toward the fire in silence.

"How did the search go? Find a job?" David asked with moderate interest as he fumbled through the cabinets. He came back in carrying two glasses of brown whiskey and handed one to Cuyler without so much as a glance in his direction.

"Yeah, at The Fire's Keeper just a couple of blocks away. I'm not sure how much it will pay, but it's something." Cuyler turned to face David. He was staring into the fire as though he might see through it completely. "You ok, Detective Burke?"

"It's just been a long week, that's all," he said as he reached to rub his neck. "I have made some interesting breaks in the Roses since we last spoke, and I think I know how we can get you back to your Sadie. It may take a while, though, and I will need you to trust me."

"What's going on? What have you found?" Cuyler's voice peaked with excitement. He leaned forward as if to urge a faster answer from his trusted counterpart.

"I have met with one of them and went to one of their houses. It was by invitation, so I knew it was safe, but Sadie wasn't there. I got some time alone with one of the girls there, and she knew her. She said she spent some time with her at a house in South Carolina." David's words were promising and yet he did not look the slightest bit pleased.

"Great! Let's go, then. I will grab my bag and we can go get her." Cuyler jumped for the door, but David didn't budge. He was still standing there, staring listlessly into the orange flame as it danced and popped; franticly trying to escape the pressure it created.

"It's not that simple, Cuyler. You don't just barge in on one of those houses. They are heavily guarded and, if we don't play this right, we will all be dead. We have to be smart about this, which is why I say you are going to have to trust me." His eyes were dark, almost hollow. His shoulders were slumped as though under a tremendous weight, such as the expression on his face testified of the solemnity of what he was about to say.

Cuyler braced himself against the stone mantle in preparation for the worst. "Ok," he managed, "tell me then. What do I have to do? How do I get Sadie home? I will do anything. Anything you tell me, I swear."

David released a heavy sigh and slouched into the chair beside him. He sat for several minutes, although it felt like hours, before he began. His eyes remained cast toward the floor as he sat with a bowed head and heavy heart. The image reminded Cuyler of an old and broken man whose joy lies in the grave of his soul mate. He cleared his throat and reached his hand across the whiskers on his chin. "Cuyler," he began quietly, "I am going to tell you a story. I need you first to not react, just listen. This is hard for me to say. I have never actually said it out loud before, so please just be patient. I am not who you think I am. I used to work for the Rose Academy."

Cuyler felt a rage that immediately set his skin on fire. Every nerve fiber wanted to throw David from the highest window, to watch him bleed slowly until the last breath was drawn in horror and agony, or something worse if he could imagine it. But, keeping true to his promise, he listened keenly and quietly. David told him of a sad and lonely man who had sold his soul for a bottle of Cognac and of an angel by the name of Eyelah who, at the hands of a slick business man, had persuaded his sell. He recalled, in startling detail, the nights he spent selecting the girls, and then training them, until he had become a full-fledged member of the highest ranks within the Academy. He then recounted a few moments of clarity when he realized the suffering he was causing them and, as disturbing as it may seem, his lack of empathy for their pain. He painted a picture of an addiction to money, sex, and power which ultimately led to his own demise.

"The day I was told I had been caught was probably the worst day of my life. All of the money I had made, the women I had gained, and the power were worthless to me at that moment. As I stared at the badge I had disgraced and the man that had been more of a father to me than anyone, with his crushing disappointment, I knew my life there was truly over. So, I did what any man would do, and got smashed on that same bottle of Cognac that had cost me so much more than I once thought it was valued." David looked at Cuyler to gauge his reaction and waited patiently for any response.

"What the fuck are you saying to me right now?" he blurted out with more intensity than he could control. "You are one of them? And you want me to trust you?" Cuyler was vibrating with anger at the man he had clearly misjudged.

"No, I'm not anymore. That is what I am trying to tell you," David pleaded. "I am different now and I want to end it just as badly as you." He sat back and Cuyler could read the fear behind his words.

"What, you found God or something? What is wrong with you? You expect me to work with you? And how do I know you won't just keep her for yourself, you sick bastard? Maybe you already have her," he was screaming at his host and the sting of his words left David crouching like a leper at a synagogue.

"I have tried to make things right with God. I have. I know what I have to do. I have to shut them down and make them pay for ruining my life, your life, and Sadie's. I realize you are shocked by it, but I am begging you to trust me." David cupped his hands together in front of his chest, "Please."

"I will work with you because it is my only chance to see Sadie again. But let me be clear when I tell you this. If I find out you have so much as looked at her I will rip your fucking throat out with my bare hands. You do not touch her, think of her, or go near her. Understood?" Cuyler watched David nod in understanding of his hostility. David's pathetic pleas were begging for comradery but his eyes remained detached and calloused. Cuyler was unconvinced of David's apology, his good intentions, or his promised epiphany. "And you can consider this friendship and my trust in you dissolved. Fuck you and your peace with God. Once we do what we have to do, we are done. You can burn in hell." Cuyler stood there gawking at his betrayer for a minute and mumbled, "I need some air."

Cuyler could not walk away fast enough. He needed the images out of head before he killed the only man who could lead him straight to his Sadie. Picturing that bastard with his hands on her made him volatile with rage. *I will find them, Sadie, and when I do…when I do…* "Fuck!" he screamed into the silent darkness of the deserted street.

"Well, hey to you too, handsome," a soothing voice called to him from his left. He spun around, startled by the sound of it. "Mind if I ask why you are screaming profanity in front of the entrance to my diner?" Serenity flashed a daring grin and waited, patiently perched on the brick wall behind her. His thoughts interrupted, he stood there dumbly frozen in the wake of her smile. Unable to say anything, he felt a grin sneak across his lips.

12

"Actually, I don't wanna know," Serenity said, jumping down from the brick wall. She landed smoothly on her feet and skipped over to where Cuyler stood still in shock with his mouth open. "You want to walk with me? I'm headed to a party about two miles from here and could use the company."

She tugged playfully at his arm, her hand smooth and warm. He had only just met her, and yet he felt like he knew her as an old friend. Her demeanor was easy and light; it brightened even this dreary night. He hesitated for a moment and tried to remember why he was so upset. The unexpected surprise tugging at him had left his dumb-founded. At last he decided he could use a night of carefree living, enjoyment, and cheery company. Perhaps it could clear his head, maybe even allow for some rest. A drink didn't sound half bad, either.

"Sure, I can go," Cuyler finally replied.

"Great! Well then, handsome, start walking," she teased, and laced her arm into his. He felt his heart jump with her tiny arm floating through his as they kept pace together.

"So, what's your story, Serenity?" he asked with genuine interest. Someone as colorful as this little pixie had to have an amazing history. He had always thoroughly enjoyed learning about the lives of others.

"I moved here from Arizona five years ago. I grew up in Phoenix, where my parents owned a manufacturing company. I have three older brothers, so you can imagine my social life was a bit stunted when I was a kid. They used to threaten every boy who spoke to me, so eventually the boys gave up." Serenity smiled mischievously and tapped her chest. "They may have given up, but I didn't. I always found a way to get what I wanted."

"Is that so? I can see you being very good at that," he teased. "Why would you leave an exciting city like Phoenix to move out here? There's not a lot of opportunity in Newland, you know."

"It may seem that way to you, handsome, but I see a wealth of untapped potential. The people are starving for something to do. I moved out here for a fresh start, and to remove myself from the crowd, the heat, and the noise. My parents are very successful, and they always expected a lot of me. Don't get me wrong, they loved me the same as every mother and father love their only daughter. But you can imagine their disappointment in having a daughter like me. I like business but not the boring kind. My dreams did not really match up closely to theirs."

"Do you still talk to them?" he asked, surprised that anyone could be disappointed in Serenity.

"Yeah, all the time. I call home at least once a week, and they try to fly out a few times a year. It's not as much as I would like, but it works," she seemed a bit sad at the direction the conversation was headed. Not wanting to dampen the moment, Cuyler thought quickly for a new direction.

"In any event, it looks to me like you are doing great out here," he said with praise. "There aren't too many people our age who have the guts to move so far away, let alone own a successful business. I'm impressed." He flashed a warm smile at her.

"Thank you darling!" she exclaimed theatrically, throwing her arms up and taking a quick bow. "I'm pretty proud of it. And I am really excited to have you. I think we will make a pretty good team, don't you?" Serenity slipped her arm back under his and gave him a gentle squeeze.

The air had lifted around him and he noted a slight skip in his step. "What kind of party are we going to, sweetness?" he flirted. He suddenly felt like he could spend all night at any happy hour, as long as she was there.

"It's just a little get-together with a few drinks, some Mary, good vibes, and, best of all, no worries. You will have a great time," she answered neatly. "And we are here. That was probably the most fun I have ever had while walking two miles in my whole life." She offered an inviting smile and took his hand.

Cuyler winced a little at the intimate touch. An arching warmth crept up his arm and fluttered through him. He tried to act casual as he climbed the two flights of stairs, hand-in-hand with Serenity. The apartments were rather old, judging from the rust accumulated on the stairwell coupled with the moss along the brick walls. The area looked a bit worse for the wear, and Cuyler guessed this was a commons for parties past. A few windows were broken out completely while others had broken blinds or no blinds at all, just sheets pinned up over them to evade prying eyes.

Serenity tapped lightly on the aluminum door. It matched the building appropriately, with its red paint peeling to reveal scratches, spray paint, and tiny dings covering its surface. As it swung open, the couple was first greeted by a cloud of pot smoke rolling in the current, happily finding a new escape. As the cloud dissipated, a friendly face appeared through the remaining haze.

He looked to be about eighteen with long dread locks dyed in alternating clumps of blonde and dark brown. His narrow-set brown eyes were squinted and red from the smoke. A long, thin face set well with his lanky body standing at least six feet, even while slouching. His baggy clothes made his thinness that much more noticeable. He was leaning in the doorway with his arms open, going in for a long embrace with Serenity.

After several awkward seconds, he looked up and noticed Cuyler fidgeting nervously behind his well-loved friend. "Who did you bring with you?" he asked. Cuyler was surprised to hear a German accent.

"Oh, yes. I almost forgot. Glen, meet Cuyler," she announced, gesturing to her accomplice. Glen looked Cuyler over, as if to study whether this stranger were truly worthy to hang here. His serious stare broke into a warm smile.

"Heya, Cuyler. Please, come in. Hang with us," he said in peaceful invitation.

The three of them stepped inside. Cuyler was pleased to see something that resembled a home. It was small and unkempt, the temperature quite warm, even for a cool spring night. Dirty dishes lined the green tile counters and matching stovetop. The floors and ceiling seemed to be in similar disrepair, with brown patches littering the sagging surfaces. The dozen or so bodies crammed in the tiny living area made the air that much thicker with sweat, body heat, and smoke. Cuyler could smell beer in the mix, and his mouth watered for one.

"Would Cuyler like a beer? Or perhaps a shot of Jager?" Glen asked him, holding a bottle of Jager in one hand and a cold beer in the other. Knowing too well the effects of any liquor in his blood, Cuyler wisely chose the beer.

"Thanks, man. You read my mind," he replied with overdue gratitude. He immediately popped the cap and took a big, satisfying gulp. "This is great. What kind is this?"

"Oh no, we make our own brew. That way, we know exactly what goes into it. Feel free to make yourself at home," he replied with unmistakable pride before disappearing into the back hallway with three other dread-locked men, a glass piece, and a lighter.

"Thanks," Cuyler said, eyeballing the last vacant spot on the couch. He walked with more than casual speed over to the corner cushion. To his surprise, a chocolate-brown pit bull leapt onto the couch just as he was about to sit. The crowd roared with laughter, accompanied by Cuyler, who now stood generously praising the animal for its cunning thievery.

He heard his name being called by a sweet voice from a few feet away. He looked up to see Serenity had secured a spot on the recliner and was gently tapping the seat, signaling for him to share it with her.

The recliner was an original lazy boy, complete with cup holders and an old-fashioned wooden lever on the side. Plopping down on the corner, he reached around and pulled the lever, sending the two of them sailing backwards in a fast jerking motion that nearly caused her to lose her drink.

"Feeling spritely?" she teased through her sunny smile.

"Maybe," he flirted back at her. "Is that okay?"

"Actually, I kind of like this better," she replied, her cheeks blushing as she laid her head on his shoulder. He hated to admit it, but she fit perfectly there. Her tiny frame felt light and soft against his masculine physique. From where she lay against him, the top of her head was only a few inches from his face. *She smells like gingerbread cookies,* he mused. *She's a gingerbread pixie.* What truly brought him comfort was the fact that she was tangibly, undeniably, there with him.

The rest of the night was a blur of laughter and beer. Cuyler could always count on complementary alcohol and weed therapies to ease his brokenness, if only for a short while. He had discovered, in light of his excellent night, that Serenity had the power to achieve on her own what it took copiously blended amounts of the others to accomplish- a feeling of untainted freedom. Spending time with her was more intoxicating, invigorating, and enlightening than a case of beer could ever be, and did not include a hangover the next morning.

The night concluded with a chatty walk back to the diner. Still a little blazed from the weed, the unlikely pair discussed everything that came to mind with an impermeable giggle. Serenity danced most of the way home, belting out lyrics Cuyler had never heard but thoroughly enjoyed. Figuring it was all in good fun, he chimed in, creating lyrics of his own. They were so caught up in their mobile showcase they almost passed the diner entrance.

"Oops, here's my stop," Serenity sang. She leaned against the door and tried to catch her breath. Finally gaining control of her laughter, she leaned back against the glass. Cuyler was staring down at her, grinning through the influences.

"You are beautiful. Did you know that?" he asked, stroking his hand across her cheek. She was so small that half of her face would easily have fit into his large, rough hand. She leaned her head onto his soft caress.

"Do you want to come in?" she asked, taking his hands into hers.

He smiled thinly into her fervently green eyes. He was thankful to spend some more time with her, knowing all too well that as soon as she left the pain he was in would come flooding back and likely drown him. Besides, he wasn't ready to go home to David Burke, afraid that if he saw him he might kill him this time instead of just walking away as he had before.

Cuyler hesitated for a moment, allowing the nippy dew to settle into his intoxicated haze. He could see the easy desire in her sodden eyes and knew that he could potentially have found a temporary bunking place. He could make a smooth entrance tonight and persuade her without objection into staying as long as he desired. He was sure of that.

A tinge of guilt attempted to surface in his dastardly plan. It was wrong to take advantage of sweet, naïve Serenity, no matter how desolate his circumstances. Looking at her sharply delicate features illuminated beneath the amber shadows of the street lamps, it was obvious she was already crazy about him, though she knew nothing of his past. He had been careful to avoid disclosing any real answers to her questions, giving vague responses to each of her carefully phrased inquiries. Still, here she stood, inviting him into her life with open arms. He could only imagine how badly it would hurt her to know that he would never love her and she was only a temporary escape from the crushing weight of his problems.

Finally, after several moments of hard deliberation, he decided it best not to squander an opportunity that may not present itself twice. "I would love to, sweetness," he said smoothly.

Her smile widened with excitement as she jumped and squeaked into the kitchen, pouring each of them a tall glass of water. "You have to work in a couple of hours," she jeered. "Sober up!" She chirped and giggled adorably, shoving the water into his palm. He was trapped inside her unique appeal, almost enchanted by the way she flittered about and danced away every second. He could find a wealth of entertainment just in watching her.

He sat down at the closest table, afraid to stumble with the glass in hand. Carrying her guitar, she sat down across from him. It was a vintage Martin with darkly aged wood, rubbed slightly lighter just below the strings from frequent heavy use. The neck was remarkably level, in spite of faded finger impressions along the frets. Resting on her tiny lap, the instrument looked enormous. Her fingertips traced the mother of pearl inlay with wistful intimacy. He could see the significance of the guitar in the way she cradled it close to her body, with protective reminiscence. He learned in later conversation the guitar had been her grandfather's and was the only remnant she possessed of the most amazing man she had ever known. He was the one who had taught her to play, to sing, and to follow her dreams. The song she sang now was for him.

He couldn't be sure if it was the booze, smoke, fatigue, or perhaps a cloudy combination. Charismatic, light, soft, and sensual, the song floated flawlessly from her lips and kissed his heart with her passion. There had only been one other voice that had moved him this way. The stinging similarities left him torn between the longing for the love he had known and the excitement of someone tangible and new.

Love's hand had given and taken, brought him life then left him shaken. With all he had been through, Cuyler knew his heart would not love any other but Sadie. Yet, seeing Serenity as he did now, with strands of red blushing against ivory skin and lips of an angel's envy, he felt heavily drawn to her. She centered him and somehow brought reason to his persistent chaos.

Since November, his world had been governed only by a few select words; words which reflected his only purpose of existing as of late: Sadie, love-lost, survival, and death. These words were really more like questions than statements, more like uncertainties than absolutes, and governed his soul as a whirlwind of doubt and sorrow. New words now crept into his stormy demeanor, words which brought a hopeful horizon, words which only came when Serenity appeared in his life: passionate, charismatic, inviting, and sincere. Thus, as the storm inside his mind retreated, Cuyler could think of only one word perfect enough for this moment: reprieve.

13

"Number 4-4-9, you are up," called an assertive voice from the hall. Sadie looked down at her wrist and read the numbers tattooed across it. She knew her number well, but she found she still looked each time it was called. Perhaps because she dreaded so much what usually came after the calling, or maybe it was the only part of her life she could still control.

She pushed herself up from her bed, if it could be called that. It was really just a piece of plywood and foam glued together and suspended by ropes about three feet from the floor. Rising quickly was necessary and left no time to deal with the splinters that always managed to pierce her skin when she braced herself against the thin, chipped plywood. The cold cement floor felt nice against her blistered feet and revived her spirit enough to ignore the aching of her sore muscles. She made her way to the well-lit hallway and stood at attention. She had learned early on how important it was to keep her body perfectly erect and completely still until otherwise instructed.

"Number 4-4-9," the newest Brethren barked, looking down at the label on her wrist. "You have an assignment. Follow me." The Brethren never looked the girls in the eye, rather their gaze always floated just over their heads. It was their way of depersonalizing the girls and reminding them of their subhuman stature.

They marched with a fast pace down the corridor, passing with nonchalance each open chamber. Sadie could hear some of the girls working as she passed by. The more experienced ones were faking their orgasms to keep the clients happy and avoid a beating. Some girls had lost their soul in this hell and seemed to feel nothing. They lay there in silence, motionless and unresponsive to every slap, cussing, or thrust. Sadie felt much like these girls and understood that sometimes the only way to deal with hell is to die to it. It was when she passed a new captive that she was reminded she also dwelt among the living. She could hear them cry and scream, even beg for mercy as the Brethren made it their personal mission to "break them in right."

One night, the constant crying from her roommate had gotten to her. The girl was only 15 and had been beaten severely for hours because one of the clients had seen blood in her panties. Sadie couldn't take the sobbing and offered to hold the girl's hand. The moment their fingers touched, however, Sadie was reprimanded. The scar below her eye reminded her how much it truly hurts to care.

From that night on she had become a model of their particular brand of sexy- silent, obedient, emotionless, and waiting. Always she was waiting. Her life had become little more than waiting for the echo of her number. Her tears had dried long ago and left her now a hollow shell, vacant until the next client filled her with his poison. Then she was left waiting once again. She couldn't remember how to smile, and no longer bothered to try. She concluded that there was only one emotion that could be kept with any real tenacity: anger. It was the only fire which still remained, the only sanity she had left.

The Brethren Young led her to a steel door at the end of the hall. Through a small window cut into the top of the door, Sadie could see descending stairs that fell into a black clandestine hole. She wondered what lie in wait for her there, and what assignment could warrant such a daunting atmosphere. She couldn't be sure, but reasonably guessed such a place could only illuminate the darkness already inside her. She imagined the consuming power of the onyx hole, the perfect stomping ground for the demons inside.

"Go down the stairs and wait. This is an important client, so behave," Brethren Young demanded. "This should break your little silent rebellion. We will see how little you care what happens to you after he is finished," the Brethren threatened. She had not spoken a word to any of the Brethren since the photo shoot. Even Dr. Scavway endured her silence. In spite of desperate pleading of the kind physician to do otherwise, Sadie had chosen to meet each of their wounding glares with a silent, indignant stare. She knew her rebellion would be quickly noticed, but had chosen not to care.

His rigid features coiled into a malicious smile. "Have fun," he said, and gave her a gentle push through the open steel door.

Taking one step at a time and in no hurry to find out what terrible fate waited for her in the darkness of the cool and musky basement, Sadie's memory kept replaying the words of Dr. Scavway. "This is the Taj Mahal of Recycling Houses," she had said. She had hoped her friendship with the good doctor would protect her, as it had for two weeks after her injuries. But as she neared the bottom of the steel stairs, the pounding of her heart told her that protection ceased to exist. Surely they would not kill her, she reasoned with herself. Nevertheless, only a fool would cast lots against death, wagering on lighter fate in the face of obscurity.

Stepping off the bottom step, Sadie tried to focus through the black blanket in front of her. She could make out no discernable shapes, save one light in the distance which lined another door. The light filtering between the cracks of the closed door did nothing to soften the darkness where she was standing, but highlighted instead the thick mix of musk and dust floating in the air. A figure moved from in front of the door, breaking the light with the size of it. She could make out the shape of a man, tall and large with skin dark enough to blend into his surroundings. Only the sclera of his eyes could be seen clearly, shining like white knives pointed in her direction.

"Come and have a seat, 4-4-9," the figure said in a robust voice, now smiling to show gleaming white teeth.

Sadie walked lightly across the dirt and mud, occasionally stepping into a puddle of cold slime, stagnant and rotting in the cool earth. She held her arms out in front of her, feeling the darkness for any unknown object which might cause her to trip and lose her footing.

"That's far enough. Just kneel where you are," he said smoothly.

She lowered herself to her knees, feeling annoyed that she should be in this position again. The skin on them had worn raw and, even at her young age, they popped and cracked each time she put any bending pressure on them. The kneeling position at one time had made her feel inferior and broken by the giants which towered over her. Now, it only made her feel more determined to never let them break her. She tilted her chin toward the ceiling and hardened her face. Her eyes created narrow slits that spat out daggers in his direction.

"Don't you want to talk to me?" he jeered, taking heavy steps toward her.

Silence thickened in the air around them, deepening the chasm between them. Sadie searched inside her frightened mind to find her gray aegis which strengthened her and gave her the courage to continue her rebellion. Fear lost its sting her when cooled by the slate of her lead curtain still cradling her stony heart.

"Not in the mood for talking just yet, I guess. Well, that's just it, isn't it? Your moods don't matter anymore, bitch. This is about what I want now, you get that?!" His breath was hot against her face and offended her senses with the odor of stale cigarettes and liquor. She flinched against the abrasive hostility in his tone as his voice became increasingly louder. She instinctively began to crouch backward to put distance between them, but caught herself mid-motion. Straightening her back and bracing her frame, she remained as any statue might- cold, hard, and defiantly rigid.

"Oh, you like it rough, huh?" he taunted, taking off his shirt to expose his brawny chest. Sweat glistened against dark skin, illuminating the bulk of his pectorals and washboard abs. His arms were larger than her thighs and appeared strong enough to kill her with one blow. Still, Sadie did not show any fear and maintained her composure. *Bruises heal,* she told herself.

Without warning, a firm hit came across her cheek and she fell to her side. She screamed out in fear and pain. The stranger jerked her arm violently until she was upright on her feet. Her knees buckled under her but he held onto her mercilessly, leaving the whole of her weight dangling from one shoulder. A second hit from the back of his right hand landed on her left cheek and she could feel his ring cut her as she spun helplessly around and fell into the mud beneath her.

"Please!" she begged, forgetting her silent strike as tears poured from her eyes inexorably. It was all she could manage through her sobbing. She couldn't stop the choked out screams between his violent blows. She tried to shift her weight to turn over. Maybe if he could see how much he was hurting her and how close to death she felt she was he would stop. As she placed her palms down to push herself up, she was shoved hard into the cold earth once again.

He was on top of her now and her legs were pinned beneath the weight of his. She could feel his rough denim jeans rubbing harshly against her bare legs and buttocks. His zipper was open and its edges constantly rubbed up and down against her; his erection intensified the friction of metal on skin.

He held one wrist firmly above her head with one hand and the other held tightly to her hair, pulling her head back so far that it was difficult to breathe through the tension on her neck, much less scream. His mouth was at the base of her extended neckline. He kissed her tenderly, repeatedly until his tongue began to massage each exposed inch from the nape across her shoulder. She could only concentrate on the burning and aching of her legs being crushed by his heavy frame. Every time he pushed against her the pain would intensify. It was her only thought that he might break them until his mouth opened and his teeth sunk into top of her shoulder. Her entire body reacted and she moaned with agony as fresh tears began to flow.

"This is my school, baby, and lesson number one is altruistic capitulation," the stranger snarled. His breathing was heavier now into her inner ear and moisture from it was beginning to bead.

"Now, hold on because this will sting a little." He chuckled deeply behind his whisper and thrust her face into a mud puddle. She was gagging and choking, helplessly trapped in the shallow slime. Nothing in her conscious mind wanted to inhale its stagnation, but she couldn't stop her desperate lungs from aspirating it between violent bouts of coughing. Her entire body began to thrust outside of her control and, just as she started to lose consciousness, he pulled her up again.

"See that, baby? I have the power to let you breathe or not. Do you want to breathe?" She gagged against the pressure of his hand sliding across her trachea. "Answer me bitch! Do you want to breathe?!" He screamed so loudly the sound echoed and left her ears ringing.

"Yes! Please!" She barely answered before he shoved her face back into the puddle. Again her stomach was thrusting to reject the malodorous gunge and her lungs burned with the deprivation of oxygen. Seconds felt like hours until she found air with the merciless tugging of her hair. Again, he pushed her face down but this time into the soft, cold earth and rested his heavy hand against the right side of her head. She could not see what he was doing when he lifted his right hand off of her and she dared not try to move. She was terrified, and the quickness of events intensified her fear and confusion. The confusion, however, quickly submitted to absolution as she felt the heat of his hard dick press against the small of her back.

His free hand lifted her hips off the ground and forced her into a downward dog position while his large, strong legs forced their way between hers, spreading them open farther than she knew they could. She felt the muscles tearing behind his force. The same hand came back up her spine and clenched her throat tightly from behind.

Her eyes flew open as he thrust himself inside her with enough force to push her stomach to the ground. Each blow came with greater exertion and effort than the one before it. She could feel him penetrate deeper into her each time, until she heaved from the depth of his violation. Her body rocked helplessly with his movement. The clots of mud felt like rocks on her open abrasions and cut into her nipples until she was sure they were bleeding also. She couldn't help but to whimper slightly with her tears, although she tried to be silent. Her whimpering only seemed to encourage him, however, and with each audible cry he would thrust harder and his grasp around her throat would get tighter. It seemed he would never stop, and her tears were as merciless as he.

Finally, he pulled out and she thought he was done. He shoved her over onto her back and held the back of her head up off the ground. "Get ready. This is what you are really good for, 4-4-9." He laughed under his heavy breathing and she felt the warmth of his cum splash across her chest. Releasing her hair and allowing her to fall limp against the earth, he stepped back to admire the mess he had made of her.

Sadie lay weakly on the ground; her muscles convulsed relentlessly. She didn't try to get up or move for fear something worse may happen. She looked up at him, watching to see if he might come back at her or if he would leave. She wanted so badly for him to just walk away and leave her in her shame. He didn't leave, though, he just stood there staring down at her and smirking, obviously very proud of what he had done.

"Baby girl, we just might make a pretty flower out of you, yet. I see real potential." The stranger said as he towered over her.

Sadie stared at the dim shadow above her and stayed perfectly still. She listened as the stranger's heavy footsteps faded and, with the latching of a heavy door behind him, the room was completely dark again.

What darkness discloses when the light is well hidden, the piercing sounds of fear and wailing from within and the tyranny of loathing. You are the love for which I still breathe; for whom I wait in the shadows of this winter's eve. Or do I wait in vain, with the scars and the pain taking all but you from me? Do you search with endless aim to restore our love, or do you sing with another in remembrance of this dark hour? Please stay in my heart with the gentle tapping of your drum, my forget-me-not. Allow me to abide in the hope that we should be together again, lest I fear that I should be the forgotten one.

14

"Rise and shine, handsome," Serenity's sweet voice broke into his dreams. He turned over to see her sitting on the corner of the cot she had graciously placed in the back for him. She looked especially radiant this morning as her cheeks blushed with healthy slumber and her emerald eyes an expectant shade of green.

He gave her a smile and reached out to pull her back into his arms. "Is it morning already? Let's stay here a while, just you and me. What do you say?"

"Well, I say that's not possible since the diner opens in less than hour and you are my only cook today. Come on, get up." She squealed and pushed against his efforts to pull her beside him.

Cuyler rolled off the cot and stretched his feet onto the cold floor. "Do you realize I met you exactly one month ago?" he asked as he watched her tap around the room. Her disposition was off this morning and seemed a bit overcast. "You ok?" he asked after a long, awkward silence.

"Yeah, handsome, I am fine," she replied flatly.

Shit, the most dreaded four letter word in the English language: fine. "You seem a bit anxious. Anything I can help you with?" he asked. He could feel the color leaving his face. Something was definitely amiss with her.

"Well, can I be honest with you?" He nodded. "I think we need to slow down. It has only been a month and you have been staying here in the diner the entire time. I love your company, Cuyler, but I need to back this up a bit. I don't want to rush into anything, and sometimes I feel like I barely know you. You disappear into some other dimension, like you aren't really here with me at all." She stopped her pacing and sat down beside him. She was nervously biting her lower lip and her eyes were pleading for something he knew he could not give her. She continued in a low, shaking voice, "I feel like the 'other woman,' you know? I really care about you and every time I think we are getting close, you shut down on me." She took a deep breath and her tiny hand cupped over his as she asked, "Are you seeing someone?"

Cuyler wrapped his arms around her, "No, Serenity, I promise I am not seeing anyone but you. I'm sorry I have made you feel that way." He knew she was right, but how could he tell her? She seemed so beautifully fragile in moments like these and although he could never love her, he didn't want her to leave either.

"I think maybe you should go talk to Detective Burke. You guys should make up already. That might make you feel better." She looked up at him with the hope she had found the root issue.

He smiled at her for reassurance. She knew nothing about Sadie and, if he could manage it, she never would. He had thought many times about David. Part of him wanted to kick his ass. Still, a much greater part of him had seen the kindness Detective Burke was capable of and the truth behind his eyes when he said he wanted to help. He had been there for Cuyler when all hope was lost, had come forth with the truth of his terrible past, then Cuyler had shut the door on the whole situation and hadn't spoken two words to him since.

Maybe it was his own fear that kept him here with Serenity instead of his anger with David. Any time he thought of Sadie, with her long hair tangled in his fingers and her ebony eyes glistening with pure admiration, his heart would break all over again. Truthfully, he was terrified of finding her. What would he find? Who would she be now that she had gone through all of this? Even worse, what if she hadn't survived it?

"Cuyler, are you still with me?" Serenity asked, brushing her hand across his cheek.

"Maybe I will try to talk to him tonight, after we close. I think you are right. It's been long enough." He was glad to see her slide a smile in his direction. "Thank you, sweetness. You have been amazing." He leaned toward her with his hand gently bracing the nape of her slender neck. Her skin was soft and smelled sweetly of gingerbread cookies. His lips met hers in a gentle seal of their reconciliation.

"I wanted to ask you one more thing," she said, her fingertips playfully petting his long auburn curls. "Will you sing with me tonight? I think the crowd would love you, and I have been practicing one of the songs you wrote." Her lips formed the perfect pout. It was impossible to say no to those lips.

"If it will keep you in my arms, then count me in. Which song did you learn?" Cuyler asked with more relief than genuine interest.

She lifted the guitar from its resting place in the corner of the storage room and took a seat beside him. Her hands delicately touched each string with grace and precision. He loved to watch her play. She was never more beautiful or vulnerable than when her spirit danced a musician's ballet, her fingertips bearing the depth of all she wanted to badly to say.

"I'm alone in the light," she began, her voice soft and smooth above the subtlety of the chords. He blinked several times, unsure if this moment was real and he was actually hearing what his mind told him he was hearing. "The rays within are searching for night," she continued flawlessly, "It's the end that we fear and the sun that has brought it here."

He stared at Serenity but all he could see was Sadie. She was lying in bed with him, bundled under layers of blankets with her pen and journal in hand. She glanced up through the skylight above them and turned to smile at him. "I am working on something for you," she told him. "And one day I want you to turn it into one of your songs, if it's worthy."

His fingers traced the contour of her porcelain shoulder. "I am the one that could never be worthy," he told her as he placed a gentle kiss on her cheek. "Let me hear it."

"Okay, but it's not finished. Here is one part I really like. Ready?" He nodded, lost in the depth of her eyes. When she wrote her eyes always glistened brilliantly, exposing the diamonds behind them which usually lay hidden.

"Please take them, my eyes, so you can see hope in fire melting the ice," Serenity's voice carried Cuyler through his reminiscence. "I'll take these, your hands, and build stars in the darkness to filter the fear. The sun smiles and night is finally clear. The end is not having you here."

Suddenly, the music stopped and he felt a tiny hand held firmly against his cheek. "Cuyler, are you okay?" a voice chimed in. He stared straight ahead, not wanting to lose Sadie again, even if she was only a memory. "Cuyler, talk to me. Why are you crying?" the voice chimed again and Sadie was gone.

Cuyler rose slowly from the cot and took empty steps toward the kitchen. His eyes were hot and his face and neck were wet, stinging with remembrance of his wilting rose. "Do not ever play that song again. It wasn't meant for you," he said in a low, chilly tone. He didn't look back to see the dismay painted on her face. The sound of his footsteps, each led rhythmically into the other, echoed through his concentration until it was all he heard and all he felt.

He moved mechanically through the rest of his day at the diner without speaking, hearing, or even seeing anyone. Every move seemed preprogrammed and somehow depressed his thoughts to a constant humming in his head.

As nightfall came, the noise of the grill and children at play gave way to buzzed conversations against the strumming of Serenity's guitar. Her voice floated delicately above the crowd without notice by anyone in the room, except Cuyler. He felt himself begin to awaken from his trance and the images of laughing congregations came into focus. Couples danced in close seduction near dark corners, men and women gathered happily near the bar and laughed in celebration of something to do in such a dead town.

A man dressed in western jeans and button down shirt caught Cuyler's attention. He watched him walk in with confidence and set his hat on the table in front of him. Scanning the room through narrowed, focused eyes for a few minutes, he finally fixed his gaze on his prey- a young blonde with teased hair, large hoop earrings, and a black leather mini. The man casually slipped his wedding band into his pocket and strutted to her side. The two of them were chatting playfully in minutes, as though they had known each other forever. Except for the obvious infidelity, the pair oddly reminded Cuyler of his immediate connection with Sadie. Their love had always been instant, natural, and easy. Seeing the couples around him, each wrapped in their lover's moment, brought the painful tightness back into his throat. He felt suffocated beneath the weight of her as though every kiss, laugh, and embrace swaddled itself tightly around the loss of his breaking heart.

Cuyler felt the heat of Serenity's eyes penetrating him. He looked up reflexively and, as her tiny frame came into focus through the smoky haze in the room, it was like seeing her for the first time. She was the image of a grieving sparrow, perched upon her stage and singing as though all was lost. Her facial features, normally brightened with excitement and life, were glazed with sadness and heavy with worry. He hated he had hurt her. As invasive as the gesture had been, it was well intended. He tried to reassure her with a smile but couldn't force his lips to turn their corners, so he just stared blankly back at her.

"Thank you so much for coming out! You guys have been great," she chirped into the microphone. The friendly pitch in her voice could not have matched less to the melancholy quiver in her lips.

Is it closing time already? Cuyler thought to himself. He glanced over at the microwave to read the time: *one a.m. I'll drink to that.* He threw back a shot of whiskey and laid the glass down with more force than he had intended. The burn swept through his empty stomach quickly and he immediately regretted not eating anything. He poured another shot as he watched the crowd file out through the back. The painful burn returned and he was reminded of his humanity. So, he took another shot. As the last customer disappeared into the darkness beyond the door, he resolved the glass was no longer needed and took the bottle instead.

Cuyler did well to put one foot in front of the other without bothering to steady his sluggish movements as he made his way to the back room. He stopped at the doorway and rubbed his blurry, drunken eyes. At first glance, he thought he saw Sadie sitting on his unmade cot, her legs folded in front of her and crossed at the ankles, with pen and paper in hand. She was running her dark, silky hair through her left hand the way she always did when lost in her concentration. He rubbed his eyes again and this time the image came more clearly into focus.

"Serenity, what are you doing?" he asked, surprised by his own disappointment. Fresh tears lay gingerly on the blush of her cheeks, freshly fallen from the emerald storm within her eyes, and her tiny mouth seemed frozen in its openly muted position. The guilt was swelling up within his chest making breathing nearly impossible. He wasn't sure what to say or do, or how to fix the awkward void between them he had created. Standing was all he could manage and even that small gesture seemed to drain the last of his energy. As this was all he could give, his very best remained frozen in front of her.

"Cuyler, I…" she paused and swallowed hard. Her tiny hand swept against the tears which fell much faster now. "I am sorry. I didn't know the song would bother you, and I just wanted to surprise you." Her lips quivered beneath the weight of her words until she collapsed her face into her hands. Serenity's slender shoulders shook behind her sobbing.

"No, Serenity. I'm sorry. I shouldn't have snapped on you like that," he said as he placed his sweaty hand on her arm and sat down beside her. "You didn't know because I never told you." He stared at her, waiting for some reply. He couldn't stand to see her so broken and small. It was killing him. "Hey, look at me," he told her gently as he lifted her chin with his other hand. She looked deep into him, her vulnerability soared with raw exposure behind the wet tips of her long lashes, and Cuyler was overwhelmed by the sincerity showcased inside them. *So this is what it feels like to make a pixie cry, steal her love, then watch it die.*

He leaned into her and kissed her gently, slowly. His sadness melted into hers, their tears sanctified the union between them and cooled the whiskey burning through his reason. As he traced the contours of her thin and delicate body, he was overcome by his desire- desire to know her, to feel her, to love her. She wrapped her legs around his waist to pull him closer and, as he slipped inside her, he closed his eyes.

Sadie was there with him now, her hair falling down around him, her eyes sparkling above a beautifully graceful smile, and her alabaster skin glowing perfectly against their crimson sheets. Her breasts pressed against his chest, their racing hearts beating in the synchronized rhythm of their tangled bodies. With each kiss and each caress the passion between them grew to mend the brokenness and pain, until they were, if only for that moment, vividly living in sensual resurrection.

"I love you, Sadie," he said as he found his release and opened his eyes to a confused Serenity. She stared up at him with complete bewilderment.

Her silence was finally broken when she pulled the gray sheets tightly around her naked body. "I want you to leave," she said in a broken, raspy voice. She fixed her gaze into the floor. Cuyler tried to touch her arm but she pulled away. "Please," she pleaded, "just go."

He picked up what was left of his life, which now fit easily into a small duffle bag, and took heavy steps toward the door. "For what it's worth you are amazing. You did everything right, Serenity. I want to give you what you deserve, but I can't. I just can't," he said as he squared himself with his own humility. The door of the diner chimed as he slipped out of its shelter into the night ahead.

The darkness smothered out the false pretenses of life like a blanket against the fire. Left ahead were only the ashes of his remains, gray and flaking reminders of the truth that is seen in all mankind when the singing of angels has been snuffed out by the wailing of demons. Their wailing fed upon him like a cancer in its vengeance, ignored and undetected until death was the only fate which could be taken. Sadie was gone and she had taken her angels with her. Each glimpse of her was the only light he had seen since her disappearance. But, in this moment of clarity, he realized that the light he thought he saw was just another train.

Cuyler lay down across the tracks and stared into the night sky. Its darkness, pure and inviting, was the closest he could find to hope. He imagined what it would feel like to ascend into that darkness and finally find his light waiting for him there. It would be the experience of the weightlessness of a soul no longer heavy laden with tears or loss, anger or grief-just unbridled freedom and joy. He felt the vibrations beneath his back and heard the smokestack panting as it pushed its cargo faster toward him. The sound brought him to a place of peaceful resolve he had not experienced before. Demons danced around him, chanting their deadly praise and as he reached for the hand of the Reaper, the clouds parted to expose a glowing white moon surrounded by stars playing in their constellations. *Sadie has come to greet me,* he thought. He listened as the train grew increasingly louder. *It's only seconds now, Sadie. I will never leave you again. I never knew love until I knew you, never felt warmth until you warmed me. I was lost without you, my love, but you have found me. Just as you and I always dreamed, we will live among the stars and create a constellation that is only ours. And now the loneliness has departed, grief and separation are a dying memory. Now, my precious Sadie, we will always be.*

Cuyler took a deep breath and relaxed completely against the cold steel rails. A sudden jolt sent him up in the air. He fell hard onto the ground. His thoughts felt scrambled and jarred; simply standing was proving too complex.

"Damn it to hell, Cuyler!" A familiar voice belted at him. "What are you doing?" A doltish and disoriented Cuyler tried to open his eyes to see who was screaming into his ear, but was caught by surprise when a large boot lunged into his abdomen with enough force to knock him over onto his back.

His assailant was on top of him now, slapping him and screaming. He could only make out fragments of what was said. "Asshole," the voice said. Then he heard, "Get it together," followed by another slap and then, "acting like a pussy." His ears rang more loudly with each slap until the screaming was drowned out completely by the ringing.

Then one phrase spoken by either foe or friend collected his senses and grounded his focus once again. "I found Sadie. She's alive." The words echoed through him with resonance. *She's alive.* Not just alive, but *found.*

The train rushed by with power and anger, nearly grazing the two men. Cuyler rolled onto his knees and gagged heedlessly on the full impact of what almost took place.

"Fuck," he spat out through the hot whiskey coming up into his mouth. "The train was… and I was gonna…Oh fuck," he mumbled. "David?"

"Yes, you asshole, it's me. Who else would it be? And you better be glad I came looking for you tonight. Damn idiot." David wasn't yelling anymore. He looked exhausted and plopped down in the mud beside Cuyler. He put his hand on Cuyler's hot, sweat-soaked back. "I found her, man."

"David?" Cuyler barely managed. "Sadie? She's alive? And you know where she is?" He threw his arms around David and collapsed into his strong chest. The sobbing came like Heaven's perfect rain, removing the tarnish and subduing the storm. All hope was not lost, but regained. Life was not in ruins, but waiting to be remade. His turmoil and despair poured from his eyes until the vacancy was filled once again with sobering renewal.

The pair stood and began to walk ahead, each man with his own reason, each step specifically determined to satisfy that reason. The sun's rising cast on them its hues of rose and amber. Cuyler stared into its masterful display and took notice of the white moon, no longer hiding in the shadows but rather fighting to feel the warmth of the new day. On the brink of the brightening dawn is when day and night find peace alike and an allowance of restitution for yesterday has been made; that mistakes be forgiven and a chance be provided to find one's way once again. Cuyler studied for a moment on the opportunity that had been mercifully afforded him. He could not squander another day, another opportunity, to save her life and his own. Testified by the Reaper and his demonic army dancing upon his suicidal plane, tomorrow is not a guarantee. He had been given a rare gift: a second chance to make things right. *There is no tomorrow,* he thought. *What was once tomorrow has now become today. What was once today has now become yesterday. And what of yesterday? Yesterday shall be as though it never was.*

15

Hugging the porcelain lid for three hours straight had exhausted what was left of Cuyler. David peered into the bathroom to check on him and could see that he was passed out cold on the tile floor. The bathroom reeked of sweat, vomit, and liquor so potently that David's nose curled, even through the door. He was grateful for all the years of homicide experience. Once he had smelled his first rotting corpse, nothing seemed to affect his cast-iron stomach.

He took a long look at the young man sprawled out in front of him. If he were to base the identification of Cuyler Byrne solely on the images enclosed in Kendrick's letter, he would never have assumed the passed out waste in his floor to be the same spirited young man in the photo. He had lost at least thirty pounds, if not more. Even at a height of six feet, the toll on his appearance was devastating. His once full cheeks now looked sunken and shallow beneath a shaggy, coarse beard. Dark bags circled his muted eyes, nearly hidden by the long, curly auburn locks which matted in tangles about his head. He also seemed to have aged significantly, appearing now to be in his late thirties.

Pathetic, David thought to himself. *Why would anyone let some girl get him that worked up? Her pussy can't be that good.* Then again, her pussy's greatness had been what had led him straight to her. In the last month alone he had heard at least a dozen reports from top-paying clients that she was the best. She had done so well, that even Ray had taken notice and planned to sample for himself what all the fuss was about.

Since the reunion with Ray on Beech Mountain, he had attended several functions at various levels of the Academy, all by personal invite and escort of Ray himself. In the beginning it was difficult to work closely with the man who had been so quick to leave him shamed in the shambles of his shattered life. Behind each handshake or candid meeting, he secretly imagined a thousand different ways to kill his esteemed and traitorous crony. At times, he would become so lost in the vision of Ray's bleeding body drowning in its own cowardice that his heart would flutter and the consequent tingle pulsate from the inside out with excitement.

Acting brashly would have taken care of Ray, but he wanted all of them. In order to do that, he needed a gathering where each patron that had spiked his crown of thorns would be present. Since he had been exiled from the NYPD for his involvement with the Academy, little had changed within the iron clad organization. The layout and all its major players were the same, giving Detective Burke a great advantage. Tracking them down had been easy enough, though demonstrating his loyalty again had proven itself a bit more tedious.

Killing the fire-eyed singer had been just the beginning. He chuckled as he remembered his panic in approaching Ray with the news. "I got a little rough with her, Ray," he had lied. "I didn't mean to take that from you, but she was done anyway. She had more holes in her than I could stick my dick into." He had tried to laugh it off, hoping Ray would see the humor. He had. Then, to David's surprise, Ray patted him on the back.

"Welcome back, Detective Burke," he said with a broad smile, reaching up to shake David's hand. "Sorry about that used up slut, but we had to see if you were really in this or if you had gone soft on us. You understand, don't you?" he asked, still beaming with pride.

"Yeah, I would have done the same thing in your position," David replied, confused by the admitted set-up.

Later that night, David had stood in the shower for hours, replaying the entire night in his head over and over again while he stared in awe of his large, rough hands. Hands that were capable once of caressing, had been equally as capable of battery, then rape, and eventually murder. Flashes of her red, mottling face kept disrupting his vision, jarring his resilience and battering his psyche. He couldn't understand why a sneering grin turned the corners of his thin lips each time he pictured those same hands crushing her tiny neck, with hope and gratitude lighting the fire behind her eyes.

It was during the same shower, nakedly unaffected by the cold water running over him, that he realized why his life had always felt amiss and voided. He had wasted a lot of time praying to the wrong God, he reasoned. Why would a God of love, peace, and sacrifice want an angry, selfish, sadistic asshole like him? He had heard of ultimate forgiveness, but does that rule still apply if your soul has already been traded to His fallen angel for a bottle of Cognac and an unlimited supply of cozy cunts? He couldn't really be sure, but his best guess deemed it unlikely any Heavenly Host would be singing his praises. The moment satisfaction sprung in his pants with the snapping of her little neck in his massive hands, he knew that he could never change.

Rather than live the remainder of his life feeling guilty and pathetic, being consumed with self-hatred, David Burke succumbed to the much more recompensing lifestyle of the Academy. He had spent the last two months touring Recycling Houses, sampling new products, and attending private parties. None of which had brought Ray and Kendrick in the same meeting place at the same time. Any fool knows the best way to take down an organization like the Rose Academy is to start at the top to get their attention, and the entire house will come crashing down. All the other drones beneath them are so mindless; they wouldn't know where to turn without their fearless leaders. They could rot in their own wondering for all he cared. All he cared about was revenge and all he needed was the opportunity.

He had basked in the memory of taking her life- the power, the freedom, the respect that was felt when he watched her soul leaving her body at his command. He achingly craved to relive the experience and it was oppressively consuming his thoughts. With his patience wearing thin, he had seriously considered settling for killing Ray and retreating into the abyss to gloat in his small victory. Then the mail carrier came through for him and unknowingly delivered the opportunity for which he had been waiting.

The note was addressed to him in Kendrick's pen, an act of promise in itself. Kendrick rarely attended socials, as he did not have the same interest in the girls as Ray. To him, the girls were purely profitable merchandise. For the note to have come from him, David understood the importance was monumental and all major players would be involved.

David carefully peeled back the envelope and slipped out a heavy card with a black rose centered on the front, as he had done several times since the note's arrival two days ago. Inside the words were written in gold scroll and read, "You are cordially invited to the commemoration of member 4-4-9. Saturday May 21, 2013. Ceremony will begin precisely at 8 p.m. Refreshments will be served. We look forward to the grace of your most esteemed company." David unfolded the crisply folded card to read once again the message written discretely inside, scripted much less formerly in lightly pressed pencil. This message addressed him directly and made clear the real reason for his invitation.

"Detective David Burke,

We are requesting your services to aid us in apprehending a nuisance that has been pursuing us hotly. His name is Cuyler Byrne and he is the boyfriend to 4-4-9. We have enclosed his picture. As you can see, he does not appear particularly threatening and, given that he has not yet found even one of us in the five months he has searched, we are assuming he is not exponentially brilliant either. However, as you know, we must not take chances. That is why we wish for you to bring him to the commemoration ceremony, so that we may deal with him directly. Thank you for your assistance with this matter. We wish you well, and look forward to seeing you in May.

Sincerely,
Kendrick, Director of Internal Affairs."

David folded the note and slipped it back into his pocket. He felt an air of excitement sweep through him and push his shoulders back. Everything was working in his favor with surprising ease. Ray and Kendrick trusted him fully, to the point they were now depending on him again. The assignment he had been given to apprehend Cuyler meant he was a full-on member of the Rose Academy again. Delivering Cuyler would certainly be easy enough, seeing as how he would blindly follow him anywhere if he thought Sadie would be there.

He had planned on smuggling Cuyler into the party somehow, to use as a buffer in case he needed someone disposable to take the heat while he was busy with Ray and Kendrick. But the open invitation to bring the sleeping sap with him meant the job would certainly be a breeze.

The way he saw this playing out was simple. Cuyler falls in behind him, ready to fight for his love while Ray and Kendrick expect him, thinking he is there to be executed. Cuyler will undoubtedly cause a scene, being the Irish man that he is, while attempting to defend his life and Sadie's. During the commotion, he will have ample time to slit the throats of his adversaries, spill a little gasoline, light a match, and make a quick exit. Or, perhaps being the lone survivor of a blazing, tumbling sex-trafficking operation would be too difficult to explain.

Plan B. It would be easier to just use the silencer and kill them off quickly. While they are busy trying to contain Cuyler, he will just slip behind them and clip them off one by one, including Cuyler. *Shouldn't take more than a couple seconds, if I do it right,* he settled with himself. *I would be the hero again, and the lovely Sadie would mine, with no one left to bother us.* David arched his back and blew out his chest, imagining all the adoring fans that would be sure to surround him. Women would be moved to tears at the sight of the man who defeated their worst nightmare. He could see the press swarming around him, begging for a photo with the country's greatest warrior. With that kind of fame, he would be unstoppable. The Detective was busy signing imaginary autographs when he heard a groan coming from the floor.

"How are you feeling?" he asked his stirring pawn. Before he could answer, David was holding out two aspirin and a tall class of water. "Here, take these. It's just aspirin but they will mend your splitting head."

"Thanks," Cuyler grunted, rising slowly to accept the gift. "And, uh, thanks for showing up last night." He looked down at the tile floor then back up at David. The shame was radiating from his face, lined by a halo of remorse for speaking so harshly with David before. Before him stood a man who had never given up the search for a woman he had never met. A man who, in Cuyler's eyes at least, stood taller than life with his selflessness and generosity.

The two men stood eye to eye for several minutes, communicating silent apologies between them the way only men do. The embarrassing exchange filtered through Cuyler's eyes and was reciprocated with a pardoning nod gifted by Detective Burke. And, in a manner only coded by men, it was immediately understood that all transgressions between them had been forgiven. They would begin fresh, without the complication ever being mentioned again.

"Take a shower," David said, moving on. "Meet me in the kitchen when you are done."

Cuyler nodded, reaching for a towel from the overhead cabinet. He squinted against the florescent light. It seemed much brighter when looking into it through a whisky hangover. Deciding he rather liked the dark at the moment, he flipped the switch and stepped under the hot water. His muscles melted under the steam and the fog was lifted long enough to remember the reason he had been brought back to David's apartment last night. Sadie is alive and David knows where she is.

He washed only the vital areas, eager not to steal a second more from her retrieval. Stepping out of the shower, the aroma of ribs and skewered veggies encouraged faster movements. Cuyler had not realized how ravenous he had become until his stomach coiled with longing for anything warm and filling and his mouth watered wildly with anticipation.

They ate to the sounds of katydids and crickets. The clanging of their forks against the ceramic plates chimed in fast rhythm against their hard swallowing. He could not remember the last time he had eaten so well and, sitting back to allow room for his belly to swell, Cuyler felt his strength returning to him. He was alive, not surviving. That was reason enough to celebrate. It was as though David could read his thoughts. He grinned and pulled out a fat joint, rolled tight and pinched together at the ends.

"After you," he said, directing Cuyler to the back porch.

The air was cool and damp with fireflies flickering against the night sky in their own celebration. Moths swarmed inanely around the porch light, occasionally knocking into each other hard enough to send one falling onto the natural grooves of the aged wooden porch. Cuyler took a deep breath and exhaled slowly, allowing only trace amounts of smoke to escape his lungs. He mind began to relax by the weed's sweet fondling, followed by his body, until he was sure he had become fixed to the chair. He allowed his mind to wonder, aimlessly taking into account every tree, star, bat, or splinter around him. The wind whistled through the trees, carrying their scent across the flapping wings of busy bats circling the great deck where two men sat in slow silence, watching a parade of moths fall among the splinters. Somehow the display struck him as hilarious, watching the moths bouncing off the light over and over, and Cuyler broke out into an unstoppable giggle. The Detective watched, dumbfounded at first, and then joined in without even being sure of exactly what had initiated the outburst.

"Why are we laughing?" he asked as best he could through the panting laughter.

"I was just thinking of what kind of story Sadie could make of all that flopping," Cuyler stated matter-of-factly, controlling himself. "She is so funny. Damn I miss that quirky laugh of hers. She will get so cracked up that she snorts sometimes. It's the cutest thing I've ever seen, I swear," he rambled, staring into space. He didn't know if his accomplice was listening, but he would have told the moths, just the same. "She has an incredible imagination and spirit about her, in spite of all that she's been through. She has been through so much, David. Her mother committed suicide and her father was an abusive drunk. That's when the morphine became such a big part of her life, but you know what? She defeated the addiction on her own. She was so brave, and she taught me how to be a better man just by being near her."

"You are one lucky son of a bitch, I will tell you that. You two really loved each other. That doesn't happen for everyone," David said, thinking of how he was sure he would never know how to love anyone. Being around Cuyler confirmed he had never really been in love with his wife. Good thing he no longer cared about such trivial matters as love, or he might actually be upset by its absence.

"And she's gorgeous, too, with those long legs and perfect lips, dark hair and eyes that are set off perfectly by ivory skin. I can't even imagine someone like that looking in my direction, Cuyler. How did you ever bag that one?" David asked, trying to keep him going. It gave him a chubby to hear all about her, like reading an article in a porn magazine. It's not as good as the real thing, but it comes in at a close second, and the end result is still the same.

"Honestly? I have no idea how I got so lucky. Oh David, you have no idea how good it feels inside those legs of hers. But, as close to Heaven as that might be, Olympus is found in her heart," Cuyler tapered his words until he was barely speaking above a whisper. "Do you want to know something really terrible?" he asked, looking up at his friend. David looked on with interest. "I can't remember what she looks like. It's like I remember her in pieces, but never the entire puzzle put together. When I try to picture all of her, the memory just gets fuzzy and she disappears again. Does that make me a terrible person?"

"No, it just means that your subconscious is helping you to cope with your loss. That's all, Cuyler. You will have the real deal back in your arms on May 21. That's less than a month. And she will never disappear again," David said in a soothing voice.

"What happens May 21?" Cuyler asked keenly.

"That is the day we take the Academy down and get your girl back," David raised his voice with excitement. "I've been doing a little work while you were gone, weaseling my way back into the Academy to win their trust. I know all of their secrets, their locations, everything about them. Best of all, I know exactly where your fair lady will be on that date because they are having a commencement ceremony in her honor. It is the perfect opportunity for both of us. Do you see how easy it will be for us now?" David was leaned on the edge of the seat, his massive size bending the plastic legs slightly forward and tilting the chair off the ground.

Maybe it was just the pot, but Cuyler couldn't help seeing a puppy in that chair, waiting anxiously for him to throw the ball. He could feel the excitement vibrating through him as well, spiced with apprehensive impatience. One month was not a long time when compared with the lifespan of most individuals. Still, when holding the fragile balance of living and existing, one month could slip life through the fingers of the beholder, slicing through life and leaving only scars of existence.

"So what do we do until then?" Cuyler asked, his eyes falling heavy with smoky sedation.

Detective Burke rested his chin on loose fists, contemplating the question as if it had never crossed his mind what to do while waiting. "You rest, lay low, and do your homework," he finally said, breaking the silence.

"What homework?" Cuyler asked, surprised. He looked up and followed David's tall frame to the door.

"You need to familiarize yourself with what you are about to walk into, and what you might see when we get there. It isn't for the weak or shaken, Cuyler. The women there go through a lot and you need to be prepared for the worst when you find her," David saw the fear once again spreading like a disease over the face of his pathetic pawn. "Don't worry so much. She will be there, alive. I wrote it down for you in a notebook. It's on your bed. Just look it over, ok? If you have any questions, I am here for you," he tried to reassure him before walking inside. Cuyler followed close behind not entirely convinced of a happy ending.

He made his way to the room Detective Burke had prepared for him and found a white notebook neatly in the center of the bed, as promised. He sat down on the edge of the down comforter and opened the book. On the first page, he found a table of contents, followed by a list of names. Ray, Owner and Dean of the Rose Academy. Kendrick, Director of Internal

Affairs. Clayton, Keeper of the First House. Anthony, Keeper of Apprentice House. Lucas, Keeper of the Third House, Recycling, and Morgue. Shamen, Keeper of the Fourth House, Recycling, and Apothecary (overseen by Dr. Lydia Scavway). Seeing their names in print saturated his buzz completely with sobering hostility. Cuyler wondered which of these men had Sadie in his custody, and in what order he would kill them.

He turned to the second page on which he found the mission statement of the organization, as written by Ray. His face grew hotter with each word as he read it aloud, "At the Rose Academy, we believe women are a gift to men, for the pleasure of men. Our mission is to shave away the thorns of independent thought, selfishness, vocal expression, and any other undesirable trait superimposed on their simple minds so as to provide the consumer with a product of perfection. It is our goal to expose her inner rose, and to please you with her delicate beauty and submission to all of your desires, thereby creating a better society, firmly upholding the natural order as it was intended."

Again Cuyler flipped the page, with more force than before, bending the thin pages. Page upon page were photos of women taken before their admission into the Rose Academy and then after. Some of them were just as beautiful, with the only difference being in the vacant expression perfectly molded into their wax-like pose. Others were images of dead bodies, badly burned, bruised, lacerated, or deformed. He stopped abruptly and stared onto the last page.

It was a photo of a young girl, possibly eighteen. She had dark hair like Sadie, which hung in thick, loose curls down her back. She was wearing a blue dancer's costume bedazzled with rhinestones and silver embroidery, white tights, and petite white ballet slippers. Her smile could light the world, as it radiated through every muscle in her expressive face from her sparkling teeth to her blazing coral eyes. Except for the highly unusual eyes, she bore a remarkable resemblance to Sadie.

Seeing her vivacity in the first picture, Cuyler found it difficult to believe the after photo was of the same girl. Her hair, dry and tangled from neglect, had been ripped out in places, exposing an exudate-encrusted scalp. She had bruises covering her cheeks, her lip was split in two places, and small, round burns covered her breasts. What was most startling, however, was her neck. Though it was slightly swollen and bruised, clearly could be seen the break in its center, just over the trachea.

The likeness between the girl in the photo and Sadie was too much for Cuyler to differentiate. He felt as though it was really Sadie's face covered in bruises, with her neck twisted sideways beneath the break. He closed the book and heaved it across the room. He threw himself back against the soft mattress and tried to shove the photos out of his memory. His concentration at last gave way to sealed eyes, victim now only to the haunting of his nightmares.

In the next room, David listened carefully for Cuyler's snoring. He picked up his cell and pressed the speed dial "2." The speaker sounded three rings before Kendrick answered.

"This is Kendrick," he said flatly.

"Hi, Kendrick. I am calling to confirm your order. It is in my custody and ready to be delivered on the date already discussed," David said proudly.

"Well, done," Kendrick replied quickly. "And we will have your payment prepared for you as well. You may have her just after the ceremony, in exchange for her boyfriend, as promised."

"Perfect," Detective Burke voiced in a shrieked whisper. Containing his excitement was difficult. He couldn't wait to have a Rose of his own, someone to call him Master and to do his every bidding. It was an added bonus that his whore would be Sadie. He had fantasized about her since the day he saw her flyer in Cuyler's desperate hands. What a tragedy to break up the couple and their perfect love. Love like that is truly a rare gem to be treasured. Certainly he would never know its true value, but who needs love when you can have servitude? It is less complicated, after all, and there is minimal maintenance required in a dictatorship.

David walked across the hall and peaked in on Cuyler, restlessly sleeping on the bed and still fully dressed. The determination and wholesomeness of his young pawn tugged at his conscience. He had done nothing to directly offend the Detective, except love the woman of David's desire. He had heard that a man cannot choose who he loves and it hardly seemed necessary to kill him. Honestly, Kendrick was right when he said Cuyler was not a true threat. He would not have the resources to find Sadie where David planned to take her and, even if he did, he would never be successful. He was also so young and could easily gain enough steam to make a full recovery with someone new. At forty-two, David did not feel he had that same advantage. In reevaluation of the situation, the Detective was confident he would not even need Cuyler to help him with the Academy take-down. There would be no need for Cuyler to share the same crude fate as those who had intentionally betrayed him.

Stepping lightly into the room, he stooped to retrieve the notebook lying on the floor. Turning the pages softly, he began to formulate a new plan. One that would achieve his revenge, allow him to escape with his fair Sadie, and leave Cuyler's fate to his own devices.

16

"Sadie, you have to eat something," Dr. Scavway pleaded. "Are you planning to just starve yourself to death? Will you really let them win like that?" she scolded in beautiful Middle Eastern dialect. At some point in the daily assessment, the same one-sided conversation always took place. Dr. Scavway would plead with her to change her obvious indifference about life. Sadie wouldn't respond at all to her begging, so the tone would consequently transmute into a soft scolding.

Sadie stared blankly at the tattoo on her wrist. She had been reduced to a number. 4-4-9, that was her only identity. They had managed to strip even her name from her, but they couldn't force her to eat or speak. She had done neither in quite a while and the effects were starting to show. Her slender build looked more like a skeleton than anything resembling feminine and her silky black hair had thinned in compliance with her soul. Whatever the consequences, those two actions were hers alone to decide when and if they happened at all.

Still, the lovely physician had a valid point. The Roses didn't care if she died or how she died. They would just replace her with someone else the next day. Lydia Scavway had been her only contact with kindness and respect since these monsters had taken her into custody. She, of all people here, did not deserve Sadie's distant chill.

"At least talk to me. I'm not the enemy here. I am only trying to help," she said, her face wrinkled with worry and frustration.

Sadie locked eyes with Lydia. Her vacant stare dissipated into an intense hopelessness. "I know," she finally replied. These had been the first words she had spoken in over a month. *I know you believe in me, even when I believe in nothing. I know you see light in me, when all that exists is darkness. I know you still have faith, but your faith has not been tainted by countless nights of rape and torture. I know that I must never give up, even if I have nothing left for which to fight. And I know that all of your hope falls in me. I know.*

"Brethren Young will be here in just a few moments, Sadie. Let us finish your assessment," she said, dropping her eyes to examine the bruises on Sadie's thin arms. "The bruises are healing nicely, and I don't see any breaks or lacerations. They've almost faded completely but, if you want me to keep giving you the morphine, you are going to have to at least stay hydrated. It's getting nearly impossible to find a vein." Dr. Scavway sounded almost irritated. She tightened the tourniquet around her arm as she talked, flicked the air from the needle, and pushed it in. Almost immediately, Sadie was released from her pain- past, present, physical, or otherwise- into a peaceful burning oblivion. It had become the greatest blessing of this life and the one feeling which still meant something to her. In a single syringe contained something to hope for, a feeling to crave.

"Thank you, Lydia," Sadie spoke in fragments through the distortion now submerging her senses.

"I know you want to give up. This is so hard for you but things are about to change. I overheard Kendrick talking to Ray last night. They have decided to promote you, Sadie," she proclaimed.

"Why is that a good thing?" Sadie asked darkly.

"First and foremost, it will remove you from the usual clients that keep roughing you up. Also, it means you will have exclusive access to Ray, Kendrick, and Shamen. I figured that once you learn the layout of the house and their routine, you can get us out of here," Lydia's eyes were wide with excitement now. Hope glimmered in her pouty brown eyes like a cheery sun in a fool's paradise.

Sadie wasn't convinced. She gave a hard glare at the physician. She had grown tired of her hope and ambition. Her words were frivolous. Worse, it tried her patience every time she placed all the responsibility of their freedom on her beaten shoulders. If she wanted freedom so badly, why didn't she make it happen? She was the one married to Kendrick, with open access to all of them. Sadie guessed she just didn't want to risk her own life, or her reputation. As a Common Hall whore, she was much more disposable than the wife of the esteemed Director.

"Just think about it, okay? I have been gathering some supplies you will need. Next time I will tell you more. I hear them coming," she whispered, squeezing her hand and helping the drugged woman to her feet.

"There's something else you should know," she whispered frantically. "Cuyler has been tracking you, searching endlessly. They know, Sadie, and they're planning to kill him at your commencement."

No sooner had she slipped out the words, the door flew open. Brethren Young's narrow frame occupied the hallway. He stepped forward in a soldier's march and pulled Sadie forward by the arm. She stole a quick glance back at the doctor, trying to process what had just been confided in her.

He had nothing to say to her as he led her from the sterile-white room and down the hall. Just as well to Sadie, who didn't wish to have her inebriated floating interrupted with doggish insults or snide comments made by a cretin on a power trip. During her escorted marches to this assignment or that, she never tired of the strange way the morphine made all of the colors around her much more vibrant. The carpeting fluffed its brilliant violet fibers between her toes, now expressively white with lack of sun or nutrition. Hues of excellence popped from the paintings as she passed them, and the sconces flooded her senses with their radiance. Sounds soured through her in melodious echoes, and she was sure she heard a familiar voice singing. *Cuyler?* She looked around slowly, but saw no one.

The Brethren Young led her to a private room with navy plush carpeting and white leather sofas large enough to disappear into. The vaulted ceilings seemed to touch Heaven, if such a place existed, with a crystal chandelier dangling its brilliance above them. Each wall was lined, floor to ceiling, with the most impressive book collection Sadie had ever witnessed. A slender man dressed in a chocolate suit walked over to them, smiling as though nothing could be more right in his perfect world. The light blue tie matched his bright eyes perfectly and made him appear safe and almost honest. Sadie noticed a gold band around his finger as he opened his left hand to greet Brethren Young.

"Welcome. 4-4-9, I presume?" he asked, turning his wide smile to her. She nodded. "Please, come in my dear. We have much to discuss, and I have some exciting news for you."

He led her to the white couches and gestured for her to sit. She lowered herself to the floor, giving silent thanks for the soft carpet which made the bruises on her knees less noticeable. She stretched her arms over her head and bowed down with perfect poise.

"Look at that," he said with enthusiasm. "She is so cute, isn't she?" Sadie could feel him staring, but she didn't rise. She couldn't move, at least not until she was given permission. "Sweetheart, that's good. You can sit up now."

She rose to see he was still smiling down at her. Sadie had gotten quite talented at reading men. The ones who smiled all the time, like this one, were the most pleasant of clients. They were usually easy to please as long as she stayed silent, submissive, and cooperative. This particular man was at least sixty, of old money, and was well-educated. This job would be an easy one.

"That will be all, Brethren Young. You are dismissed. I wish to be alone with her." The man spoke with kind authority.

"Yes sir, Keeper Shamen. As you wish," Brethren Young stated. He turned on his heels and marched rhythmically out of the room.

"I suppose now you know who I am. Pity, I was going to surprise you. Damn it all to hell," Keeper Shamen snarled. His face was red with frustration. "That's alright," he said as he recomposed himself, "I still can because I have an even better surprise that maggot doesn't know about. Ha!" He took a seat on the leather sofa in front of her, twisting his brandy glass between his hands and gleaming with excitement. He waited in silence for a few moments before he anxiously inquired, "Well, aren't you going to ask me what it is?"

"Yes, Master," Sadie replied smoothly. "What is your surprise?" she added with due inflection to mimic interest.

"Your little tight ass has just become my number one best-selling item in my warehouse!" He surprised her with a tight hug around her tender shoulders. "Why, I have clients from all over the world bidding on you right now. I have made more money off you, a recycled whore, than all of the best-trained girls in the Academy. I am ringing with excitement here and I just had to share it with you." His tight grip pulled her by the waist to her feet. He pressed his hand against the back of her head, burying her face in his tailored jacket. The thick fibers and tight grip made it difficult to breath. Finally, he pulled her back and looked her squarely in the eyes, "My dear, you have just opened a new market here at the Rose Academy. We must celebrate and you will be my headlining event!"

Sadie's heart raced wildly in her chest. She didn't know how to react to this strange and happy man who was not groping her, but embracing her all because she was the best whore? How was she supposed to react? With the last memory of her headlining event still burning the coils of her anger, she wanted nothing to do with this so-called celebration.

There was also Cuyler to think about. The more she replayed her last seconds with Dr. Scavway in her mind, the more certain she was that she had heard the words correctly. Cuyler had not given up. He was still looking for her, tracking her relentlessly, even willing to take on the Rose Academy to save her. And they were planning to kill him. She couldn't let that happen. *I will do whatever it takes,* she decided. *I will keep him safe until I can escape.*

Just the thought of his name brought back the strangling ache in her chest. She had rehearsed abstinence of his memory to the point that his existence seemed to her only a lie or, at best, a lucid dream from long ago. She never wanted to forget him, but his memory crippled her and kept her raw. Under the circumstances, there was no other alternative for coping. Now she stood in startled realization that, although his name rehashed the pain, she couldn't remember his face clearly. Had she hidden him away so tightly that he had smothered behind the mask?

"I know all about your little mishap in Asheville, sweetheart. Don't worry. This party will be fun and involve no needles. I swear it." He looked at her empathetically and brushed the scar under her eye with his thumb. "If all goes well, then things will change for you. I want to see you succeed, my dear. But, if it doesn't," his voice trailed and he turned to refill his brandy. "If it doesn't," he continued in a low voice, "there will not be enough left of you for the rats to enjoy."

Sadie felt knots rising in her gut, the dread churned through her lungs and lodged in her throat. These men were even more soulless than she, and she could not mess this up. With deep regret she understood how ruthless they could be. Most of them would probably enjoy seeing her cut up into tiny pieces. She could imagine them laughing over the dinner table about how she bled like a stuck pig. It was a conversation she had overheard more than once while serving them in the dining hall.

He bellowed with laughter at her cowardice trembling. "I don't want to ruin the mood with all that scary talk, do you?" She shook her head slowly. "That's better. You're okay, sweetheart. Now, don't you want to thank me for this wonderful opportunity to advance your career here at the Rose Academy?"

Sadie nodded and tried to smile but her eyes kept trying to cry. She swallowed back the growing lump in her throat and lowered herself to her knees once again. Master Shamen sat down in front of her.

"That's a good girl. You are quite graceful. You almost dance when you move, like a weeping willow caught in a gentle summer breeze," Shamen observed as he followed her long, gentle body with his lustful gaze. She was grateful for the black satin robe draped elegantly over her otherwise naked flesh. Though she was sure his eyes had already undressed her.

"Yes, that is what I will call you. Willow. It suits you, don't you think?" he asked as he unbuttoned his slacks.

She closed her eyes and sealed her lips around his dick. *Willow,* she thought to herself, and the image of Cuyler standing beneath the weeping willow by the river flooded her mind. The moment she had realized how much she truly loved him, he was standing beneath a willow tree in Elizabethton, TN. The river hummed gently behind them, swirling below the wind that kissed the willow's low branches. A melancholic enlightenment rumbled through her as she once again realized her love for him was stronger than any circumstance, any pain, or any reality they could bestow on her.

She felt her heart warm as she could recall every strong feature of his face, the depth of the ocean in his eyes, and the kindness of his smile. *It's actually kind of perfect,* she resolved. *You will be with me always, Cuyler. And I will keep you safely in my new name, Willow. So that when we are together again, as I know we will be, and you ask me what is in my name I may justly reply, 'You are.'* She embraced her new identity with a single tear as it trickled down her cupped fingers and onto her Master's skin.

17

April came to a close peacefully. Cuyler was glad to see May's rainbow breaking through the storm. Blooms of cherry trees, dogwoods, and lilies were in abundance, greeting his morning with their fragrance through the open window above his bed. Robins and squirrels frolicked alike, side by side, on the trunks of the dense forest surrounding him. Taking a deep breath, he took notice of the bustling activity just outside his door. The energy rode in on the back of spring and invigorated everything in sight, including him.

He stepped out of the cabin with coffee in hand. He couldn't help but to think of Sadie and how much she would love the secluded tranquility surrounding him here. David had left for another week-long outing with Ray, insisting that during his absence Cuyler stay well hidden. He understood well enough the reason he couldn't be seen coming and going at David's apartment. He loved the idea of being so close to nature also, with plenty of time to decompress and prepare his rattled nerves for the slaughter of Sadie's captors.

Stretching his long arms over his head, Cuyler prepared for what promised to be a glorious day to hike. David had insisted he stay inside so that no one would see him but it was difficult to imagine anyone else being this far off the grid. Even if he did pass a lone hiker, there would be no need for formal introductions or suspicious behavior. He would just act casual and keep on the trail. The sun peaked over the tip of Raven's Rock, illuminating the path through low hanging branches with shadows of ambient gold, sprites of pink, and lavender kisses. That was all the encouragement he needed to explore. Cuyler slipped on his black vans and blue bandana and headed for the trail.

Once across the river, it was only a thirty minute hike to the natural stone shelter of Raven's Rock. Two oversized boulders towered at twenty feet over head and protruded from the face of the mountain to support a sixty foot stone slab shelter. A stone fire pit lay heavily sunken into the earth just in front of the shelter's overhang. Any remnant of use had long since washed away, leaving the place with a ghostly loneliness. He stood in awe of its size and uniqueness that lured him inside. Though the mouth of the cave was massive, it was deceptively so, as its expansive exterior lead to a disappointing 30 foot cavern, unremarkable by all accounts. His heart sank as he walked passed its rounded, wet edges, brushing his hand against the cold mud walls in hopes of finding something interesting. When his efforts left him empty-handed and without adventure, he resolved to sit by the vacant fireplace. The view was breathtaking from its staggering form edging the cliff of a mile-high drop.

If nothing else the cool moisture in the air brought clarity to his thoughts, as he had hoped to find on his hike. He felt strengthened and alert like he had not experienced since her disappearance. He longed to share this view with her, and he was sure of what she would say if she were standing next to him.

"I want to fly," she would tease him with her arms held out like wings. Then, he would wrap her in the safety of his arms, and hold her there. No harm would come to her when she was harbored in his protection.

With so much beauty here in the states, why did they feel the need to leave? He couldn't remember now what the urgency had been. All that came to his memory was the last words she spoke to him, "Hurry back, I will miss you." He was sure she was missing him now; his entire body could feel her pulling him nearer to her with each passing moment. And, although he had hurried, he had not moved fast enough. Now, with every splitting cell of his being, he missed her more than he ever imagined possible.

Rising to his feet, he squinted at the midday sun now directly over him. Its upright position allowed its warming smile to touch each crevice, valley, and mountain top equally, eliminating dismal shadows in favor of illuminating the vibrant craftsmanship of God's hand. Endless variances and shades of the spectrum testified against the lull of a pale blue sky, proclaiming their lustrous mystery for all to ponder and admire. He looked out onto miles of ranges and thought for a moment he saw true freedom. No twisted thorns of roses weeping petals to the ground in candid tyranny could retain the spirit dwelling here. In standing abreast this canvas all fear is abolished, hope restored, and justice realized. Freedom, then, gains adornment in place of vague sentiment and the dweller thrives in happiness not pursued but achieved.

Descending the face of the mountain, Cuyler took time to admire each undiscovered diversion of the overgrown path, just as he imagined Sadie might. He imagined her picking items of interest and snapping her camera from various angles insatiably. When they were together again he would have to bring her along this same trail, so they could take the photographs together. The images were much more gratifying when seen through Sadie's lens.

He skipped into the cabin, unaware of the excitement in his step. His thoughts were bouncing brightly with ideas on how they would spend their day on Raven Rock- the hike, the enjoyable adventure she would undoubtedly find, and the stolen frames of life's greatest moments captured timelessly on digital film. Lost in his imagination, Cuyler almost didn't hear his cell phone buzzing in the bedroom.

The phone had been loaned to him by David, to be used only in case of emergencies, and always answered by the third ring. It was a system they had arranged as a means of communicating without drawing attention to David, in case Ray were to walk in and see him on the phone. The fewer the questions asked by Ray, the better. He also explained that he would only call once to ensure Cuyler was still safe, so it was vital that he not miss the call. There were times when he doubted

David's sincerity regarding his safety and entertained the idea that David's call was placed to ensure Cuyler stayed where he'd been dropped. He wanted to trust him again but had seen two distinctly opposite faces worn by David. One portrayed a man of remorse who sought justice for those he had hurt. The other was calculating, manipulative, and successful at weaseling his way back into any severed relationship. Either way, Cuyler decided it was best not to dwell on the specifics of David's intentions. Sadie's rescue was tomorrow and it was a call he could not afford to miss. He ran as fast as he could to answer the buzz.

Unfortunately, it was not David calling. The voice tinkling through the receiver threw him into a tailspin of reactions, all colliding at once and causing a paralyzing crash of activity. For several minutes he was completely mute in disbelief that she could have this number. No one was supposed to have it, save David and Cuyler. The point of buying the disposable cell phone was privacy and security. That plan obviously had some leaks, a matter to discuss with David later. Once the continuous crashing began to reside, Cuyler was able to respond in broken thoughts. What could she possibly want with him? He didn't know where or how to begin this conversation and, truthfully, he would not have answered at all if he had bothered to look at the caller ID.

He cleared his throat and pushed out the only word that would form, "Hi."

"Cuyler?" she asked with hopeful intonation.

"Yes, it's me," he managed to his own surprise.

"This is Sere-" she tried.

"I know," he shorted her. Realizing the harshness in his voice, he tried to rephrase. "I recognize your voice. How have you been?"

"That's why I am calling you," she began again nervously, ignoring the interruption. "I need to talk to you, but I would like to see you first." She waited for a moment and when Cuyler didn't reply, she continued. "I realize it has been several weeks, and you are very busy with David, but this is urgent. I wouldn't have called you if I had any other choice."

"How did you get this number?" he interrogated. He could not explain why he suddenly felt so angry with her. Was it the way she was tip-toing around what she needed to say? Or was it the distraught, hero-deprived tone of her voice? He wanted to crush her desperation into a stone-cold death, and he couldn't even begin to understand why. He shuttered at the thought of actually killing her.

"It's a long story," she started in a whispering squeak.

"Never mind," he interrupted again. "Why not just say what you need to say now?" Of course he realized that she should be treating him this way and not the other way around. He was the one that had used her, taken advantage of her vulnerability, and left it exposed and bleeding at the call of another woman's name. Yet, once again, she had interrupted his daydreams about Sadie.

"I just can't. Cuyler, I know you are going through a lot but so am I. Meet me at the diner tonight." She paused and he could hear her breath trembling. Had she been crying? "Please, I need you," she said with desperation.

He had never been good at turning away from anyone who needed him, even if that person had been more of an enemy than an ally. Certainly, he could not do it to the woman who had opened her home, her heart, and her legs to him when he needed them most.

"I can't meet you there, but if you can find a way to me then I am open to meeting with you," he replied with sincerity. "Just come alone and watch for tailing lights, okay?" He didn't want to frighten her, but couldn't risk being seen either. It was a bad situation to throw her into, but she is the one that called him. Apparently, David had approved of their contact or he wouldn't have given the number to her in the first place. Their meeting seemed fairly justifiable under that umbrella of thought.

"Thanks, Cuyler. I'll be there at six," she replied, sounding relieved. A gentle click came into the receiver and he closed his phone.

Six o'clock came faster than expected. He hadn't prepared anything for dinner; nor had he cleaned up around the cabin. His intentions should be clear, and he didn't want to mislead her by going out of his way to spruce up a nice dinner by candlelight. On the other hand, she had been quite generous over the last couple of months, so he didn't want to be rude either. Finally, after pacing the floors for several minutes, he decided it would be best to compromise and prepare as if the meeting were with an old friend.

He picked up the jackets and boots from the living room floor and tossed them into his bedroom. It should be the safest room in the house to hide his mess, as he figured she would be nowhere near his bed tonight. He then took the leftovers from last night's supper and threw them on the stove to reheat. Baked beans, chopped steak, and grilled zucchini looked sufficient for the occasion.

The gentle knocking at the front door startled him. He dashed to the door, not wanting to leave her out in the broad daylight for too long. She looked disheveled in her sweat pants and baggy sweater, her hair was flat and slightly tangled on the ends, and her skin was bare of the usual make-up and glitter. Her bright green eyes were red and puffy from crying. Without her even trying, however, she had a beautiful glow in her cheeks and looked more radiant than he remembered.

"Come in," he said gently. Her pitiful display tugged at his heart in spite of his best efforts to ignore it.

"Thanks," she spoke softly, not yet making eye contact with him. In her hands she was nervously wringing a white handkerchief, occasionally touching it to her nose or cheeks. "I am sorry to barge back into your life like this, and I won't stay long," she said, stepping through the threshold and stopping on the door mat. She stared down at it, as if contemplating the irony of the word spelled across the front. This situation felt anything but welcoming.

"Have a seat. I have some food warming up. It's not much, but you are welcome to it," Cuyler said passively. He took quick steps toward the kitchen, expecting her to follow. She didn't. When he looked back she was still standing on the mat, wringing the dirty handkerchief.

"Like I said, I'm not going to stay," she repeated assertively.

"Then what did you come to tell me? Are you sick?" he questioned, observing her slouching stance and heavy-hanging eyes. He could recognize exhaustion and worry like that which she wore and at least feel empathy for her.

"No, I'm not sick. Well, not exactly," she hesitated.

"Just spit it out, Serenity. I know you didn't drive all the way out here to dance around bushes." He felt his cheeks getting hot as he lost patience. If there was one thing he could not stand for a woman to do it was to give him three drops of paint and expect him to paint the entire mural from it.

"I'm pregnant, Cuyler," she blurted out, breaking out into a sob.

He stared blankly at her, without blinking, wincing, or moving. He knew the meaning of each individual word, but together in a sentence they just sounded like jumbled jargon. Her crying seemed the most heinous sound possible in those long, frozen seconds. He couldn't think with all her noisy sobbing and repeating of what sounded to be the same sentence. Pregnant?

She tried to reach for his arm, her tiny, shaking hand still holding the handkerchief. He reflexively jerked back and narrowed his beady eyes at her. Pregnant? His glare traced her body once again from her rosy cheeks and sodden eyes to her swollen breasts and slight bulge beneath her baggy sweater. The full reality was too much to take in at once and a shrill transgression filled the space between his ears. His vision was blurry, his ears ringing, and the pounding behind his eyes made him stagger.

"Pregnant?" he finally managed to ask, his voice bellowing with more harshness than necessary. "What am I supposed to do now?" The cabin suddenly smoldered him into a fast sweat and started to close in on him. He had to get out, had to get away from her. "No, no, this can't be," he mumbled, heading quickly for the door.

"It's not like I wanted it either," she started defensively.

"You don't understand. I can't have a baby with you. It's supposed to be Sadie. I am supposed to rescue her tomorrow and we are supposed to be together again. Not you, not a baby with you, not anything with you. I don't want you, I want her. And I don't want that unless it is with her. Don't you get it?" he snapped at her.

She stood firmly planted on the mat, her mouth gaped open. "You don't have to do anything," she said finally, the color leaving her rosy cheeks. "I just thought you should know." She stepped toward the door, solemnly droning each step. Stopping beside him, she stood only inches away. The sweet smell of gingerbread tickled his nose and made his heart beat faster.

"Here," she said, handing him an envelope. "There's a letter inside, but don't read it until I have already left. I don't want to make your life complicated, Cuyler, I promise. All I wanted was to make sure you had a chance to know." Serenity's melancholy gaze bore into his own as he stood dumbly frozen with his hand still on the threshold. She slipped gracefully by and took light steps toward her vehicle. He could hear the engine turn over and the gentle rumble of her Jeep fading into the distance. Still, he couldn't move.

Unsure of how long he had been standing there, staring incomprehensively through the open door, Cuyler tried to process if Serenity had really been there. Had the news been real? Had any of it been real, or just a very vivid hallucination? The letter in his hand was proof that she had indeed been there. He fell heavily into the couch, unfolded the neatly pressed seams, and read each word slowly.

"My Dearest Cuyler,

"I am only writing this letter to you in case something goes wrong during our meeting, as I expect my news will not be well received. All I can tell you now is that I am sorry for complicating your life. I realize fully that your heart belongs to Sadie, and your life is made of meaning only when you are with her. The guilt has been tearing at me inside, knowing that I cannot ask you to be with me and yet I cannot face this alone.

"I have given a lot of thought about how I can handle this situation. There are options available to me, I know. I could be another number here, taken at the welfare line while my unborn child demands the best of me that I cannot provide. I could also place him for adoption and live the rest of my life wondering who he is and if he thinks of me, too, or just wastes his life hating me. There is, of course, abortion. I hate to even think that word, knowing all too well its accompanying life sentence of wondering what might have been or, worse yet, who might have become from all of this. Please understand I have deeply considered every avenue. I promise you.

"Yet, all of these options leave either one or both of us dead in some way or another. I see the children of single parents walking barefoot in front of my diner every day. They are starved for the opportunity to be like everyone else, or at least a fraction of everyone else. Alienated by poverty and shamed by welfare, they fill their idle curiosities with mischief and resentment at the hand they've been dealt. Eventually they become another burden on society, not having been taught any other way. Their lives are limitlessly dead, trapped in the judicial circus. How can it be right to doom innocence that way?

"If he is adopted, he could end up having a long, blessed life with a family who loves him and spoils him at every turn. That is what movies would have us believe. The reality is, however, that he would most likely become a warden of the state, bouncing from one foster home to another. God only knows what living situations could arise from that, and if he survived it with any sanity, I am left to wonder in which home hope finally dies?

"I cannot just kill him in my womb and leave me alive to go on like nothing ever happened. Taking his soul in that way would take mine as well, condemning me to some sort of hell on earth. That is why I have to do what I believe is the only right choice. Since we are one life now, one cannot die without the other. Yes, Cuyler, the unborn life inside me and I will die together. I am asking that you do not pursue us, or try to contact us. No doubt that by the time you come to your senses and read this, it has already been done. Or at least you could not reach us in time.

"Here is what I want you to know. When I first saw you in my diner, I already knew I would hire you. It wasn't out of pity, or generosity, it was because of the color of your aura. From the moment you walked in, it was like a rainbow shown around you, surrounded by a beautifully balanced white. I knew you were an amazing person, and I was hoping to find some way to get to know you. The job offer was a perfect way to do just that. And I am smiling, even as I write this, because I had the best two months of my life with you in that very diner. Thank you for that, Handsome.

"Also, I realize that you never really loved me, and I want you to know it is okay. I'm not upset because I understand what it is like to love someone so much that no one else exists, even when they are standing right in front of you. When you think of her in a picture, she is the only part of the image that comes clearly into focus, and you know it will be like that until the day you take your last breath. Every moment will be lived for her, every action revolving around your attraction to her happiness. I know these things, Cuyler, because I love you in this way.

"Lastly, I wish to give you my blessing. I hope you find your Sadie, and that the two of you will live happy lives together. I will be picturing you truly at rest in her arms, and that image will give me the courage to let you go. Don't let anything stop you from saving her. And when you do finally get to hold her again, never let her go. Shower her in your love, as it is only she who deserves it. Don't worry about me, or our unborn, because we will be at rest, too. We are ready for our next adventure where death has no meaning and loneliness does not exist. Pain cannot touch me, fear cannot burn me. We are free, Handsome, as we should be. And, now, so are you.

Forever Yours,
Serenity"

A single gunshot echoed through the dense forest, announcing its grievance from every direction. Then, in the heart of one man sitting alone in a small cabin sunk in the darkened hills of North Carolina, there was only silence.

18

"Good morning, Willow," he said, slipping tainted fingers between the sheets. His hand rubbed the inside of her thigh tenderly, arousing her from her light dozing. She opened her tired eyes and looked down to her legs where his hands disturbed the surface of the blue satin sheets. Lying perfectly still, she hoped he would assume she was still sleeping and give up. Her lack of recognition only made him rub faster and harder, his smooth palms creating a tingling burning sensation along the tender skin of her inner thigh.

"I want to celebrate your ceremony with you, Willow, and show you how proud I am," he continued in a low, seductive tone. His soft lips caressed her neck with warm, passionate kisses as his hand found its way between her legs and continued its steady rubbing. "And I have an idea for a game we can play."

She still didn't answer. It was pointless to struggle, cry, protest, or even pretend to like it. After their initial meeting in April, Shamen had insisted she live in his suite rather than the Common Hall. At his word, she had been moved and had not returned to her pressboard bed and concrete cell. She didn't miss the splinters, drab gray surroundings, or the noisy clients in the slightest, but she did miss the privacy. He had wanted to keep her close, so that he could enjoy the best she had to offer any time the desire struck him. Unfortunately, she was surprised at just how often the strike of desire landed right upon her cheek. He was much more aggressive than she had expected of a man in his sixties. Her face stayed swollen, bruised, or cut with a new mark added almost daily. Experience taught her it was usually best to just be still and eventually he would be done.

She tried to take her mind elsewhere, as she often did during sex with Shamen. This morning, however, she was too tired to think of any other place. He had kept her up until nearly daybreak, performing various role play exercises and dances. He was as indecisive as he was old and couldn't make up his mind which he liked best for the ceremony. At one point he had even brought in another whore from Common Hall and made them perform together. She cringed at the thought of the girl's nasty vagina in her mouth, the skin broken and loose from the frat boys who had paid a little extra for a train just a few minutes before there forced charade. Sadie had brushed her teeth twice but still tasted their ejaculate on her tongue as well as she had last night when it dripped back out of the teenage girl and into her mouth.

"Ask me what the game is girl. Beg me to tell you," he demanded in a hot whisper. His penis was hard and rubbing against her back now. The thick gray pubic hair acted like a scouring pad scrubbing her buttocks.

"Please, Master Shamen, tell me what game you want to play." Her lips formed the words in a sort of high-pitched plea. *Please, God, give him a heart attack or a stroke. Anything would look natural at his age.*

"It's called Cavity Search," he growled, climbing on top of her with more speed than she thought he was capable. The sudden shifts in weight against her belly made her yelp out, inspiring a heckling cackle from her aggressor. In another quick movement he had heavy ropes tied tightly around her wrists. The other end of the rope was tied to each bed post. He moved to do the same thing to her ankles and Sadie tried not to fight against it. She was so close to being rid of him, she didn't want to ruin her chances again by losing her cool. After he had tied her, she lay sprawled helplessly upon the bed, arms and legs open and entirely vulnerable to him.

He walked to the side of the bed and tapped his fingers along her torso, giving extra attention to harden her nipples with a slight pinch and roll between his fingers. He then grabbed both breasts in his hands and pressed against them for support as he climbed back onto the bed, straddling her and chuckling with anticipation. His erection threatened penetration, but he quickly withdrew.

"Hmmm, I wonder if you are hiding anything in there?" he said as he shoved two stiff fingers into her vagina. Sadie squirmed reflexively, birthing a sardonic expression into his eyes, which spread like cancer through his entire body. The ropes tugged at her ankles, burning them with their constant friction as he pushed her legs farther apart, ripping painfully at the muscles in her groin. Sadie focused all of her attention into her hands, trying desperately not to cry out from the shredding pain he was inflicting.

"Are you having fun, my precious Willow?" he asked. Sadie nodded her head, not wanting to upset him as long as she remained bound in this vulnerable position. His left hand pushed up and back against her leg, causing the ropes to pull tighter at her ankles, as he pushed a third finger in, then a fourth. "I can't hear you, darling? I need you to tell me how much fun you are having," he said calmly. His eyes penetrated her with sadistic charm, unaffected by the agony he inflicted.

"I am having…" she struggled through the tears in her throat choking the words, "so much fun," she tried again. Her mouth opened to scream, but she stifled it to a whimper. Tears began to soak both sides of her face and into her ears as he pulled out his four fingers and forced them in again, repeating the motion until she thought the pain alone would kill her. It can be shocking how much one person can live through and how much torture a single psyche can endure. She could feel the distortion creeping in, distorted fragments of thoughts that distanced her from reality as it unfolded.

"It does me well to see you enjoying yourself so much, Willow. But, I still haven't found what you are hiding," he said playfully as he withdrew his fingers. "I think I need to search elsewhere," he continued. Lowering himself to the floor, he untied the ropes around her ankles then reached for her arms.

"Don't do anything stupid, girl," he warned sternly, untying her right arm and pulling it over to join the left. Her arms were now bound together securely so that she could barely move her fingers. She could feel his rough hands bending her knees and pulling her farther down on the bed, stretching the ropes tighter around her stinging wrists. The tension heightened against her torso and made it difficult to breathe. The constant air hunger drove her anxiety until she thought she felt her soul begin to slip through the knot which bound her body.

"Please, Master Shamen," she started to beg. His wide-eyed expression stopped her from going any further with her plea. It was hopeless. There was no physical escape from this nightmare and she prayed silently that perhaps she could die rather than experience this.

"Please what? Please keep going? I'm just trying to make our last morning together special," he said as his voice grew increasingly louder. Sadie nodded weakly to his rambling, desperately seeking to deafen herself to him. She closed her eyes and searched for the soothing gray that had numbed her before, but found nothing. Instead, all she saw were the demons dancing, swaying in their laughter, and tapping about the room with flamboyant mockery.

Sadie's mind narrowed on that one thought. If this was to be their last morning together, that must mean she would be leaving again to another house, another Master. This was never going to stop. She stopped her sniveling and strained to ignore his repetitive probing. Her mind searched sharply for a new solution. *It's now or never,* she decided. *I have to get out of here tonight or I never will.* Her eyes were focused and searching for anything that might help her escape. The room was completely clear of any sharp objects and the only item with any weight was a wide screen television mounted to the far wall some twenty feet away. She knew she would never reach it in time and the attempt would surely cost her in more than bruises, cuts, or scrapes. She closed her withered eyes and tried again to pray, imploring any god to take her away from the suffering forced on her.

His hands pushed roughly against her face until his left hand was behind her head, pulling her hair back so that her neck was extended and threatening to break. His right hand moved to pry open her lips. She wasn't sure what she should do or of his plans for her until he forced his fingers into her throat. Sadie gagged against his rough nails scratching her uvula, and hot bile began to climb around his fingers and into her mouth. He pulled back and looked at her as though contemplating what to do next, tapping his bile-stained finger against her cheek lightly. Sadie stared up at him, her eyes animalistic with scornful abhorrence. Her jaw clamped tightly with her angst building against the chains around her freedom.

"I don't think my fingers can reach back there far enough," he said, still pondering. "Perhaps I need something longer and harder to make sure you aren't hiding anything down in there." He rose up to his knees and walked them forward until his scrotum scraped against her neck and his dick rested on her wet lips. Sadie prayed silently that he would not do what she was sure he was about to do. Of all the things she had been through, and all the clients who had beaten her, raped her and degraded her, she had not experienced this level of inhumanity. Even as it happened, she could not believe it.

"This is how I would do a cavity search if I were the prison guard," he said with excitement. "Watch and see, you will love this idea." With that he leaned up and bent his dick downward into her mouth, impaling it all the way into her throat. Her eyes became wide with terror and she tried to scream, but her attempts were blunt against the occlusion. She was choking on it until even the vomitus had no way out and burned backward into her lungs.

Perhaps it was the thirst for air which drove her, as a purely physiological response empowering her with adrenaline. Maybe it was the snapping of the conscious from the subconscious mind that led her, and the response was consequent of a trauma-induced mania. Or perchance the demons dancing around her were more than hallucinations conceived by hatred and in her vulnerability became opportunistic parasites. Whatever the cause, her body fell limp against the mattress and Sadie was lost in transcendence. A viscous claret river flowed beneath her feet as she stood amidst the foaming fog around her. Her body was made new again and the returning strength pumped vigorously through her, elating her to new heights. Consciousness was a subjective state in her enlightened mind as the escape for which she had been begging became as real to her as Cuyler had been. If only he could join her here among the tranquil rolling fog, bathed in the strength of the mystic red river, she thought with yearning. She looked around her subconscious but felt the quiet cry of pining as the river changed its course. Wind funneled around her, bringing chaos into sight. Through the lashing of her future as it could be, Sadie resolved that no one could imprison her unless she allowed them. No one could take her again without her permission. Her thoughts versed the seduction of her misery as she sought her way back to life.

Signals racing, bullets chasing arrows from my mind; stained with the blood of a thousand thoughts and dreams we left behind. Now angels dancing, their moves enhancing love across the crimson sky. Then I see, in spite of me, the receding voice of reason left to die. The quiet still poised against the noise of the ever changing tide- a confliction of quick decisions directing worlds collide. Embracing fear of detectable shear I prepare to take my dive; each direction a new collection of the fight to stay alive.

The past in shadows cast, encased within your light, to laugh upon the grave of fate that I should die this night. I look ahead where sorrows bled and find lain across a latent shrine a way to irritate the hands of fate- leave light and darkness intertwined. So brief the relief is the stolen breath of time; a small delay of the debt to pay for a captive of the crime. Ceasing is my civil right justly laid upon the waling wire; though my act of will could leave me still caught in the crossfire.

No sooner had she understood her truest heart's desire, Sadie lost herself to the crimson veil which blinded rationality and fed the instincts of survival and revenge. Sadie bit down at the base of his penis. No longer would she do as she was told. His body tensed and she pressed her teeth closer together. Never again would she let them touch her, rape her, or insult her. His hands were smacking against the top of her head and her arms. Sadie sank her teeth deeper into his skin. Blood began to trickle into her mouth and the taste of it made her crave more. She would not be sold, traded, abused, or trained by one more of these sadistic creeps. She bit down again, this time with the full force of her jaw, and the blood flowed even faster. Not now, not ever again. *This ends here.* The wailing against her arms stopped and Shamen's body slumped over.

Still cloaked in the warmth of the devil's fire, Sadie didn't take time to think. She rocked her shoulders until his body collapsed onto the bed next to her. Finally able to breathe, Sadie swallowed the last of the blood in her mouth. The texture was warm and smooth, bitter to the taste buds yet metallic on her tongue. She became intoxicated by the smell of it all around her and pulled forcefully at her arms to break free of the ropes. Her right hand finally found freedom and untied the left. Sadie rubbed the sores on her wrists and stared at the mess she had made on the bed.

Pulling the corpse into the floor, she struggled to shove his dead weight under the bed. He was almost too tall to fit neatly and as she struggled with his head, she noticed his pale blue eyes were iced over just like his soul, frozen forever in fear and agony. Sadie smiled brightly, knowing the devil had collected his soul to slaughter. She imagined him writhing and wailing from the depths of a flaming lake, drowning in his own personal torture for all eternity.

Finally, his head popped behind the bed frame with one last push. She was glad she had gotten him moved before rigor had a chance to set in. Working through the intense shaking that threatened to smother her completely, Sadie's gut wrenched violently against Shamen's life sinking heavily in her stomach. She raced to clean the blood spills from the walls and frame with straight bleach. The broken skin on her wrists burned as it was reduced to slough, but Sadie continued to scrub relentlessly. Heat radiated through her face as she scrubbed and tugged at the sheets in desperate strain to conceal his death. She snatched a heavy black satin duvet from the closet and spread it over the soaked sheets, adorning pillows to ensure there would be none showing through and fluffing out the skirt so that it draped low against the floor. She stepped back to observe the space. Nothing could be seen of Shamen's blood or his body.

As she looked around, she caught glimpse of a mirror hanging above the bed. She was shocked by the woman staring back at her. Dried blood caked across her mouth and down both sides of her chin, covering her neck and pooling between her clavicles. She stood stark naked and panting like a dog in heat. Her bright, wild eyes were open wide over a full display of rabid teeth.

Hearing footsteps, Sadie turned quickly and headed for the bathroom. She closed the door behind her and leapt into the shower. Turning the water on fully, she didn't wait for it to warm to her liking. She began to scrub her face and neck vigorously with the bar soap. It ran into her mouth and eyes, but she hardly noticed. The last of the blood vanished down the drain when the door flew open. The startled Sadie pressed her back against the wall and waited.

"Willow, where is Shamen?" an angry voice called out to her.

Sadie closed her eyes and tried to sound innocent. "He was gone early this morning, sir."

"Why are you in the shower so early?" he demanded.

"My Master will want me to look nice for him, sir. I was only planning to surprise him," she answered softly. Sadie couldn't move and was grateful for the hot water flowing down her back. It helped to keep her calm and hide the trembling in her voice.

"Well, that's real sweet but you have to get out now," he replied condescendingly. "Lydia needs to finish preparing you in her office."

"Yes, sir," Sadie answered. She reached down and turned the water off. Her wrists were already starting to bruise badly. Her ankles bore similar marks.

She walked down the hall, wrapped in the security of an oversized black towel. Its cotton fibers felt soft and warm against her skin. The hallway usually chilled her to the point of shivering but, at least for now, she remained comfortably cozy. The walk was a pleasant one, without conversation or small talk. Just silence, except for the rhythmic marching of Brethren Young's steel-toed boots. Sadie skipped along slightly behind him, without notice of his glances in her direction.

"What are you so happy about? Are you that excited for tonight?" he asked with suspicion.

"Yes, sir, I suppose I am. My apologies if I have upset you," she said sweetly. She kept her eyes cast to the floor, hoping it would help to conceal the brilliant grin which shone through them without containment.

"Lydia, here she is. You might want to check her head, though. She's acting a little off," he whispered behind his hand into Dr. Scavway's ear. The physician peered over his shoulder and looked Sadie over.

"Yes, I certainly will. She will be ready, Brethren," Lydia confirmed officially. Dr. Scavway stood perfectly poised until he disappeared around the corner. Closing the door behind her, she turned her attention to the grinning young woman fidgeting in her office. "Sadie," she said cautiously, "Are you ok?"

"Oh yes, doctor. I am quite well," she answered darkly. Redness still cloaked the room from where she stood. The only difference was the demons were no longer playing outside but were rejoicing from within. "I am sorry for how I have treated you. My eyes are completely open now, and I am not scared anymore. I have just realized you have been right all along. It was always meant to be me, and I am here to set us free," Sadie said smoothly. Dr. Scavway leaned closer and locked her eyes into Sadie with keen interest. Sadie looked up through her long, dark lashes. Her eyes appeared completely black, as though no iris existed beyond the pupil. Her dark hair had loosely fallen into her face and flirted with the edges of her slanted stare. Her lips twisted into a seductive leer and the tip of her tongue danced along the smooth edges of her perfect teeth, luring the physician closer.

"Are you ready?" she whispered, entranced by the dark temptress standing before her. Their lips were almost touching; moisture beaded along their edges from their hot breath being exchanged at such close range.

"Make me beautiful," Sadie whispered back.

19

Cuyler stared at the back of a silent cell phone lying on the nightstand. He flipped it over and checked again for any messages or missed calls. No new messages or calls, just the time displayed in large white letters- 5:14 p.m. He took fast steps to the bedroom window and peeled back the blinds to look out. David's car was not yet in sight. He was two hours late without so much as a text message explaining why.

He paced nervously around the room, down the hall, and back around the room again. His nails were chewed to the quick an hour ago and he now bit nervously at the skin around them. When his fingers started to bleed, he pulled at his long curls instead. His hair was uncharacteristically loose and twisted carelessly around his neck and shoulders. He was wearing the shirt he had been wearing the night he first met his love in Bethesda. That night his hair had been down also. He wasn't normally superstitious, but he figured he could use all the luck he could get. Besides, it might bring Sadie a little comfort and help her to see things were going to work out for them, just as they had years ago.

Cuyler stuck the phone in his pocket and stomped outside, letting the screen door slam hard behind him. He looked out over the mountains and thought briefly of Serenity. There was no sign of her jeep in any direction and thought perhaps had just imagined the gun shot. For a brief moment he entertained the idea of looking for her to be sure. The entire evening felt like some terrible nightmare and he thought it was possible the meat had spoiled or the mushrooms had gone bad, resulting in vivid hallucinations of the whole affair. Either way, he didn't have time to investigate. He couldn't leave and go traipsing about in the woods. What if David showed up before he made it back to cabin? Nightfall would be coming soon and David would not bother looking for him with so much to do tonight.

He pulled out the cell phone and checked it again, looking mostly to see if there was a strong enough signal to receive calls. The signal was moderate at best, but should allow calls or texts to come through. There had been no trouble receiving David's call this morning. He had said to be ready to leave at three and he would call again when he was on his way to the cabin. David had finished with brief instruction to rest well but eat even better because he would need his energy in case the situation got out of hand. He had done just that, polishing off two chicken breasts, a generous portion of broccoli and cheese, and three rolls. He felt rested, motivated, and strong enough to kill ten people with his bare hands if he had to. The only thing missing was David.

Truthfully, he wouldn't even wait for David if he had the address where Sadie would be. He would have already left to find her himself but the reality was Cuyler did not have the address. David did. He didn't even have a state or city to search. All he knew was David was to pick him up at three and it was well past time. He looked at his phone again and read the numbers displayed: 5:29. Cuyler could feel his cheeks getting hot and his fingers beginning to tingle. Patience was a virtue he proudly possessed under normal circumstances. Today, however, was anything but normal and his patience was spent.

Although he tried not to consider any negative connotations, he couldn't stop his mind from entertaining the thought that David had planned this whole thing to keep him out of the way. He had been very chummy with Ray and frequently visited the houses. David had confessed to sleeping with the girls, explaining that if he didn't Ray would be suspicious. Cuyler had always suspected David did it out of enjoyment, at least in part, rather than obligation. Perhaps David had other plans for Sadie than her release. What if it was part of his plan to leave Cuyler out here as a diversion so he would have plenty of time to take Sadie even farther away?

He keyed in David's number and waited. After one ring, the phone went straight to voicemail. Cuyler no longer wondered why had not heard from him yet. It's hard to call someone from a phone that is turned off. Cuyler was burning with anger as he began to pace faster across the porch. He was sure that he had been deceived and cunningly placed far out of the way, and then left here to miss the only chance he might have at saving Sadie. Picking up the chairs, which leaned against the front of the house, he threw them into the dense woods. They smashed against a large oak tree into several splintered pieces. He still wasn't calm, and taking the phone out of his pocket, he started to throw that, too. Before he let go, however, he reconsidered. He might need it to get a ride out of here.

He keyed in a different number this time. His shattered nerves deflected the tremor in his hands and vibrated against the phone as he dialed the one person he knew would never turn him away. He hated to drag her into his drama, but it was a matter of life and death. After two rings, he pulled the cell away from his hear and listened closely. Somewhere, faintly in the distance, he could hear Serenity's ringtone echoing against the mountain ranges around him. He listened closer, his heart banging frantically in his chest, for the direction of her cell phone's singing. The events of last night were not a nightmare or the hallucinogenic effect of bad mushrooms. She had been there to bring awareness to him, the unborn child they created was real, and the conclusive gunshot was a deadly fact. *What have I done?*

Cuyler took off running into the thick woods. Branches slapped into his eyes and against his bare legs. Dense shadows surrounded him so that he couldn't see where his feet would land next, but he didn't care. He pressed forward into the blackness of the setting sun, determined to reach her. Hopes that he was not too late, that their unborn might still have a chance, and Serenity might continue to bless the world with her wonder fell to a crushing end when he tripped over something cold and rigid sticking up through a thicket. Losing his balance, he was lunged forward into the air and landed sharply against a brightly colored vehicle. It was Serenity's jeep, recklessly parked and left desolate.

Rubbing his jaw, which had taken most of the impact, he looked around in the dirt to find what had caused the crash. He knelt down on his knees and took out his cell phone for extra light. Bright red hair shook against the wind and he followed the tufts of it with his hands. Moving back the leaves, he uncovered the crystalline face of Serenity. Her eyes were open and her lips parted slightly. Blood that had trickled out of her mouth was now dried hard against her cheek and corner of her lips. He reached out to touch her face and retracted his hand. Cuyler had never been so close to the dead before and the cold stiffness of her cheeks surprised him. Their rosy color, gifted by the pregnancy, was completely gone now and her flesh was opaquely white.

Remembering the reason she had come to him, he laid his trembling hand gently against the small bulge of her abdomen. The unborn inside was as still and lifeless as its mother. Cuyler began to weep, knowing how little he done to stop this and wondering what it would have taken to change her mind. He felt the immense weight of responsibility tearing him open inside. How much loss would it take before he stopped hurting everyone around him? First he allowed Sadie to be taken, tortured, and sold. Then, dismissing his quest for Sadie had brought him to this lovely and energetic woman. He had used her and left her broken. She had tried to reach him, and perhaps he could have saved his child if he had bothered to listen. But, he hadn't, and now both mother and unborn were dead. The misery of guilt lies barren when compared to the suffering of the true fault found in it.

Falling back into the leaves beside her, Cuyler held his knees close to his chest and rocked. His eyes caught focus of her jeep, abandoned at the tip of the trail it had created the night before. The last of the sun touched its chrome edges, so that he could see the silver lining through the dense forest embedded in him. He may have let these two die but that didn't mean Sadie had to die as well. Cuyler walked cautiously around the vehicle to find the driver's side door still open and the keys lying on the seat. Taking one last glance at the corpse of a woman who loved him too much to live without him, Cuyler felt a changing burn surge through his veins. *I will make this right,* he decided and started the engine.

He struggled to back the vehicle down the steeply graded mountain side, moving slowly so as to dodge the large oak, pecan, and pine trees that leaned into the freshly cut path. He could not imagine how she managed to get the jeep this far up the mountain without wrecking, especially with the limited visibility provided by the evening sun. Cuyler did not even have that luxury. The sun had crept behind the ridges, turning its shift to the moon and stars as the only source of light.

By the time he had reached the gravel road at the bottom, the clock on the dash testified it was already half past six. He hated himself for trusting David. He had wasted too much time waiting around and worried his chance to save Sadie had set with the sun. Getting the vehicle out of the woods had taken a lot of precious time but now that he was on a main road he could drive much faster. Even so, he knew he would not reach David's apartment until after eight. David would be long gone by then, if he wasn't already.

As he pressed the accelerator to eighty, he pictured David's massive frame hovering over Sadie's sacred body. He wondered angrily if David had paid for her with cash, because he certainly didn't seem as wealthy as the clients described in the notebook he had read on the Rose Academy. Drugs could have been the negotiated currency, and he would have ample access with his position at the police department. One thing of which he could be certain was that David would come home eventually. He was a creature of habit and order. Everything in his life had an order, purposefully displayed and fine-tuned to David's liking. He could not survive without it. A wicked grin crept across his haggard face. "You will have to come home," he reasoned aloud, "and when you do, I will be waiting for you." Cuyler reached beneath the seat where Serenity kept her only weapon while they were together. It was still there. He pulled out a twelve-inch fixed blade bowie knife with a comfortable bone handle. "I will be waiting," he repeated darkly and made the hard right onto the final stretch of road that stood between him and his fair Sadie.

20

Master Shamen's celebratory gathering included only the most exclusive guests. She had been bathed and groomed, prepped and costumed to their liking then shuffled into the back bedroom. Sadie sat quietly on the king-sized bed and waited for her cue to enter the party. The purple lace corset was stiff and tight, forcing her to keep her back perfectly straight to catch small breaths. The cups of the corset pushed her breasts up so much they were hardly covered. The bodice ended at the tip of her hips, where black lace trim matched the garter and stockings, and the outfit was made complete by black stiletto heels to accentuate her long legs.

Dr. Scavway had taken a considerable amount of time to tease and style her hair, making it rigorously wild and yet surprisingly elegant. Layers had been cut into it, which fell seductively into her painted onyx eyes. Lavender gems sparkled at the corner of each eye, shaped in roses as her crowning honor. She could feel her skin pulling under them when she blinked and the inside corners were stinging from the close proximity of the glue to the tear ducts. False eye lashes had also been applied and, though her eyes were threatening tears from their recent irritation, she dared not touch them for fear of smudging the doctor's masterpiece.

Special attention was also given to her lips and they were still tingling from the collagen that had been injected that morning. Pale pink lip gloss highlighted their new pout and she wondered how she would work without smudging it. In light of the circumstances, she felt she must look her best for the high-ranking men on the guest list. In attendance were familiar faces- Kendrick and Ray- and unfamiliar ones as well- one called Lucas, and the other Anthony. Sadie thought of Clayton and felt disappointed he had not been invited. It was of his own choosing, according to Dr. Scavway, that he stay home to monitor his child bride and the baby inside. She could hear those who had arrived talking through the door, expressing boisterous excitement for the festivities to begin, speckled with occasional impatient remarks regarding the tardiness of three others- Shamen, another called David, and Cuyler. Cuyler's perfect name rolling off their spiked tongues pierced her indifference, allowing her hatred to seep through the rehashed wounds. Perfection was key on this special night, above all else, to gain their lust so they may perish in it.

Sadie walked quietly over to the standing mirror and observed the stranger staring back at her in silence. Her last basking stare into a mirror had been the night before she came to this place. She had worn a red satin dress then and had not looked as beautiful as this. If it was perfection they were seeking, then she was sure they would be pleased. She admired every curve accentuated by the costume, and ran her fingers down its tight satin fittings. She could understand fully their interest in her and wondered dimly why she had never seen herself in this light. Clearly, she was an object of desire. Temptation had found its living vessel.

And now I see in a mirror, dimly, but then face to face. Now I know in part, but then shall I know just as also I am known. Sadie's lips twisted satirically at the mocked reflection on the sermon her father had given the last Sunday before her departure to Tennessee. At the time, she had dismissed his ramblings but, in this new light, it was becoming clear to her what could be known within a mirror no longer shattered and what truth could be revealed when the layers of perception had been taken away. Her heart fluttered when she remembered the fear of her first November night with the Academy, chained among the rats with her bleeding side teasing their instinctual drive to feast. The distortion had been overwhelming and left her vision broken in shards, slicing that which had been known into fragments seamed by the inevitable unknown. That had been a time of great uncertainty, when the threat of death lingered heavily as a noose around her neck. Her single imperfection had been that she feared death. Now she knew with conviction that death had no dominion over her and she found the flutter was not of fear, but of excitement. What could be found in fear except restriction that disabled action birthed by dreaming? Though this was not a dream, reality was a distorted image through the crimson cloak burned into her retina. Sadie was no longer afraid.

Her gaze fixed upon the shadows beneath the bed where Shamen's body still lay, in full rigor by now. The metallic taste still tickled her tongue with delightful recall of his life's blood between her lips. The image of Shamen jerking in agony then collapsing in death at her demand was sharply in her mind and made her wet. She reached between her legs where delight had begun to surface and pushed her finger lightly inside. Her fingertip grazed the dagger Dr. Scavway had given her for protection. Lydia had been very specific about not using any weapon except as a last resort. She had been hesitant to lend it to Sadie at all, but once convinced she gave strict direction that it was to be worn inside her bodice and only drawn if desperately needed. The demons frolicking in her fearless heart, however, had other plans for the men laughing in the next room, especially Ray and Kendrick who had initiated her misfortunate turnabout. The dagger, she decided, was much more useful when fitted snugly in her snatch.

Her cheeks flushed from pink to red as she burned with anger at the image she had become. She had forgotten who she was, where she was from, and to whom she truly belonged. Where was the woman who had overcome addiction, had traveled the world, and found strength and peace in love? Where was the poetic writer whose hand would cramp from all the stories she could tell, but still never tell them all? And who were these assholes to take her life from her, to turn her into some slave begging for crumbs from the Master's table? At times she thought that perhaps this is all she had ever been, that the other life was a vivid and long-lasting dream. Cuyler had been the heart of that dream, giving her life with every beat of his being. And yet, Cuyler was not here and still she stood breathing. Breathing and waiting. *Waiting, breathing, serving, and waiting. I am tired of waiting.*

Shortly after she had met him, Cuyler held her as she writhed in pain, impatient and crying with the morphine leaking from her system. During her withdrawal, there was little more she could do except wait for her body to adjust. Cuyler had told her then that waiting was a skill to be mastered, and only in mastering that skill could one truly find themselves reflective of patience and understanding; find themselves made new. "The trick," he had told her, "is to think of the time spent waiting as an introspective key. This key unlocks any door that you choose, whether it is your innermost subconscious or completely new worlds. The same key can solve problems or create new ones to solve later. Learning to wait is learning yourself and what you are capable of." The patience she learned on Cuyler's bed while going through the pain of abstaining was so very different from waiting on her soul to finish its dying under the sword of many men. Still, she had perfected the skill of waiting and had been made new, as promised, not in love and understanding, but in something more powerful. Her renewal was created by anger, birthed by death, and made complete by payment of souls owed to her. *Hell hath no fury like a woman's vengeance,* she thought wryly.

"I am tired of waiting," a deep voice explained with a distinctive southern lag over the first syllable of each word. "I am going to get my part done so I can go on."

"Aren't you coming back for all the fun, camera man?" An unfamiliar voice replied.

Sadie heard light footsteps tapping in the hallway behind the door. The tap-click sound made her think this man was wearing loafers, probably with a nice suit. The deeply southern draw made her sure of her first visitor's identity- Kendrick. The was the same Kendrick who flattered her with compliments and tugged at her heart with photo-shopped pictures of his beautiful family, soon to be separated by his failure if she didn't help him. And he was the same man that that had pushed her through a fire escape into her new and terrible life. Since this horror had begun with him, it seemed fitting that tonight's delight should also begin with him. Sadie tip-toed to the bed, sat down gently, and waited.

The crystal knob began to turn. Her heart began to beat wildly into her throat. Just as the door cracked, a long and lanky shadow blocked the light and covered her. He paused. "I'm probably going to go out the back after this anyway. Lydia and I have plans," he said with blatant disinterest. The disappointed taunts and teases increased in volume as the door swung open.

Kendrick was sharply dressed as the poster child for sophistication and style, just as he had been when they first met six months ago in a crowded airport. He was wearing a tailored, dark gray suit and black loafers, as she had predicted. His salmon button down matched perfectly to the handkerchief cornered into his lapel and complemented his harvesting green eyes perfectly. Sandy blonde hair sashed loosely over long lashes, making him appear well-educated and successful, yet still young and mysterious. During their first meeting, this look had led her to believe he was a man of genuine interest and eager candor simply by his wistful gaze. Sadie knew the truth of him too late, but even as he stood here now with the truth fully exposed to her, she could find no threat in him. Sadie searched his eyes for anything resembling the monster he truly was but found nothing.

"Hello, Sadie. This shouldn't take long," he said, closing the door behind him and locking it. He walked casually over to the bed and placed a briefcase next to her. With two small movements, the briefcase clicked open to reveal an expensive-looking camera. She observed in silence. Her exterior displayed a calmness that could not be more opposite from the rambling activity of her mind. *He's not going to touch me,* she thought in a panic. *He doesn't even look remotely interested.* Realizing all of her weapons were on her body, she thought quickly of a way to bring him closer to her. She would not be satisfied until she had all of them.

"Just lay back on the bed, Sadie. Put your right arm over your head and your left by your side." His orders were direct, but coolly polite. He showed no signs of aggression whatsoever. She did as she was told in contemplative silence.

"Bring down your right hand and touch your breast with it," he directed apathetically.

Sadie didn't move. The fingers of her right hand were tangled into her teased hair, feeling for the syringe taped to her crown.

"Are you deaf? Move your right hand to your breast," he demanded. He peered over the tip of the camera with impatience transferring into his white-knuckle grip on its sides. She lay in stillness, closing her fist around the cylindrical plastic barrel. With her thumb, she pulled back on the plunger until she felt the stop. Her eyes remained fixed into his. "What are you doing? I have other events planned for tonight. I am not in the mood for your games, woman," he barked angrily tossing his camera onto the bed.

He lunged closer to her, reaching for her right arm. His peachy skin was molten red with frustration. This was a man who was accustomed to being obeyed as the Master of the submissive Lydia Scavway. Sadie's disobedience peeled his cool exterior to full exposure of his repugnance. Her eyes narrowed against him, meeting his rage with equal offense.

Satan's minions held tightly to her hand in her hair, shrieking their thrills into her ear. *They have come to help me*, she thought pleasantly. A naughty grin took hold of her as darkness cast its spell between them. Sadie could smell his blood pulsing through his bulging jugular as he hovered above her. Kendrick, already taking hold of her right wrist in blind anger, noticed her malevolent glare too late. Her hand pulled free much easier than expected, causing his eyes to fly open in surprise. In his periphery, he saw the needle point aiming quickly at his throat. He tried to dodge her but the reaction was halted by a sharp and searing pain as the needle pierced through his skin. Lanky arms twisted and flailed in its direction to no avail as Sadie pushed the plunger quickly into his vessel.

Kendrick stumbled backward against the wall, grasping his chest and panting. His mouth mangled with pain. She stood over him as he crouched on the floor. His lips continued to twist and his right hand squeezed into a fist over his heart. "You look pathetic," she observed aloud. He looked up at her with shock and small tears began to trickle from his dying green eyes. "The thing is," she continued coolly but quietly, "I have an amazing family. I was afraid we could be separated forever if I failed one more time. It has been threatened so many times before, that I knew this was my last chance." She stooped to the ground so that her lips nearly touched his. His breath was cold and dry, pumping through small, whimpering pants onto her cheeks. She reached up and traced lavender around his lips with her fingertips as she whispered. "You know, you have the perfect face for a portrait. I was hoping you could help me out."

Sadie stood and stepped gracefully to the bed. When she returned to him, she held in her lovely hands his oversized camera. He was weakly reaching for the needle in his neck, still fighting with some dim hope against imminent, encroaching death. "No, no," she warned, clicking her tongue and moving his hand back down to his side. "It adds interest to the photo. All I want you to do is relax and act naturally." The fist that had clutched his heart collapsed into his lap. His lips seized their twisting and fell open as his breathing was increasingly restricted by the collapsing of his lungs. "That's very good," she taunted. She held the camera to her eyes and peered through the lens, adjusting the focus so that his entire body could be seen clearly. With the closing of its shutter, Kendrick drew in a quick breath and relinquished his life, captured now in high resolution.

Feeling satisfied, Sadie checked his carotids for a pulse. When she couldn't find any sign of life in him, she reacted quickly to get rid of the body. She would only have a few minutes left before the rest of the ceremony began. Grabbing Kendrick by the ankles, she tried to pull his dead weight across the floor. Even with his thin frame, he was too heavy for her to move very fast. She looked around for the closest hiding place. The bathroom was by far the closest, but it was at least twenty feet away. Sadie took off her heels and tried to pull him behind her, thinking the process would be faster without the inconvenience of balancing on stilettoes, but she still barely inched forward. The dagger was scraping her from the inside, as the straining was pushing it downward with each heaving step. Sweat began to cluster above her brow, dripping into her eyes and down her cheeks. The bodice was not as flattering in this particular moment, as it crushed into her ribs and restricted her to a fast pant.

Finally, Sadie reached the bathroom and turned to drag Kendrick inside. She paused when she heard rustling in the other room. It sounded as though the men were arguing outside. They were running out of patience, and she was running out of time. With a grunt stifled behind clenched teeth, Sadie pulled one last time and his body slid just beyond the door's clearance. Straightening her spine, she glanced into the bronze encased antique mirror mounted above the sink. Luckily, the sweat had not damaged the jewels or the flawless make-up on which Lydia had spent hours perfecting. Her hair looked a bit tussled from the scuffle, but nothing she couldn't fix. She tried to breathe as deeply as possible against the corset's stiff hugging as she combed the messed up strands back into place. She calculated that with Shamen and Kendrick dead, and David and Cuyler still tardy, she had only three men left- Ray, Lucas, and

Anthony. *Three men*, she thought with reservation, *and only one weapon*. One tiny dagger shoved between her legs.

I am outnumbered, she thought fretfully, *I need something more powerful than a dagger*. She stooped to search the fresh corpse on the floor. His body was still warm and moved without resistance as she tugged and shifted his torso in search of anything that might be of use against three large, cruel men who would not hesitate to kill her and feed her to the rats. Sadie shuttered at the thought of hundreds of rats, with their sharp yellow teeth and wiry whipping tails, tearing through the cold-cut chunks of her remains. At last she spied what she had been hoping to find. Tucked into the backside of his expensive gray trousers, was a 9mm semi-automatic pistol. She pulled it out and released the clip, which was full with seventeen rounds of hollow tipped bullets. Pushing it back in again, she listened for the click that told her it was secure and turned off the safety. Sadie held it warmly in her right hand, stroking the chrome barrel and admiring the custom comfort-grip handle that seemed to mold into her palm as she held it. She pulled back on the slide to make sure it was hot and ready to fire.

The argument was escalating quickly, their voices clearly audible now. "Let's do this already, I have a red-eye to New York in two hours," one of the men shouted.

"Where is Shamen? It's not like him to be late," Ray inquired with more suspicion than concern.

"I don't really care where the old bastard is," the third said in a low voice. "He probably went outside and stroked out or something." The third voice was sounding more frustrated and authoritative with every word. "I say we just call the bitch out here and at least see some entertainment. I have whores of my own to look after. He's almost half an hour late."

"It's possible Shamen crawled off and died but, let's face it, he's in better shape than most of us. And where is David? He was so excited about tonight. He wouldn't miss picking up his blushing bride," Ray's suspicions were growing stronger. Sadie watched him through the crack below the door. He was standing with his head tilted to the side; attentively eyeing the oversized grandfather clock leaned against the wall beside him. "Something isn't right. Has anyone seen Kendrick?"

The three of them fell quiet and looked around at each other, shrugging and shaking their heads. Ray took out his cell phone and flipped it open. Sadie ran to where Kendrick lay in the bathroom floor. She searched his pockets frantically for his cell phone. Pressing buttons until the main screen lit up brightly, Sadie paused with disappointment when she saw that it was password protected. Opening his phone to silence it would take too long, and she could hear Ray dialing the numbers already. She pressed a manicured nail below the back of the phone and popped out the battery. She waited silently, holding her breath and listening closely for the men to react.

"It's going straight to voicemail," Ray said, contemplatively.

"He did say he had plans with Lydia tonight. Maybe he doesn't want to be disturbed," the first man said. "Let's just screw the bitch and get out of here. Her own Master is late getting her home, so she can't be that special. I don't want to miss my flight for something that is just alright."

Sadie felt her spirit stir with contempt. How much could one woman take from them? How many had they killed, or beaten and left for dead? How many had they used, abused, and discarded? Sadie knew all too well the suffocation of their imposed submission and diminishment, painted white and stained with a permanent smile designed to ease liability. She stared into the barrel of the pistol and wondered how the paint might crack if she pulled the trigger. Could that be the only way to penetrate the many faces they painted on her? Behind them would she find the girl she used to be or the one they have made her see? *The light in me has been snuffed out by their terror and darkness. The silence drove me to madness, and that is the mask adorned to me now. I must remove the madness from my restless spirit and lift the crimson shade to see clearly, allowing light to penetrate the darkness in which I hide behind this mask of borrowed pride.*

She walked over to the doorway with quick, stealthy steps and reached a clammy palm toward the crystal knob. The door pushed open with force enough to slam against the wall behind it. Their arguing hushed as the three of them looked onto her in disbelief. "Never again will you hurt us," she asserted, drawing the pistol from behind her back. Her arms did not waiver with any detectible fear. She held it straight before her, aiming at the one called Anthony. He sat leaned against the white leather loveseat where Shamen had first called her Willow. The name corroded her most sacred of memories and infuriated her.

Sadie felt stronger than she ever had as she looked directly through the front sight, centering his smirk with the muzzle. She remembered the first time she had held a gun. It was also a 9mm Cuyler had selected for her. He stood beside her now, so vividly imagined that she could feel his warm hands wrapping around hers to steady her grip. "Squeeze the trigger like you are making a fist," he reminded her patiently. "If you try to pull the trigger, the gun will move before you fire. That will cause you to miss every time and, if someone intends to cause you harm, you don't want to miss." His voice sounded so closely audible and even his breath collected hotly against her neck. "Don't be afraid of it Sadie," he reassured her. "You are in control."

"Never again will any of you steal an innocent soul for your vile pleasures," she stated more harshly and, gripping the gun firmly in both hands, she pulled the trigger. Anthony didn't move, but dropped his smirk-spoiled mask to expose his cowardice. Ray and Lucas hesitated to react. Their jolly, round jaws jiggled as they whipped around to see their comrade coughing and spitting out his own blood. She had hit him directly in the center of his throat, the hollow shell mushrooming out to collapse all the structures within.

"The fear tastes good, doesn't it?" Sadie said smoothly. She inched closer down the hall with short steps. Her body had gone completely numb, as though she stood on its outside, controlling its movements with invisible strings. "You will not keep me here any longer," she demanded with heat radiating through every syllable. She turned her attention to Lucas, who was still leaning over Anthony's blood-bathed body. Again, Cuyler's hands wrapped around hers and held them steady. She tensed her arms so that they were focused and straight behind the barrel. She squeezed the trigger a second time; and Lucas slouched over. His head fell quaintly into the lap of his partner. A clean shot to the chest left less blood splatter this time so that it trickled quietly into the plush carpet.

Sadie took long strides so that she stood only a few feet from Ray. He was feeling for his own weapon, his eyes largely open and fixed upon the muzzle aimed into his head. She stared at him and took in his small presence with curiosity. He was relatively short with black hair and a scruffy black beard. His waist line was hidden behind a roll of fat hanging over his belt. This was the man with the black gloves from the airport, the same man who had held her mouth and laughed boldly at her fear. He was not so intimidating now, with his fat jiggling in a fearful shiver.

"Okay, let's just slow down, eh?" His northern accent was as thick as the cologne he was wearing. She tilted her head and tried to process the delight she found in his quivering.

"You took me from the only person who loved me," she whispered coldly. Her eyes flinted with the memory of his hand shoving her into the ice, away from Ireland, away from her happy ending, and away from Cuyler.

"I'm sorry about that, I really am, but he's on his way here. He's coming to get you. Maybe we can just talk until he gets here," he stuttered.

"No, I don't want to talk," Sadie said calmly. The gun dropped to his knee and she squeezed the trigger a third time. Ray fell to the ground, moaning and crying. She stared at him as he squirmed like a slug caught in a salty soak. Blood was spilling from the entrance wound. There was a surprising amount considering the small caliber of the bullet. "Actually, I have something for you," she said softly as she stooped to join him on the floor. Sadie shifted the gun to her right hand and held it to the crown of his head. With her left, she retrieved the dagger from between her legs.

Ray squinted away his tears. "What are you going to do to me?" he cried between short breaths.

"Shhh," she said, placing the muzzle against his lips. Ray closed his eyes and started to pray. "God won't help you, Ray. What have you done to deserve any help from God?" Sadie asked rhetorically. She took the dagger and stabbed the tip into the intercostal space on his right side. Ray yelled out and fell onto his back. His contorted face writhed in agony. It was a mask she rather liked him wearing.

"Sadie, please just go. Just leave," he pleaded through choked out gasps. He tried to hold onto his freshly wounded side, but the blade came down again, this time into his the hand that protected it. He yelled out again through bitter sobs as he withdrew his crippled hand and attempted to grab the knife from her with his other hand.

"Oh, a fighter, eh?" she said to him with a sneer. "I know just the place for you, where you can never hurt anyone again," she said darkly, stabbing the dagger's merciless tip into the flesh just below the clavicle. She swept the blade against his left wrist, admiring how quickly his soul drained in stains of red from her infliction. As the scent of fresh blood filled the air around her, Sadie was intoxicated.

The steel blade snapped smoothly into his flesh, tearing it open at her command. His body twitched under her control, slicing at defensive hands, sniveling eyes, and wherever her all-pervading hatred could diffuse into his body at the tip of her dagger. "Never again," she kept repeating. His life spilled over between her fingers and thighs, sprayed her eyes and cried upon her chest, driving her madness with each repeated thrust to replenish an insatiable thirst for more.

Finally, he was limp against her thrusting and Sadie realized the last soul had paid penance. The dampness of her eyes surprised her with the weeping of cogent tears. She gazed around through the haze of reality. No longer seeing the crimson veil before her eyes, the light was blinding, as a halo for the wicked. Tired and weighted by freedom, she collapsed against the corpse. Each extremity seemed to be knotted, hard and heavy against the noise inside her mind. Sleepy thoughts were disorganized and detached flashbacks feigning recognition against the roaring white light before her eyes. The silence she craved was disrupted by echoes of footsteps running through the room, a voice of reason pled with the dead and negotiated with the deadly. She was too weak to react and resorted to only listen as best she could as the voice beckoned her to stand, to answer, to show some sign of life behind the blank expression fixed upon her flawless face.

He arose from the ashes of her dreams as though sent by God's angels to save her. Arriving too late, he found her cast against the shadow of her own creation. Levitating through the room in the arms of her angel, Sadie felt nothing but peace as the door to hell slammed shut behind them, sealing in the evil within those walls. He rested her gently onto the backseat of his Explorer, covered her warmly with his jacket, and shifted the vehicle into drive. Sadie closed her heavy eyes and allowed the darkness to swoon her.

Sadie had once described freedom as a lovely sunset that marks closure for the afflicted and the guarantee of a new day to come; one of hope, of promise, and of a silver lined future. She now understood that such a guarantee could not be upheld, even by the most optimistic of spirits. In fact, it could just as easily be taken as it could be spoken. Freedom now held a greater honor than the silver lining adorning whimsical daydreams. It is the strength to stand when they have taken your legs, and the courage to fight when they have stolen your will to survive. True freedom is the gift of seeing through the red and finding white, and remaining poised against the noise of the ever changing tide.

Breathing with ease, in spite of the oppressively snug corset she still wore, Sadie was lost within her own imagination and dreaming soundly. She had not really seen the driver to identify him, nor had she asked, as she had been completely lost in her own illusions. Neither could she see where it was the driver took her, or the sly grin he wore as he pulled into his destination. And, swayed by the peace she felt in entering his arms, she could not predict her angel's blackened intentions to char her freedom and disable her white dreaming.

21

"Do you remember how it happened?" David Burke spoke with a voice that was solemn with only a trace of shallow concern. He was much less interested in how she got here than what he would do with her now that she was.

"I remember so many things," she whispered. Her gaze was absent and her chalky lips cracked and trembling. Her mouth barely seemed to move with the words she spoke but through their weakened part he could see the straight, white edges of her teeth. He wondered if those perfect teeth had been exposed by her smile in some distant past. She seemed so frail and void of expression now. Her skin was a frosted white and smooth with youth. Her pallor was striking against her dark brown eyes and coal-black hair that hung loosely over her exposed narrow shoulders. She sat with her knees held closely to her chest. Her half-starved body curved outward against her back in such a way that made her vertebrae so evident they could be counted through the laces of her deeply purple bodice. Her long, slender legs were a flawless example of God's craftsmanship. Crossed ankles exposed a tiny tattoo of a black rose on the inside of her right foot, which was bare and tainted slightly with dirt. She posed as a porcelain doll upon a shelf, a delicate masterpiece. Her vulnerability excited him.

"Can you elaborate a little bit?" He was careful to keep his voice soft and added only the due inflection to make him appear more inviting. It was his unique and unsurpassable ability to convince people to tell their story that had landed him this beautiful woman. It eased his frustration to recall the ease with which his skills at building rapport had enabled both Ray and Cuyler to trust him completely. Ray was eager to resume their partnership, especially since the organization had taken new root so close to David's office. Taking her from under Cuyler had also been easy, as David imagined Cuyler was still sitting out in the middle of the woods, completely stranded and waiting helplessly for a ride that would never come. A part of him regretted betraying Cuyler so badly. He was a nice enough guy with the best of intentions, but this world, he rationalized, had little room for nobility.

Still, he had spent almost three hours with this crazy bitch and couldn't get any more than a simple, disconnected phrase from time to time. His patience was wearing thin and it was showing in his coarse expression regardless how hard he tried to hide it. "Ok, you don't want to tell me right now? I can drive back to Berea Police Department and we can talk there. Does that sound more appealing to you?" He waited for a moment and listened to the silence. Her absence was unwavering despite his crude statements saturated with sarcasm. He inhaled deeply trying to relax his facial features. "You do realize you're going straight to prison without my help, don't you? I promise I only want to help. I'm not here to hurt you, but you have to trust me. Do you understand?"

Truthfully, he did not need her to tell him anything. This case was solved long before he had found her, and he had no intentions of taking her to any police station. He simply loved to play the cop and prisoner game. He could remember when his wife would play this game with him. Sometimes she would even let him handcuff her before the interrogation. The game would always end up a little more aggressive than she had intended, but he believed she always enjoyed herself. Playing the same game with Sadie, without her even knowing, made it much more exciting. Never had he tried it with someone who had no idea of the end outcome. Her innocence in the situation was empowering and hearing the violence spill from her sweet lips promised to be just as tantalizing as if he had been the one to kill them. He could feel his chest pushing out with full-bodied authority as he imagined how intimidating it must be for someone caught in the act to be face to face with a detective as large and strong as he.

He wiped the sweat off his upper lip and brow line with the rag from his shirt pocket. He couldn't help but wonder why these small roadside hotels never had air conditioning. Was business so bad they couldn't afford the unit? Damn. Even at this late hour the humidity was nearly unbearable. Under normal circumstances, David would prefer to drive the short three hours and stay in his own bed, with the thermostat set comfortably at sixty-eight. However, Sadie was in no shape to travel, even that short distance. He needed her stable and ambulating so there would be no need for questions or raised eyebrows in a town where eyes and flapping tongues get far more exercise than necessary. He could see sweat beginning to surface on her alabaster shoulders and trickle down her left arm. He watched it fall slowly over the smooth traces of bruises which painted her body with various shades of greens, blues, and lavenders. Everything in her demeanor cried out with a victim's sorrow. Yet, he was the one who had found her covered in another man's blood, and the scene had been horrific. He had seen what she was capable of doing. There was something about her he loved to hate. Her lack of cooperation only made him want her more. He could hardly wait to force her into submission.

"It was just...I just...had to stop...to stop it." She spoke in a choked-out whisper. Her eyes widened as though she was watching the climax of a horror film. Her pupils were large enough so that they seemed to blend into the darkened iris surrounding them. Darkness was all that could be seen in her expression. Her chest began to rise and fall quickly; she was panting with restless intensity. Each breath made her breasts press firmly against her knees, encouraging them to expose their rounded edges through the ripped seams of the corset tightly formed to them. The moisture that had budded from her long and graceful neckline moved faster with her rapid respirations and formed a small, steady stream in the cleft of her breasts. Her breathing continued to intensify and he noticed her white-knuckle grip on metal frame of the chair. Her muscles were clenched and her body stiff. Even her teeth were grinding together, this made obvious by the straight part of her tense lips. She began to groan slightly under the agony of her prolonged stress and it seemed as though her entire body could explode from the increasing pressure within. David stood up slowly and cautiously began to walk over to her. He wanted to keep a careful distance in case this was some clever trick to try to escape. Edging closer to her, he stretched out his large rough hands. He had almost reached her when her body went completely limp and collapsed from the chair.

"Sadie, are you okay?!" He kneeled over her with both knees to the ground and his hands fumbled through her long black hair to find her carotids. She had a pulse but it was faint. He turned her body over so that she was flat on her back and he could see the blood trickling from the right side of her hairline. He reached for the rag in his left shirt pocket and held it firmly against her bleeding head. Listening closely for the sound of gentle breath escaping her lips, he watched her chest for movement. She was breathing. Slow, shallow respirations caused a gentle rising of her chest against his cheek. He could not resist his urge to touch her and found himself fully fallen into the pits of temptation with her helpless body unable to stop him. The air buzzed all around him and made it too loud to think clearly. The game he had been playing became obsolete as he was captured by her helplessness. Desire possessed him and carried the current above all else as his hand slid gently on her inner thigh. Her skin was as soft as he had imagined, cold and wet from perspiration yet tender and subtle to his calloused hands. His right hand continued to the lace trim of her corset and moved medially until his fingertips grazed against her black thongs slightly and he could feel himself getting harder. A pounding on the metal door of his room resonated loudly through the small, dingy suite. David quickly removed his hand in a smooth jerk and tried to pull himself together.

"Everybody ok in there?" The hotel manager yelled in a panicked, squeaky voice. David stood up and took quiet steps to peak through the blinds. He was very young, twenty years old tops. He had red hair that he kept in a military issued buzz cut in an attempt to add masculinity to his baby face with innocently clear green eyes and thin lips. He stood only 5'8" tall and roughly 120 pounds. He was the type of over-zealous rooky everyone hated to work with. David knew they type well from years of training them at the Police Academy in New York. This type was always by the book and the first to snitch on you for taking a nickel bag from the evidence room.

David's lips and mouth were dry and cold from his recent arousal and he could feel his face start to flush with warmth. He shook it off and slid his tongue through his lips to moisten them so he could speak. "Yes, we are doing well. Thanks for asking," he yelled back through the door.

"I heard a loud thumping noise and need to check it out, please. Could you open the door for me?" The manager sounded persistent and David knew he wasn't going to leave until he had a chance to look around. He looked at his sleeping bride-to-be, lying cold on the floor and wearing nothing but a torn piece of lingerie. This would not go over well at all with the over-zealous worm outside. David grabbed his sleeping Sadie and tucked her snugly into the sheets, turning her head to the right to hide her bleeding. She moaned slightly but didn't try to fight him. Her face was burning hot beneath the clammy perspiration. Prior to joining the force, David had spent three years working as an EMT and he recognized the symptoms immediately. His blushing bride was going through withdrawal. Luckily he had just what she needed in his bag, but the pounding on the door told him it would have to wait.

"Of course," David said calmly, opening the door. "My name is Detective David Burke," he denoted, holding out his badge for the young stiff to see clearly. "The loud noise you heard was just me. I was trying to figure out how to pull out that couch so I could turn in for the night and I'm afraid I wasn't doing a very good job at it." He chuckled slightly, trying to appear somewhat embarrassed.

"Is she ok?" the manager asked, unconvinced.

"Yes, she is just sleeping. I am transporting her back to my home office for some questioning in a murder trial. I am not allowed to discuss the details but I will tell you she was pretty shaken up and exhausted. She's been through a lot and I am just glad to see her resting finally. Poor girl cried herself to sleep." David rested his hands on his hips and shook his head sympathetically.

"Oh, I see," said the manager much more softly. "I am sorry to have disturbed you, Detective. We have had some issues around the hotel and I am trying to put a stop to all that."

"Absolutely, I understand," David replied. "I wish we had more model citizens like you in this world," he said with obvious pride. "Maybe there would be a lot less cases like the one I am working now." He wanted to pound his face in for interrupting, but maintained his cool composure. This was really not the place anyway. Under better circumstances he would have her, of that he was sure. His time alone with her would come soon enough and there would be no interruptions where he was taking her.

"Thank you, sir," the manager replied, sticking his chest out boastfully. "Have a good night, then." He smiled and turned to leave.

"We will do our best and thanks for all you do," David said convincingly, laying a hand on his shoulder to direct him across the threshold. He waved as he watched the young man strut back into his office and close the door behind him.

Back inside, David looked through his overnight bag until he found the two syringes and vial of morphine he had packed for Sadie in case she needed it. He stepped over to the bed where she slept, completely still. Taking her small arm in his large hands, he wrapped one hand tightly around her upper arm to create a tourniquet and the other carefully inserted the needle. "You will feel better soon, my dear," he whispered into her left ear. He reached back into his bag and pulled out the first aid kit he had also packed for her. Inside the kit, he found a generic and outdated version of a suture set. "This might sting a little but you must stay completely still for me, Sadie," he whispered again as he rotated her head toward him. Her eyes were moving behind the lids as he hooked the needle under her torn flesh and threaded the first suture. Her lashes fluttered slightly but she didn't wake, so he continued until the gash on her head was reduced a seam held together with six neatly tied stitches.

He sat back to admire his porcelain doll. He couldn't help but to pat himself on the back for a job well done on finding such a lovely bride. The day had been eventful and turned out even better than expected. Sadie had done the killing for him, and his hands were clean of their blood. She was too weak in her current state to resist or ask questions, which would make the transfer to his apartment much easier in the morning. He picked up the two plane tickets off the dresser and held them fondly in his lap. In just two short days, the pair would be resting on a beach off the coast of New Zealand. She would be so excited about a new start and a chance to escape a life-sentence for murder she would have to no choice but to leave with him. He was sure that once they arrived and had some time alone, she would fall in love with him. He smiled, picturing her doting affection pouring over the hero who had saved her from death's clutches. If she didn't fall in love with him, however, it was of no relevance. She would take care of him regardless. After all, where else would she go? Assuming, that is, she could even get past his massive stature.

His spirit still sailed across the tide with her by his side as his tired head hit the pillow. He wrapped his strong arms around her and drifted in and out of sleep. His mind was too jumpy to sleep soundly. Each time she would move or moan, he would tighten his grip and look over to make sure she was still there. He was not about to lose her after all the planning and patience it had taken to gain her. She had spoken very little to him and he couldn't be sure of her state of mind. At times he would begin to dream and be jolted awake by nightmares of her standing over him with a blade in hand, slicing his throat or piercing his heart. The vivid nature of the nightmares would leave him gasping and clenching at his wounds when he awoke. At last he came to the conclusion that all sharp or potentially dangerous objects would be kept in a locked cabinet. Otherwise, he could guess with certainty that it was be his blood that covered her next, just like Ray. At least until she had a chance to grow comfortable in her new home. In finding a solution to his nightmares, David finally relaxed enough to slide into a dreamless slumber.

Morning broke through with the sun peaking across the room. David opened his burning eyes once again to see Sadie's dark eyes staring fiercely at him. Her cheeks were burning with anger and confusion. He could see the questions racing through her active imagination and considered, for a moment at least, the fun he might have if he tried to interrogate her again. All things considered, however, he didn't wish for her to pass out again and she didn't look stable yet. There would be plenty of time for games when she had a chance to recover and gain her senses.

"In case you have forgotten, my name is David Burke. I am a Detective from New York," he began. "I know you are a little confused right now, and that's okay because I am going to tell you exactly where you are and where you are going." She offered him only a hard, cold stare. Occasionally, she shook her head in disbelief as he described the blood bath in which he had found her and the trouble she was sure to face if she stayed here.

"Don't worry, my love," he concluded with a firm hand against her cheek, "I have a ticket for each of us. I have to stop by my apartment first to tie up some loose ends, but then we will catch our flight and be in New Zealand by this time tomorrow. I won't let anyone take you to prison, or anywhere else. You are mine now and forever," he leaned in to kiss her but she jerked her face way. His short temper began to surface into tensed muscles and a clenched jaw. If this had been his first wife, she would have paid dearly for such a transgression. He caught himself before overreacting, bearing in mind the excitement of the past twenty four hours. "You might want to reconsider that attitude of yours, because I can just as easily take you back to Berea and turn you over to the police." He looked down at her with his finger pointed, as one might if they were scolding a small child or puppy. He grabbed a brown bag off the floor and handed it to her, smiling. "As much as I love your ensemble, you can't go outside like that. No one sees your body but me, from this day forward. Here, I bought this for you to wear."

She opened the bag carefully and looked inside. She didn't speak or express any significant emotions. David stared at her as she dressed slowly. Her body was thin and malnourished and she moved slowly behind weakened muscles. She winced often, most likely from the multiple bruising and lacerations that covered her entirely. He was disappointed by her lack of excitement, fear, or even interest. In spite of all she must be thinking, her affect remained completely flat. It made him feel uneasy and arose in him a sour desire to know what she was planning behind her silence. She stepped into the jersey-knit sweat pants shakily, stumbling under her weakness. He placed a strong hand across her prominent ribs to stabilize her as he pulled the loose-fitting t-shirt over her matted hair.

"Thank you," she said with a tremble. The cotton fabric felt soft and warm across her body and there was comfort in being modestly dressed for the first time in months. She wasn't sure of the man in front of her, but couldn't deny the gratitude she felt in being adequately clothed in something comfortable. He did not appear angry or abusive, but most didn't in the beginning. She had learned that, more often than not, violence was sure to follow, and since she could not avoid the violence, she chose to enjoy what kindness might be offered. Sadie traced her tired gaze along his daunting figure. He stood well over six feet and was built to kill. She shuttered a little at the thought of her neck snapping under his powerful strike.

"Are you cold?" he asked, interrupting her thoughts. "You won't be where we are going. New Zealand has one of the best climates in the world, and a beautiful coast we can enjoy together forever."

She smiled at him shyly. Her lips were sore and her cheeks still bruised from the harshness of Shamen's temper. "Can I use the bathroom before we leave?" she asked timidly.

"Sure, just be quick. We have to check out soon and I am starving for some steak and eggs," he replied with enthusiasm. He watched her walk softly into the bathroom, limping slightly on the right side.

Sadie stepped into the small, dingy bathroom and closed the door behind her. She stood frozen before the mirror, staring in search of some fragment of her soul which might shine through at last. Her dark hair had lost inches in the matted tangles around her scalp. Blackened eyes opened into a hollow casing where her life had been, matching with elegance the scars she adorned as her painful reminder. Lips silenced by the knights of lament were worn cracked and left bleeding by the devil's kiss. Sin had taken form inside her ivory skin, and showcased its sacrifice in all her shameful glory. She might consider crying, but tears are reserved for those who care to reason with life; who preserve wishes painted among the stars. She now knew such constellations could never exist, even with love as the artist's brush, though she was sure she had seen them in a distant past. Emptiness cannot paint as love can, nor can it create as it is only love which dreams of possibilities for its canvas. Taking a razor from the sink, she wondered if the stars might be revealed to her in some other way, if she could dance among them in death since she could no longer see them as she existed now. Perhaps Cuyler would be there as well, or maybe she could see him from her prancing perch in the night sky.

"Sadie," David called through the door, startling her. "It's time," he said with marked enthusiasm. Sadie broke off the razor from its handle and slipped it into the hem of sweat pants as she pulled open the door. David was standing at its threshold, hovering over her impatiently and blocking the exit. He reached out for her and his hand landed gently against her tangled hair. "You are going to be okay now, Sadie. I will take care of you and you will take care of me. I don't know how to love anyone, but I am confident you will love me if for no other reason than to save your own skin. If ever you think of leaving me just ask yourself what your life is worth to you. I cannot promise you anything but this one vow. I will kill you if you try to escape," he said sinisterly as he stroked her arms. He was sure he could see the glare of Al Satan flash through her eyes before her gaze dropped to the floor. He stepped aside and gestured for her to walk ahead before continuing. "Let's get you in the shower when we get back to my apartment. I think I got most of the blood off of you last night but you look terrible." He looked her over teasingly. "A hot shower fixes everything, in my experience."

Sadie chose not to answer. She was stirring restlessly against the liberty she longed for and the prison which was guaranteed to her. No amount of bloodshed would stop these men from taking her and there would be no escape from the spiked chains of her existence. Climbing into the silver Explorer, she found the stillness of resolution. Liberty may remain colorless behind lock and key, restricted only for those more fortunate than she, and love the perfect shade of pink just beyond her reach. But freedom could be swooned in a claret sea of release controlled by the silver blade of mercy she smuggled at her hip.

She rode in silence, deaf to her driver's lulling conversation and boasting. Her mind was flooded with memories of a time when love had a name and hope was something achieved rather than sought after. His laughter and whimsical day dreaming could fill her days with joy unknown to her now. She imagined he was there with her, taking her on some undisclosed adventure where waterfalls stacked against a weeping mountain and the many beautiful faces of nature smiled their fragrance into the mist of the water around them, just as they had done so many times before. It was a time of innocence immersed in consecrated beauty and shared only in each other's eyes. The difficulty with innocence, however, is that it lacks gravity, continuously floating higher above understanding until the fall is too far to survive should its consecration become dismantled. Silently, she was a rotting sea of corruption, hatred, and insanity. None could be more dismantled than she, but it was not death she feared the most, as David believed. She smiled slightly at the scrape of the razor's edge against her hip and thought of the demons' claret choir rejoicing for her as they chanted their reassurance into her focused ears. *You cannot kill what is already dead.*

22

Shadows streamlined the apartment through the sleepy haze in Cuyler's eyes, creating images which howled and wailed against the walls surrounding him. He crouched low beside the fireplace in a sulking slouch with his back leaned heavily against the wall. Scattered about him across the floor were items he had found during his long wait. Among them was the letter he had sent in March with a naked picture of his beloved folded into its seams. The invitation to Sadie's commencement ceremony in South Carolina had also been revealed inside David's jacket. After reading it several times, Cuyler had found a hidden message requesting his deliverance written inside. Cuyler must have read them all thousand times. Each time his anger would poison the gaping wound inside his heart. By this early hour, as he read the invitation yet again, the infected wound had turned septic and now coursed through every vessel, causing such a tremor that reading was nearly impossible. He reached for the picture of Sadie, which seemed too heavy to be a real image, and the heat from it burned tears into his eyes. Hot and strangling tears flowed sorrowfully over its edges.

Cuyler's soul felt pulled out of his body, ripping him apart with its downward flight. The agony in her eyes, the hopelessness in her lifeless arms, posed heavily against her thin thighs. He wondered what he would see when she came through the door with David pushing his desires on her. Would she be dead already or could he still save her? He deliberated if her body would be bruised and her spirit eternally broken, or could love salvage her remains? There was a part of him that yearned to believe in fairy tales, the same part that craved confirmation that love could mend all things, but what if he was too late? What could be said of a loveless fate?

Footsteps clattered against the stairwell outside, jerking Cuyler fully awake. He brushed up his gathered items and slipped the photo into his shirt pocket, firmly held closest to his heart. David's deep voice rumbled from outside the door and Cuyler could hear jingling keys fumbling for the lock. His heart raced wildly as the sepsis spread further out into his nerves, vibrating against every tensed muscle fiber of his body. His face was burning with rage, and his eyes narrowed on the door as his right hand squeezed a white-knuckle grip into the bone handle of his weapon, ready to slaughter the predator just beyond that metal barrier.

Cuyler held his breath and positioned himself to lunge as the lock finally gave into the key and the handle turned to open the door. He stopped cold as a frail and beaten girl walked through first. Her exposed arms were scarred with needle tracks nearly covering their small anterior surface. Her pallor was so strikingly white against her matted black hair that it looked painted on, like a mask. The dark and soulful eyes he had remembered had lost their luster and were as flat as the expression donned on her face. She walked with a limp, exposing the prominent ridges of her hips. He blinked several times, trying to decide if this moment was real. Surely this pathetic, half-dead creature could not be his Sadie who had been the very image of life and happiness for him the last three years. The shock strangled inside him, restricted his airway and wept into what remained of his heart. All of his hopes disintegrated into ash, and left him glossed and frozen in his own shadow.

David walked in behind her, strutting proudly as he led her into the bathroom. Cuyler heard the shower running and music streaming from David's bedroom. "I will be back in a few minutes to check on you, my dear. I have to call the office," Cuyler heard David call out. There was no reply from his unwilling guest. David strutted back into the living room and fell heavily back into the couch, stretching out his full length and placing the phone against his ear. As he hung up the phone, Cuyler rose and took slow, silent steps until he was standing directly behind David's head. The air was dense with humidity in the small apartment and sweat reamed from every pore. His shirt was stained with the evidence of his emotional lability and his palms wept with excitement for what he was about to do.

"Welcome home, David," Cuyler spoke with deep sarcasm. David jumped to full attention and whipped around to face his intruder. His eyes bulged open and his mouth was gaping with surprise. Immediately, he regained his composure and curled his lips into a grin.

"Well, I'm so glad you could stop by," he said, matching the sarcasm. "It's always good to see an old friend." David stood and took strong steps toward Cuyler. He topped Cuyler by at least three inches and outweighed him by more than he cared to measure. David's body was tense and ready to fight, his stance bold and powerful. Cuyler could see he was not easily intimidated, but that was just as well with him. He was not there to intimidate, but to eradicate.

"I should have killed you the night you told me about your involvement with the Rose Academy. I trusted you, David," Cuyler spoke grimly. He took a deep breath and locked eyes with David. "Look what you have done to my Sadie. She looks like the living dead." His voice grew steadily louder. "I have had all night to think about how I would kill you," he warned. He could see David reaching behind his back for his gun.

"Yeah? And what did you come up with? Something good, I hope," David jeered. He thought of pulling his gun, but was rather enjoying this new game. He knew he was much stronger than Cuyler, even when he held such an impressive blade by his side. David was confident he could have the trigger pulled before Cuyler even raised his arm to strike. "Tell me, Cuyler, what terrible fate lies in store for me?" he teased.

Cuyler didn't reply. His eyes penetrated through David as though he could see straight through him. He didn't blink or even twitch for several minutes. The cold indifference to David's jeering gave him chills. He wrapped his fingers around his gun and started to pull it free from his belt. It was caught against the loop and David tugged harder against the snag. His chest began to feel tight with panic. Sweat beaded above his brow as he broke eye contact to look for an alternative. Cuyler still hadn't moved; his body was locked and loaded to strike at will.

"Look me in the eyes, you faggot," Cuyler demanded at last.

David was trying to hide his rattled nerves and cocked back his shoulders. Cuyler was fearless and raged beyond reconciliation, but David was stronger and a trained officer. He chuckled and stepped closer so that the toe of his oxfords touched Cuyler's bare feet. He leaned down and breathed hotly into Cuyler's flaring nostrils. "Is this close enough for you? You little shit, what do you think you can do to me?" David taunted through his chuckling. "I am an officer of the law and you are in my home. I have every legal right to kill you where you stand." His eyes rolled with his head and his hands clapped hard against Cuyler's head, leaving his ears ringing painfully by the sudden strike. "Actually, I think I will, but not here. I think the little bitch in the next room should get to watch, too. Don't you agree Cuyler?" David tried to pull Cuyler forward but he wouldn't budge. He stared evenly into David, as he had before, with pungent indifference.

Cuyler rotated the handle inside his palm, unnoticed by the arrogant fool holding onto him. His mind raced with all the ways he had considered killing him. Evisceration seemed to be a deserving choice, to leave him as gutless on the outside as he was on the inside. But standing at this close proximity, the blade would never slice him the way Cuyler had imagined.

David pressed harder against his ears, disorienting his senses and making it difficult to think. He had to get David's brooding body off of him somehow and raised his left had to punch in the direction of his blurry offender. David's heckling resounded above the ringing in his ears and fueled him to strike harder.

"I thought you were going to teach me something, boy," David teased. "When does your big plan start to happen? Don't let me miss it," he jeered as he thrust his knee into Cuyler's groin. Cuyler fell onto his knees in agony, but David lifted him again by his long curls. Cuyler pulled back the knife and swung hard in David's direction but his arm blocked the blow. Startled by the abrupt stop, Cuyler attempted a second time to cut the massive man wide open. He was stopped again, this time by a hard punch to the throat, directly over the trachea.

Cuyler's airway felt collapsed as he struggled to find his footing. Reason and focus were slipping through the spotty haze in front of him. Cuyler staggered and fell onto the floor, paralyzed and gasping for air. Pulling fiercely at his long auburn locks, David forced Cuyler into the sofa beside him. His face was pressed down into the woven fabric and Cuyler could feel the suffocation of its fibers further aiding in his strangulation. His chest was building pressure as he tried with all his remaining strength to shake David off him. He was sitting with his knee in Cuyler's back, pressing his face farther into the cushion with one large hand held firmly against his head. With the other hand, he grabbed the knife Cuyler had been wielding and pried it free from his weakening grip.

"Don't worry, Cuyler," he whispered in his ear, "I will take good care of my sweet Sadie." With that, David pressed the tip of the blade into Cuyler's vulnerable neck. He admired how the young lover's life poured easily into woven sofa and blended nicely with the burgundy fibers. He scooped Cuyler off the couch and carried him as a bride might be carried over the threshold on her wedding day. The screen door was open and David thought it to be the perfect place to rest his weary soul. *After all*, he thought with his own brand of sympathy, *the sun is always shining here and at night, he will see the most beautiful constellations.* David laid him gently on the wooden porch and walked inside.

The shower was still running and David was ready to leave. He knocked on the door but there was no answer. "Sadie," he called out assertively. She still didn't answer his call. He felt irate after all he had just done to ensure they could be together and she wouldn't even speak to him. David reached to open the door and swung it open with furious intensity. Lunging for the shower, he ripped back the curtain.

Sadie was lying beneath the running water; a stream of it was tinged pink and trickled from her open wrist, still embedded with the razor deeply lodged inside. David began to fluster as he again assessed her for a pulse and normal breathing. If he could fix her this time, he was definitely going to lock away all sharp objects. Sadie moaned lightly and tried to push him away as he lifted her from the tub. He laid her gently on his bed and held pressure to the site above her wrist. The razor he removed slowly, followed by the fast application of a pressure bandage. As he worked to revive her, he spoke in a soothing voice and stroked her wet hair.

"Sadie," he began, "please don't leave me. I know you are sad about Cuyler. I know that you love him very much."

She looked up to meet his eyes. The mention of his name brought her back to life. "How do you?" she struggled to ask. Her throat was tight against the tears.

"I know all about him, sweetheart, and I know that he loved you, too. He and I looked for you everywhere, and he never gave up on you. Until his very last breath, Sadie, he never gave up," David looked down upon her with as much compassion as he could muster.

"Is Cuyler? Is he?" she couldn't force herself to say it aloud.

"Is Cuyler dead? Yes, Sadie, he is dead. He died trying to find you but he made me promise that if anything ever happened to him, I would take care of you. And that's all I am trying to do, sweetheart. It's what he wanted. Do you see now why you can't leave me?" David asked his sobbing Sadie. She couldn't answer him through her desperate wailing but he knew she wouldn't leave again. He pulled her closer to his broad chest and rocked her as she cried. "There, there, it's okay now. I won't ever let you go. I will always be here, Sadie. I promise," he whispered as his lips turned their corners into a smile.